Praise for Jessica Chiarella and *And Again*

"*And Again* is a moving and beautifully crafted novel about the frailty of identity, the illusion of control, and the enduring power of love. A fantastic debut."
—Laila Lalami, Pulitzer Prize finalist and author of *The Other Americans* and *The Moor's Account*

"Chiarella's characters are well drawn, and their anguishes ring true. Do the people who love us in sickness and health really love us, or do they act out of a sense of duty? The SUBs have gotten a reprieve; what will they do with their second chance? Chiarella expresses their deep desires and yearnings with poetic compassion."
—*USA Today*

"Chiarella is also a pioneer as a writer, spinning a plot that's as groundbreaking as the medical procedure Linda, David, Connie, and Hannah undergo."
—*Chicago Review of Books*

"*And Again* delivers a stunning journey challenging the nature of identity, weaving four stories into a cohesive narrative. . . . As Chiarella gradually reveals the characters' pasts in tandem with their present courses, she illuminates the reality that their bodies—and our own—determine identity far more than expected."
—*Paste*

"*And Again* is a fascinating and disturbing glimpse of a medical technology that some believe the future may hold for our society."
—*San Diego Book Review*

"[Jessica Chiarella] does an amazing job moving from character to character and delving into their inner thoughts. The idea of creating human clones is already a controversial subject, but this book offers an eye-opening view to the mental and psychological strain that it can cause. The vulnerability and self-consciousness of the characters makes them easy to relate to and endearing."
—*RT Reviews*

"Chiarella provides a finely nuanced look at four people whose return to the living feels miraculous but provides no magical answers or happy endings in the long run. The body transfer serves easily as allegory for any major life change; we are called upon in life to remake ourselves at some point. Strength and resilience abound in this deeply felt debut." —*Shelf Awareness*

"Contemplative . . . Chiarella's entrancing prose and fully fleshed characters should garner widespread, enthusiastic praise."
—*Booklist*

"Chiarella's engaging writing creates so many haunting moments that readers will find themselves moving quickly through the story, as well as awaiting her next work. This is a novel about what it means to be human, with all the flaws and vulnerabilities that implies, and whether we can ever truly begin again."
—*Kirkus Reviews*

"What a stunning first novel! *And Again* was continually haunting me, and just when I thought I knew these characters, who are so vivid and singular in their desires and frailties, and yet so universal in their humanity, they surprised me once more until the pages were finished and I was left pondering our lives, our future, and how love still works. Jessica Chiarella has so much talent."
—Susan Straight, author of *Between Heaven and Here*

"It was the unique premise of *And Again* that pulled me in, but it was Jessica Chiarella's luminous writing that kept me reading page after page. The characters were gorgeously observed, the world fully believable and utterly absorbing. I never wanted it to end." —Rebecca Johns, author of *The Countess*

ALSO BY JESSICA CHIARELLA

And Again

THE
LOST
GIRLS

A NOVEL

JESSICA CHIARELLA

G. P. PUTNAM'S SONS
NEW YORK

PUTNAM
— EST. 1838 —

G. P. PUTNAM'S SONS
Publishers Since 1838
An imprint of Penguin Random House LLC
penguinrandomhouse.com

Library of Congress Cataloging-in-Publication Data

Names: Chiarella, Jessica, author.
Title: The lost girls : a novel / Jessica Chiarella.
Identifiers: LCCN 2021017432 (print) | LCCN 2021017433 (ebook) |
ISBN 9780593191095 (trade paperback) | ISBN 9780593191101 (ebook)
Classification: LCC PS3603.H536 L67 2021 (print) | LCC PS3603.H536 (ebook) |
DDC 813/.6—dc23
LC record available at https://lccn.loc.gov/2021017432
LC ebook record available at https://lccn.loc.gov/2021017433

Printed in the United States of America
1st Printing

Book design by Tiffany Estreicher

This is a work of fiction. Names, characters, places, and incidents either are the
product of the author's imagination or are used fictitiously, and any
resemblance to actual persons, living or dead, businesses, companies, events,
or locales is entirely coincidental.

For Matt and for Susan

When it most closely allies itself to Beauty:
the death, then, of a beautiful woman is, unquestionably,
the most poetical topic in the world . . .

—EDGAR ALLAN POE

THE LOST GIRLS

ONE

The world is full of lost girls. Scores of them. Girls who disappear into the night, who inject heroin and fall off the map, who love other girls and come home to find their parents have changed the locks. Girls who run away, girls who are taken. Girls full of sin, ones who like boys more than they love Jesus. Girls who are locked in basements and held until they give birth to more girls. The weight of them could drag a fleet of ships to the ocean floor. I know all about them. I've made it my business to know.

The recording plays over the sound system of the crowded theater in midtown Manhattan. The house lights are momentarily down, and onstage a logo of a retro radio mic, lit up in purple neon light, hangs above the proceedings. The crucifix in this particular church.

People look for some of them. Sometimes there are police investigations, sometimes candlelight vigils, volunteer phone banks, pleading parents on local news. No one bothers to look for others. If they were rotten, or ruined, or from the wrong place, or from the wrong sort of family, they are allowed to slip away. For others still, no one even knows they are gone. Because no one cared for them to begin with. My sister was lucky in that way, at least— she was loved. We looked for her. I don't think I will ever stop looking.

I'm standing at the bar to the left of the audience when a man sidles up to me. I can feel it without having to look, like a little static pulse at the hairs on my arm. The kind of sixth sense you develop when you've had a life like mine. It's my talent, the one my friends would tease me about in college, saying I was a little bit psychic beneath it all. I'm not, of course. I just pay attention.

By my count, my sister was the sixteenth girl lost in the hundred-year history of Sutcliffe Heights, Illinois. One of two kidnappings, though the other was a six-year-old, taken across the Wisconsin border by her father during a custody dispute in 1973. That girl was returned—unharmed—two days later, as soon as the police put out an APB. Most of the others were runaways. Factory girls who worked in Chicago's nearby industrial yards in the early forties. Bright teenagers sucked westward by the promise of California in the sixties. Nothing like Maggie.

He orders a drink, a SoCo and Coke, and it clings to the ice in his glass with the stickiness of syrup. I know who he'll be without looking at him. If he'd ordered an IPA, he'd be one of the young producers, with a tweed blazer and an encyclopedic knowledge of audio equipment. Whiskey, and he'd be talent, an investigative journalist with a voice for radio, a bit better at talking than he is at writing. But Southern Comfort and Coke? He's an investor, the sort of guy who puts up the funds for a production company because he read that podcasts are becoming increasingly lucrative and he doesn't have the head to navigate the tech industry.

> *Maggie was lost on October 16, 1998. She got into a car with a man. Perhaps she knew him. Perhaps he had simply spotted her walking home that day. These are the things we don't know. Even the car was a mystery, a sedan that might have been blue, or gray, or silver. It was twilight and difficult to tell, especially for an eight-year-old. Especially a scared one. I took off as soon as Maggie let go of my hand. She stayed where she was, and I ran for home. I ran because she told me to. It was the last thing my sister ever told me to do.*

Applause begins as the audio fades, and onstage, the words "JANE DOE, Nominee, Best Debut Series" appear on the screen. Above it, gold lettering reads "APA Annual Awards Gala" in a thin, looping script. It would all be elegant if the floors by the bar weren't still tacky from the rock concert held here at the venue last night.

"That one's going to win," the man beside me says, sipping from the little cocktail straw floating in his drink. He's wearing a blazer with a V-neck T-shirt underneath it. His hair, cut in a high fade, slick with expensive pomade, shines a bit too much in the light from the stage. The soft pudge at his waist rests on the buckle of his belt. I guess the gym can't quite keep up with all those sugary drinks.

"What makes you so sure?" I ask as he slides his forearm along the bar so it's almost brushing my elbow. It seems he has no intention of getting back to his seat any time soon.

It's the fucking dress that's the problem. Andrea's dress, the one she convinced me to wear, insisting that *someone* should still enjoy her pre-pregnancy clothes. The dress I took without even considering that I'm already three inches taller than my co-creator in flats, and I'm not wearing flats tonight. It's short in a way that implies intention, like I'm in a nineties legal drama, trying to make a point about fashion and empowerment. I've resolved to try to stand as much as possible through this interminable event, which leaves me hovering by the bar, ordering refills at a pace that's ambitious, even for me. And apparently looking as if I've been waiting all night for the attentions of a man whose chest hair is poking through his organic cotton T-shirt.

"Everyone loves a dead girl," the man says. "People eat that shit up."

"Missing. Missing girl," I reply, and the man gives a surprisingly high-pitched giggle, licking some errant SoCo from the webbing between his thumb and forefinger.

"She's totally dead. There's no way she's not dead." He takes a long pull on his drink. "And it sucks, because the show my company produces is so much better."

"Oh yeah? Which show is that?" I ask, my voice flat, as I sip my dirty martini. Here I am, a girl in a short dress with cropped hair, playing her part as much as everyone else. Wearer of smudged eye makeup. Drinker of astringent drinks. Cool and sly as a War-hol superstar.

"*The Chuck Hoffman Show*," he replies. I've heard of it. Chuck Hoffman tries to be Ben Shapiro but falls more into the Alex Jones tier.

"This is the award for Best Debut," I reply. "I'm pretty sure your show is in a different category."

"Whatever," the guy says. "It's still better. No dead girls."

"Maybe you guys just aren't trying hard enough," I reply, and the guy bursts into another round of tipsy giggles.

"That's cute," he says, as if it's a delightful surprise, my wit. He takes his forefinger and traces it, almost experimentally, down my arm. "You're funny."

I indulge momentarily in the fantasy of smashing my glass into the bridge of his nose. I wonder what would break more eas-ily, the stem of the martini glass or the soft tissue of his face. It would be bad timing, though. Onstage, a woman in a sequined dress approaches the podium. Words materialize on the dark screen above her as she reads off the names into the microphone:

BEST DEBUT SERIES

THEATER OF THE ABSURD

CHAMPIONS UNSCRIPTED

TELL ME LIES

JANE DOE

"What's your name?" the guy asks.

"Marti," I reply, because I can't use my go-to alias here and there's nothing else to do but go with the truth. A ripple of applause breaks out in the theater.

"See, what did I tell you?" the guy says.

"What?" I ask. He motions to the stage. On its screen, "JANE DOE, Winner, Best Debut Series" is written in that same gold script.

"So what do I get for being right?" He seems awfully proud of himself. I fish the olives out of my martini glass and down the rest of it, fast and hot in the back of my throat. Just for fun, I drop my skewer of olives, still dripping with brine, into his drink and give it a little stir.

"The fuck?" he says, his lips curling.

"Congratulations," I reply as I head for the stage to collect my award.

THE TRUTH IS, despite what I told Mr. SoCo and Coke, all of this actually did start with a dead girl. Jane Doe #4568, who arrived at the Cook County Medical Examiner's Office on April 17, 2018. Jane had been left on the street outside of Illinois Masonic Medical Center during an early-season thunderstorm, her veins full of heroin and mono-ethylene glycol—more commonly known as antifreeze—according to the medical examiner's report. She was between the ages of thirty and thirty-five years old. She'd had her tonsils removed, and she was slightly anemic, a condition that was likely the result of the fact that she'd recently given birth. She had a large tattoo of a lizard on her right thigh. And her hair was blond.

My friend Andrea and I were out to lunch when I got the call. If Detective Richards had still been with the CPD, he probably would have reached out himself. But he was already in his forties when my sister went missing and had retired from the force in

2017. The detective who'd replaced him—some kid who'd just been promoted from an undercover gig in Vice—apparently didn't see fit to pick up the phone when the body turned up, even out of courtesy. Luckily, I'd bought the receptionist at the medical examiner's office breakfast every six months for the past decade, so when the file came across her desk, she remembered Maggie well enough to reach out.

It was plenty, after all. The age, the hair, the tonsils. The receptionist didn't even know that Maggie's favorite stuffed animal was a blue iguana our father bought her at the Lincoln Park Zoo when she was seven. The other details were enough already to raise the possibility that Jane Doe could have been Maggie.

It was Andrea's idea to record what happened. She and I had worked together before, when she'd interviewed me for an episode of a true-crime podcast she'd produced for a few years. And we'd been friends since college, where she'd studied journalism and I'd dabbled first in criminology, then sociology, then finally landed on English literature. We were sitting at a French bistro in Lakeview when my phone chimed, because Andrea claimed that all she could keep down in her first trimester were croissants with lots of unsalted butter. She must have sensed it was about Maggie when I got up from the table to answer the call, must have seen it in my posture as I hovered near the bistro's sunny entrance, leaning against the whitewashed brick. Maybe I looked stricken. Maybe I pressed my hand to the door, unsteady; maybe it left a crescent of white fingerprints on the glass. I can't remember anything from that moment. Still, Andrea must have known, because she already had her recorder running, set on the table between us, when I returned.

"What's going on?" she asked, and then held up a silver-ringed hand to stop me from answering right away, ever the journalist. "I'm taping this. Just so you know."

"Yeah," I replied, feeling the blood begin to drop from my head, the prick of nerve pain in my fingers. As if I'd slept wrong and just awoken. "So, I guess there's a Jane Doe at the morgue."

I picked up my fork and speared a couple overdressed leaves of lettuce before I realized that there was no way I could bring them to my mouth, chew, or swallow. Andrea's dark lipstick disappeared as her mouth tightened.

"They think it's Maggie?" she finally asked. Straight to the heart of it, in a way that reminded me of the affinity between us. She knew that I would bristle at being coddled. That I was never more vicious than when I felt pitiable.

I listed off Jane's vitals. Andrea was familiar enough with Maggie's case to understand, to draw her own conclusions.

"So this is the first new development her case has had in . . . what?" Andrea asked.

"About eight years," I replied, thinking back to the last sighting, the last Girl Who Might Have Been Maggie. It used to happen more often, when her disappearance was fresh. But after twenty years, nobody else was looking for her anymore. Nobody knew what to look for. "She's got a tattoo on her thigh. A blue lizard, according to the coroner's assistant."

I remember how Andrea's hands flew to her face, pinkies meeting against her lips, the rest of her fingers splayed along her cheeks. Peering at me over her fingertips, lines appearing in her high forehead.

I knew what she was thinking. That I also had a tattoo of a blue iguana, a tribute to my missing sister's favorite toy, across the ribs of my right side. That surely, the world could not manufacture such a stunning coincidence. That it had to be her. Finally, my sister.

WE RECORDED THE six episodes that became our podcast in the week that followed, starting with the muffled recording of our conversation in the bistro. First with the intention of pitching it as a follow-up to the older podcast episode we'd recorded about Maggie's case, and then under our own steam, when the hours of material proved to be more than one episode could contain. We went through every detail of my sister's case and gleaned what we could from Jane's autopsy report. I spent hours on true-crime forums online, sharing details and soliciting advice from the other obsessed amateur detectives and retired policemen and bored college students who were all trying to solve unsolved cases. Andrea tracked down the hospital orderly who'd found the body and peppered him with questions while he ate his lunch at a little bakery across from Masonic. And I talked, just talked, for hours at a time. Speculated about why Maggie might have been lost for so long. About what it would mean if Jane Doe was really my sister. And what it would mean if she wasn't.

A lot of reviewers pointed to those discussions as the greatest strength of the podcast, after we released it. Listeners loved that it was my story as much as my sister's, an honest portrait of childhood trauma, a detailed rendering of survivor's guilt. I talked about the death of my father, my fractured relationship with my mother, my lingering nightmares. The years it had been since I'd allowed myself to hope for an answer to my sister's disappearance, because hope could be a terrible thing, apt to turn leaden inside you and drag you down if you let it. When I listened to the podcast, after Andrea cut together our conversations into a coherent narrative,

I couldn't even remember saying some of it. I couldn't imagine being willing to put into words the things that had been roiling inside me. I could hear it in my own voice, how desperate I was for an answer. Grappling for anything. I was still drowning, then.

Of course, I didn't tell them everything. There are things I couldn't bring myself to admit, about what happens when your sister gets into a car with a man and is never seen again. I was so young when my sister went missing that I grew up convincing myself that maybe she was okay, out there in the world somewhere. I imagined all the lives she might have been living, instead of imagining all the things that might have been done to her, as others did. When I was eight, I thought she might have run off to Hollywood to become a movie star. I would ride my bike to our town's little video store and search the faces on each VHS cover for my sister. Or there was the alien abduction. The amnesia, or the witness protection program, or the secret, star-crossed boyfriend. The vampire lover. The religious cult. An owl, stuffing our chimney with invitations to someplace magical. All the conceivable reasons a girl might disappear and never say goodbye to her sister. Never drop a line to her family. Never reassure them that she was okay, somewhere else.

I would never admit out loud that, twenty years later, I was still letting myself believe those things. Numbing myself against the darker possibilities, cobbling together a normal life in the negative space between thoughts of Maggie. It's what allowed me to finish high school, go to college, get married. To go through the motions of everyday life, pretending I wasn't always pulling against a hook dug deep into my chest, its tether rooted always to that moment in my eighth year.

And then there was the darker truth. That if Jane Doe #4568 was my sister, it would be the end of all that dreaming. It would cut short all the lives I had given her over the years. It would really be the end of her, in a way that she had ended for so many other people already.

Of course, the Jane Doe was not Maggie. A DNA test proved that. Since the prevailing theory at the time was that Maggie was a runaway, the CPD had never seen fit to take DNA samples from our family home. So instead they tested Jane's DNA against a swab they took from my cheek. Looking for a familial match. It took them three days to get the results, and we recorded the season's last episode when Detective Kyle Olsen, the hotshot detective newly assigned to my sister's case, called me with the results. I still haven't been able to listen to that final episode, even all these months later, even after the podcast became one of the most popular of the year. Even after all my hope brought me to the ground.

I don't want to hear the thread of relief in my voice in that moment, the part that's so obviously grateful that the mystery of my sister hasn't yet been solved. I don't want to hear what other people must hear—the gratitude of a woman who is still allowed to hope that her missing sister is alive. Because the truth is, I don't hope she's alive anymore. I don't think I'll see her again. My relief exists only in the part of me that would rather imagine her out there somewhere, living a life separate from mine, so I'm still allowed to hate her for it.

I'M STILL A little drunk when I head to the airport. It's early—barely six in the morning—and I made the mistake of attending both the award show's after-party at the hotel bar as well as the after-after-party at a watering hole a few blocks away. I only had time to stop at my hotel and change out of Andrea's dress—now rumpled and smelling of spilled vodka—before I had to catch a cab to the airport.

The award is heavy in my carry-on bag on the flight home. It's one of those pointy, engraved-glass affairs. The sort that looks like it could be used as a weapon, under the right circumstances. Like in the third act of a slasher film, to impale the killer in one last rally by the bloodied, willowy protagonist. I'm a little surprised they let me bring it on the plane.

There's no room for it in my apartment, of course. That place doesn't even have enough bookshelf space to hold my books, much less an award. A far cry from my old condo, with its three bedrooms and its built-in shelving and its vintage-Chicago stained glass above the back door. No, I'm sure the award will go in Lane's office; she's the head of our production company. Andrea certainly won't want it in her house, not when she's about to have a toddler . . . well . . . toddling around.

I sleep most of the flight, despite the man next to me, who is watching a superhero movie on his laptop with the volume all the way up, to the point where I can hear every explosion hiss out of his headphones. I take my phone out of airplane mode as soon as we touch down in Chicago, and a voicemail pops up on the screen. Eric. Saying something kind about my win, no doubt. Lane and Andrea and all the rest of the crew were on the phone the minute I was off the stage, but Eric has always been the sort to go to bed early, even on weekends. The sort to sleep in his running clothes and rise with the sun. He's also very good at being the compassionate ex, still supportive, still wanting the best for me. Despite the things I've done.

I'm too tired and far too nauseated to catch the Blue Line at O'Hare, so I opt for a cab instead. I figure my win has earned me at least one more ride expensed to our production company. After all, it's my sister's story that put them on the map.

My apartment is a tiny one-bedroom in Uptown, above a head shop and across from one of the best pho places in the city. The sort of place you move into when you walk out of your marriage and take nothing with you except your BA in English literature and your extensive employment history of tending bar. Eric offered me more, of course, because Eric has never been anything but incredibly decent. But I couldn't imagine taking any of his money with me when I left, considering that he was the only one working a serious job in the five years we were married. Since we split up, I've been bartending most nights at a goth club in Avondale while pushing the podcast by day. *The Best Debut Podcast of 2018*, I think as I unlock my apartment door and drop my bag— award and all—onto my thrift-store couch.

The apartment isn't so bad, really. It's just in an area of town where no one has yet bothered to start remodeling old buildings and rebranding them as "vintage." So the paint on the walls is yellowed and thick with a hundred years' worth of fresh coats between tenants, the hardwood floors battered and discolored in sections from damp springs and the occasional leaky pipe and the scrape of a century's worth of furniture. The windows are so heavy I can barely lift them and have to prop a block of wood under one to keep it open. The radiators popped and hissed and rattled all through winter, and now there's nothing but humid, hot air in summer. But it feels honest in a way that the granite countertops and Sub-Zero refrigerator of my condo never did. Or, perhaps, it's just that I'm more honest now than I ever was living in my pristine marital three-bedroom. That's the thing about grief. It forces you out of your habit of lying.

My phone vibrates in my pocket as I head to the kitchen, leaning over the sink and drinking water straight from the faucet, Brita filter be damned. The mixture of my hangover and the flight has left me feeling wrung out and achy with dehydration. My head feels like it's full of grit, the tight pain in my skull shifting slightly with every movement. Twin notifications pulse from my phone, and I glance at the screen to see a voicemail from a number I don't recognize and a text from Andrea: **Heading over. Munchkin in tow.**

I cross the room and drop onto the couch, resting my feet on my carry-on. One of the great advantages of this apartment is its proximity to Andrea. She shares a place nearby in Andersonville with her wife, Trish, an interior designer who was overjoyed at the prospect of this apartment, despite my nonexistent decorating budget.

"It just has so much potential," she said the first time she stepped into the space, which still smelled of eggshell paint and drywall dust. "Any designer can make an amazing space in a brand-new rehab with a twenty-thousand-dollar budget. This is a challenge," she said, her eyes gleaming. Already seeing what it could become, once she had her way with it.

So, for the past six months, Trish has scoured Chicago's secondhand stores and estate sales on my behalf, coming away with what has become a charming—if eclectic—collection of furniture. At first it seemed to be a ploy to get me out on weekends amid the fog of my crumbling marriage, but even since the podcast has taken off, Trish still texts me two or three times a month with pictures of pieces she's found across the city. A lime-green rolltop desk we could "easily refinish" or a china cabinet I'm certain would never fit around the hairpin turns of my building's staircase. And as much as I appreciate her help, I still wonder if she expects me to stay here, in this cheap, poorly maintained rental, for longer than I hope I will.

I text Andrea a thumbs-up emoji and listen to the voicemail. The fuzz of static on the line sounds for a moment like a recording might kick in, telling me I've been selected for a Hawaiian vacation. Or worse, it could be one of the calls I've been getting since the podcast aired. Blocked numbers, dead air. The faint sense that someone is breathing on the other end of the line. But instead a low, careful voice begins to speak.

"Hello, I'm trying to reach Marti Reese. I apologize for calling on your personal line, but your production company was hesitant to put me in contact with you, and I was able to get your number through a mutual friend. My name is Ava Vreeland, and I believe I have information about a crime that may be connected to your sister's case."

This isn't the first call I've received since the podcast began. At minimum, it's probably the fifteenth. Plenty of people have been reaching out with tips or suggestions, to the point where Lane has been talking about hiring a private investigator to track down as many leads as possible, considering that Andrea and I are suddenly in way over our heads. But something about the coolness, the depth, of this woman's voice sets her apart. She doesn't try to be tantalizing like the rest, the barely covered excitement in their voices evident as they tell me they "know someone who might be involved" or "could break the case wide open." She doesn't sound like she knows she's in competition for my attention with every other person who has a theory on what happened to Maggie. In fact, her diction sounds almost formal, like the overly professional cadence of an MBA on a job interview.

"I would love to set up a time to speak with you, at your convenience," she says. She leaves her number. I don't write it down. Sleep presses inward, making my attention drift. The calls—Ava Vreeland's and all the rest—can at least wait until I've gotten some rest. After all, Maggie isn't going anywhere. Maggie isn't anywhere at all.

CHAPTER
TWO

I wake to the sound of a key turning in the dead bolt of my front door.

"Marti?" It's Andrea's voice. I raise my hand from where I lie on the couch. A moment later, two sets of eyes are peering down at me. Andrea's, large and brown beneath a knot of curly hair atop her head, and Olive's, round and pale hazel amid a face pudgy with baby fat. I raise both my arms, making an exaggerated grasping motion with my fingers, and I'm rewarded with my prize when Andrea pulls Olive from her front pack and deposits her in my hands.

"So where is it?" Andrea asks.

"In my bag." I hold Olive aloft above me for a moment, watching her beam down at me until a little droplet of drool collects on her bottom lip, and I sail her down onto my stomach before it has the chance to drop onto my face. Olive giggles and squirms as I wipe her chin with my sleeve. She smells of peach skin and baby powder.

"May I?" Andrea asks, motioning to my feet, which I raise off my carry-on long enough so she can pull it from the couch and unzip it. She rustles in the tangle of my clothes and finds the award, in all its cut-glass glory. "I can't believe I missed this. I'm going to kill Trish for having to work." She pushes a stack of junk mail to the side on my coffee table and sits down. She's wearing overalls, in a way that only Andrea could wear overalls. In a way that makes them look chic, cuffed above brown leather work boots, over a green cap-sleeve turtleneck. Like she's come from a magazine shoot about motherhood, one whose aim is to sell denim. Or to make twentysomethings want babies.

"So how was it?" she asks.

"Stodgy," I reply, scowling theatrically at Olive, who grins back at me.

"Define 'stodgy,'" she says, using the throw on my couch to rub an errant fingerprint from the award.

"There wasn't anyone there I wanted to fuck," I reply, because I know the reaction I'll get.

"Please don't say 'fuck' in front of the baby." She whispers the word as she says it.

"My sincere apologies," I say to Olive, all seriousness. "There wasn't anyone there I wanted to . . . play with."

"See, maybe that's progress," Andrea says. "I seem to recall a time when there wasn't anyone you wouldn't . . . play with."

"Ouch," I reply. But it's true. Studies show the best way to ruin a perfectly good marriage is to fuck everyone in sight. And, since the Jane Doe, I've done the research to back it up.

"Have you eaten anything?" she asks.

"Ever?" I reply, though Andrea's mother-hen routine is one of my favorites.

"God, it's like I have two children," she says, rolling her eyes and getting up, setting the award reverently on the coffee table as she heads to my little kitchenette. I can hear her rustling around in my fridge and do a mental inventory of what she must be finding. A bottle of dry vermouth, a half-empty jar of Dijon mustard, a limp bunch of green onions, and about fifteen old takeout containers. Not exactly the makings of a gourmet meal.

"Okay, fuck it," she says, slamming the fridge. "Grab your coat, we're going to Pick Me Up."

"Andrea," I say with mock horror, clasping a string of imaginary pearls around my neck. "Don't say 'fuck' in front of the baby."

"THE PROBLEM IS," Andrea says as soon as the waiter drops off my tofu wings and Andrea's omelet, "you know all Lane cares about is how to sustain this." Olive clucks her agreement from her high chair. The table between us is covered with little cutouts of *Star Wars* characters beneath a coating of epoxy. The Pixies play over the murmur of conversation around us.

"Where do we even start?" I ask, spearing a piece of tofu and dunking it in ranch. God, I'm hungry, I realize with a suddenness that's actually surprising. "My phone has been ringing off the hook with people reaching out. Leads about Maggie's case."

"Mine too," Andrea replies. "But there's only so far we can take a case that's been cold for twenty years, and trying to craft a whole season out of these cranks is going to start feeling like squeezing water from a rock."

"So, what?" I ask. "We should pick an entirely different case?"

"Maybe," Andrea says. "This is Chicago. There are a lot of missing women out there. And a lot who aren't getting the kind of attention they should be. A lot whose families don't have the resources yours did."

"I know that," I reply. It's pure selfishness, I know, to ask Andrea to keep our focus on Maggie's case. Still, I can't stop thinking about last year, the prayer I offered up as I gave the DNA sample to Detective Olsen. *Give me another chance. One more chance to find her.*

Andrea folds her hands on the table in front of her. Even Olive pays attention, seeing the seriousness of her posture.

"I'm saying, maybe it's time to shift your focus onto something that won't take such a personal toll."

"I'm fine," I reply, though my voice is threaded with a raspy note. "Don't I look fine?"

I address my question to Olive, who gives me a smile and claps her chubby hands in affirmation. She's the only one who thinks so. I'm pretty sure I don't look fine, still recovering from the open bar and wearing yesterday's eye makeup. Wolfing tofu wings like a sleepwalker who has just awakened, ravenous.

"I'm just saying," I continue, "the Jane Doe fell in our lap. We weren't even looking for Maggie. Think of what we might find if we actually looked."

"Fine," Andrea says, though I can tell she's just placating me. I know that this will not be the last time we discuss shifting our focus onto a different case. But I'll take whatever little victory I can get, for now. "Then we need to find one lead. The most credible one, and start there. Do some research, pitch it to Lane."

"Good. Now, did I mention I didn't get much sleep last night?"

I ask, because my head is still throbbing a bit, despite the influx of food.

Andrea ignores me.

"If we start trying to tackle all of them at once, it's going to look like we're letting the mob direct the course of the show. We have to be deliberate about where we take this next, or the audience is going to drop."

"No sleep, actually. I got no sleep last night."

Andrea sets down her knife and fork, wiping her mouth on her napkin, and then leans forward, to the point where her overalls are dangerously close to brushing her eggs.

"Marti," she says, her voice so low it's like she's doing an Elizabeth Holmes impression. "I have an eight-month-old child who doesn't sleep through the night and depends on constant sustenance from my tits. I'm not allowed to have coffee. And I'm not allowed to drink. So I'm going to need you to suck it up right now with your hangover and your one sleepless night, okay?"

"Right, sure," I reply, giving her a halfhearted thumbs-up. "So what theory are we thinking? Mafia lady?"

I give Andrea a teasing grin, testing the waters. The Mafia theory is my personal favorite, from a woman who called four times, saying she was once married to a member of the Carlotti crime family. Saying Maggie looked just like the girl who was dating the youngest son of Vito Carlotti—*il capo di tutti capi* himself—back in 1998. Ignoring the fact that Maggie was definitely not commuting between Chicago and New York before she disappeared, the theory has a panache I like.

"I'm being serious," Andrea replies, unsmiling.

"Yeah, well, serious is the guy who thinks my sister starred in a Ukrainian porn video he helped film back in 2005," I reply.

Because that's the nightmare scenario right there, the one that drove my father into an early grave. Maggie getting into that car and being taken to a rest stop on I-94, forced into someone's trunk or the bed of a truck. Then into a shipping container. Into a pipeline of girls just like her, facilitated by the burgeoning mainstream use of the internet, chattel to be rented out to vicious, voracious men.

The sex trafficking theory is one that's been cropping up more and more since the podcast went viral. It's the most likely scenario, for a girl of her age, from her background, disappearing without a trace. That was the theory that pushed me from wine with dinner to vodka whenever I needed it. To stop my brain from moving. To keep me from imagining it.

"And let me tell you," I add, "after four days of looking through that shit? It's no wonder Eric and I stopped having sex."

"Come on, you guys stopped having sex long before that," Andrea replies. "But I get your point."

Olive starts to squawk from her high chair.

"Is she hungry?" I ask.

Andrea shakes her head. "Just fussy."

"Give her here," I say, and Andrea lifts the little grump, handing her across the table to me. I sit her in my lap, kissing the downy hair at the crown of her head. Breathing deep, letting her presence chase all the darkness out of me.

"So, fine. We need something more serious than Mafia lady," Andrea says as I bounce Olive on my knee. "But maybe avoid anything that has us looking for a needle in . . . you know."

"In the dark web," I say.

"Right," she replies, and I can hear the relief in her voice. Because I know that if there's anything worse than imagining

Maggie's disappearing into a shipping container, it's being the mother of a daughter, raising her with the knowledge that one day she will escape your grasp and the world will have her. And there will be nothing to do but hope she doesn't get lost.

"What about the runaway theory?" Andrea asks as Olive grips my hoodie's drawstring and begins to gum the knot in its end. It's the most popular theory behind sex trafficking, that Maggie ran from the cloistered, repressive wealth of her upbringing and disappeared into a world that would more readily accept her for who she was. The theory was bolstered by a report from a classmate named Lauren Price that she and Maggie had, on numerous occasions, had sex in the basement of Lauren's house. They had even discussed running away together, she said, though neither of those claims had ever been substantiated. She did report that they'd broken up a year before Maggie's disappearance, however, and had fallen out of touch, so the girl couldn't provide any additional practical information about Maggie's potential whereabouts.

But the runaway theory is a compelling one, especially considering all the terrible alternative possibilities. And it's made even more compelling by the fact that, in the weeks leading up to her disappearance, Maggie took large amounts of cash out of the checking account my parents had set up for her, totaling over six hundred dollars. No one knows what she did with the money, only that it wasn't left among the rest of her things in her bedroom at our house.

"Who's the man in the car, then?" I ask. Because the runaway theory depends heavily on my getting that part of the story wrong. That there wasn't a man driving that car. That Maggie was not afraid. That she did not tell me to run. And I, unfortunately, am not wrong about any of it.

"Okay, so what if she was pregnant?"

A riff on the runaway theory, and just as obvious in its naming. The argument that Maggie, despite being involved in a treacly high school–sweetheart relationship with a boy named Spencer Talbot at the time of her disappearance, had gotten pregnant by an older man. The man in the car.

The theory sort of ends there, though. Because regardless of the likelihood that a teenager could get pregnant in the sex-ed desert of the nineties, it doesn't explain why she dropped off the face of the earth after that. Which means that the pregnancy theory becomes the matricide theory, which leaves Maggie as dead as most of the others do.

"It's just basically 'the man in the car killed her,'" I reply. "There's no way she was afraid enough of disappointing our parents to run off to have a baby and then stay underground for all this time. Like, my mom's scary, but she's not *that* scary." I think of the last conversation I had with my mother, the two of us shouting at each other over the phone. About my divorce. About my airing of our family secrets in public. I've taken the brunt of my mother's anger and her grief, over the years. And if I—the accidental, late-in-life baby—am still standing, then Maggie, the golden child my mother planned her life around, would have been too.

"It always comes back to the man in the car," Andrea says, running her fingertips through her hair until they meet at the bun at the crown of her head. Andrea always plays with her hair when she's feeling stymied. The problem here is that, well, I'm the problem. Me and my inability to remember anything specific about the man, or about the car. Other than the fact that I hadn't ever seen either before.

"So we look into anyone who has called or written us with a theory on who the man is?" Andrea asks.

"I guess it's a place to start."

Olive, who has no doubt realized she won't be getting any food from the pull on my hoodie, starts to whimper on my lap. Within a moment, it's a full-on wail. "Oh god," I say, lifting the little girl and handing her across the table to Andrea. "DEF-CON One."

"Yeah, she's all cute and cuddly until she's screaming in your face," Andrea says, rolling her eyes. I can't tell if it's at Olive or at me.

THREE

I intend to sleep the rest of the afternoon, even though I've promised Andrea that I'll look through "the cranks," as we're calling them—the calls and emails from podcast listeners—before the production meeting next week. I'm working tonight though, and the last thing I can handle is tending bar on the little sleep I got on the flight home. The cranks will have to wait.

Except, the dreams have begun again.

She stands before me, as she was at sixteen. At my feet, something heavy or sharp. Just beyond us, in the darkness, a man. A man I do not recognize, whose face seems to shift the more I try to see it. He says nothing. He doesn't have to say a word; I know what I am to do.

I pick up the object at my feet. A piece of glass. A knife. A length of metal pipe. I put it to work. Cut her throat. Cave in her skull, soft as clay beneath the heavy crush of a brick. Tell her I have to. Tell her I have no choice. I have to save myself.

I never wake from them suddenly. The dream is so thick around me, it takes a long moment for me to pull myself back to the surface. My hair wet, my bed too. My body going haywire, reacting to the dream like it's an infection. Trying to burn it out.

I'm groggy and disoriented, like I'm not where I'm supposed to be, even though I'm in my own apartment. Sometimes I get this feeling like I'm always facing the wrong direction, as if the life I should be living is oriented a different way from the life I'm living now. Never more than when I wake in this little apartment, my semiconscious mind instead expecting the condo I shared with Eric or—worse—the house I grew up in. As if my mind is trapped somewhere back in a younger version of myself, unable to comprehend the path my life has actually taken.

I can't sleep anymore. Not after one of the dreams. So I pull on a ratty old T-shirt and shorts, grab my bike from my entryway, and carry it down the stairs. I head south on Broadway, the Saturday-evening traffic light, the air almost cool, the sky tinted orange with sunset. Skirting lingering cars, waiting to pick up the afternoon bar hoppers and the early dinner crowd. I pray for a breeze off the lake, something to lift the sweat from my skin as I ride, but there's nothing but stale, briny air around me. That's the thing about Chicago—fall air is like taking in a mouthful of cold sky, and in winter, in certain parts of the Loop, the air is redolent of chocolate from a nearby candy company. But in the summer, the whole city reeks of exhaust and asphalt and sewer gas. It's almost enough to make you wish for a chill.

There's always an evening cohort at my gym, even on weekends.

Shift workers, mostly. Blowing off steam, like me, before going in. Or decompressing after a Saturday spent on the clock, watching other people enjoy themselves. It's a boxing gym, very old-school, mostly men, not really what I'm used to. Still, it's better than nothing. I lock my bike out front and duck inside, where it's humid with sweat and the blare of hip-hop gives every movement a rhythm. I wave to Randy at the front desk and go to the mats to warm up. Just a few jumping jacks, some push-ups, mostly upper-body stuff, since I biked here. Then I wrap both hands and take my place at the heavy bag.

My fingers ring out in tingling pain with the first connections of my fists with the tight-stretched canvas. Then my arms, waking up, adding their protests bit by bit, as I get into a rhythm. Fast. I have to be fast, because I'll never be strong enough.

That's a lesson you learn quickly, as a girl. It's why I only box to keep fit, and to keep my edge against an opponent. Boxing isn't much use to me otherwise—mostly because it's a sport designed for men. Its rules even the playing field, advantage those with more weight and upper-body strength. It rewards the people with the most reach, the most power, when standing two feet from their opponent and trading punches. I only started coming here because it's close to my place in Uptown and because I can't afford my old gym anymore.

When I was with Eric, I used to go to Bucktown Jiu-Jitsu for training. The serious kind. To practice joint locks and chokeholds, to grapple on the mat, where the referee of a boxing match would never allow the fight to go. In a boxing ring, I don't have a prayer against any of the guys working out around me. That's why the sport has weight classes—put a heavyweight into the ring with someone my size, and you're not going to get much of a fight.

But take the rules away, take the fight to the mat and let me use speed and leverage and technique, and I could have them tapping out no matter their size if I'm fast enough. If I've practiced enough. Out in the world, being able to punch someone twice my size does me no good. There is no referee to determine if the fight is fair. Out in the real world, I have little hope of being able to do actual damage to a man who seriously outweighs me, no matter what the movies say. But can I take him by surprise, buy myself a few moments to run? That, I know how to do. Still, I think as I punch the heavy bag, it does feel good to just fucking hit something, sometimes.

I SPAR A little with one of the smaller guys in the gym and then grow tired—as I always do—of not being able to get close and sweep his legs out from under him. There is no moment of triumph for me in this. Even landing a punch is unsatisfactory. I want him helpless, not mildly bruised. I want to imagine that I could escape him, if I had to. If it came to that.

When I'm sufficiently wrung out, I turn to find a familiar man watching me from the side of the room. Coleman. I figured it was only a matter of time before I ran into someone from my old life, but still, seeing him out of context brings with it a rush of disorientation. The last time I saw Coleman, I had sex in the upstairs bathroom of his town house with a member of his dinner party's catering staff. I hope beyond hope he doesn't know about it.

He tips an imaginary hat in my direction when I catch him staring and approaches as I step out of the ring.

"I didn't recognize you at first," he says, motioning to my short hair. "It's been a minute."

"Yeah," I reply. Coleman, on the other hand, looks exactly the same. Broad and short, like most of the guys at this place. He is a guy who loves MMA and his job in finance equally, because he's the sort who always needs to feel like he's going into battle with someone, even when he's wearing a suit. I wonder how much Eric told Coleman about our separation. The two of them never struck me as particularly close—no more than casual work buddies. But still, perhaps Eric might have confided something, even in passing. I wonder how Coleman must see me now.

"How's work?" I ask.

"Good. We've been killing it this quarter," he says, as if he's relaying important information. "And Cindy's pregnant. Due in October."

"Congratulations," I reply. "You must be so excited."

"Yeah." He nods. "I asked Eric to be the godfather. I thought, you know, it might be good for him."

"That's really nice of you," I reply. I guess Eric and Coleman are closer than I thought.

Or perhaps Coleman overheard the little tiff Eric and I got into at that party last year, over whether I should have ordered a gin and tonic at the bar. Eric, being Patron Saint of Perpetual Responsibility, felt the need to quietly remind me of the statistics regarding fertility and alcohol consumption. At any other point in our marriage I might have rolled my eyes and acquiesced, if only to keep the peace around Eric's work buddies. Or looked him right in the eyes as I sipped my gin, daring him to get angry with me.

But this wasn't any other point in our marriage. This was two weeks after the Jane Doe showed up in the morgue. After I'd given the police my DNA, and then gone out for a run late that night and fucked our favorite bartender in the storeroom of our favorite bar. After I'd spent days lulling myself to sleep at night thinking of Detective Olsen and the clutch of attraction I'd felt when I met him at the police station. The man whose job it was to care about what happened to my sister. Whose job it was to try to find her.

In the days since Olsen had called to tell me that my DNA was not a match for the Jane Doe, I'd begun to realize that, no matter what I tried, I couldn't go back to the way I'd been before. By the night of Coleman's party, everything I'd been keeping at bay to appear normal—to act like the good wife, the patient daughter, the devoted, resilient sister—was slipping out through seams I'd once stitched so tightly. And Eric hadn't noticed yet. He didn't realize that I had spent the past two weeks wild and invincible with grief. Eight years old again, but no longer allowed to scream at the top of my lungs, to kick, to drop to the floor. If he'd known, he never would have insisted on going to the party that night. If I'd told him what had happened, he would certainly have watched me more closely.

But I hadn't told him. And he didn't notice. So instead, I handed him my gin and tonic and went out to the back patio to bum a cigarette from the group of waiters taking a smoke break.

I remember letting my posture slacken as I joined them, abandoning the air of age and respectability that came with putting on an expensive floral dress and attending a catered cocktail party with my husband. Trying to let them know that I was really one of them, underneath it all. After all, I'd bartended for three years in college to pay for jiu-jitsu, because my mother wouldn't have dreamed of financing something as unbecoming as martial arts training.

Two of them clearly didn't buy it, looking at me like I was a *21 Jump Street*–style cop, sidling up to a group of kids in hope of narcing on them. But the third one just grinned, pulling a pack of cigarettes out of his back pocket and extracting one.

"Of course, ma'am," he said with faux deference, offering it to me on his palm, like a tray of hors d'oeuvres.

"And a light?" I asked, adopting the lofty-eyebrowed posture of a finance wife. It was a windy night, and both of us had to cup our hands around the cigarette to get it to light. Hunched toward each other, as if we shared a secret.

"What's your name?" he asked when we finally leaned apart.

"Maggie," I replied, and the name came out of my mouth in a perfect white cloud.

I burn with the memory now, as Coleman crosses his thick, hairless arms. He probably rolls up his sleeves during business meetings, hoping the web of tendons beneath his skin will make him appear intimidating.

"Well, it's been a rough year for him," Coleman says, his usual friendliness cooling before my eyes.

He knows, I think. *At least, he knows enough to hate me.*

"I keep telling him he's better off in the long run," he continues. "So he can be with someone who'll appreciate him. You know, for all that he can offer a woman."

"I'm sure he will be," I reply, undoing the fastenings on my boxing gloves. "Better off."

"I keep telling him that only a fucking idiot wouldn't see him for what a great guy he is. Only someone really, irreparably damaged would treat him that badly."

"He's lucky to have such a good friend," I reply, and because I can't resist, I give Coleman a little bare-knuckled punch to the shoulder. Just a little too hard to be playful. "Good to see you, Coleman. Good luck with the baby."

"Go fuck yourself," he mutters over his shoulder as I elbow past him and head for the door.

THE BIKE RIDE home eases some of my anger, but not all of it. I stop for a moment after I lock my bike to my building's back gate, pulling out my phone, Coleman's voice like a pressure headache as I open the Find My Friends app. It takes only a moment for the blue dot to appear on the screen. Eric is at home. Our old place, which he keeps offering to sell and I keep insisting he keep. I don't want strangers in it, that place that was once a home.

I'm running late, so I shower quickly and make a box of macaroni and cheese that I find in the back of a kitchen cabinet. I eat sitting on my couch while simultaneously doing my makeup for work tonight, John Oliver talking in the background from my little TV. Something about Russell Crowe, though I'm not really following it. I have two distinct collections of makeup: One is the shimmery corals and dewy CC creams I collected during my marriage. I still wear them for things like production meetings, or when I really don't want to look as hungover as I am. And then there's the rest of it, the wine-colored lipstick and the pale powder and the black false eyelashes—the stuff I wear to the club. I apply it like a mask, like it's Halloween and I'm going as Morticia Addams, except the wig I pull on over my pixie cut is a dark chin-length bob with bangs. And then there are the clothes. Open my closet and you'll find a section that looks better suited to a dominatrix than a podcaster. Leather skirts and black lace camisoles and choker collars with heavy buckles. Tonight, I pick a lace shift with combat boots, fishnets, and a leather jacket. Morticia Addams meets Joan Jett.

It feels good, putting on this clothing, the makeup, the wig. It's why I took a job at a goth club when I could have applied for a gig at a bar closer to my apartment or an upscale place in Fulton Market, where the cocktails have eight ingredients and the tips would be massive. I wanted to do this five nights a week instead. Put on armor. It's the same feeling I used to get with other men, like the bartender in the storeroom or the waiter in Coleman's bathroom. The excitement of slipping into someone else's skin. Giving them a name that isn't my own. Becoming someone else.

It's no coincidence that I had a habit of giving Maggie's name to strange men. Even during the years when I thought I'd ridden myself of my sister, really there was nothing—not the things I enjoyed or the man I married or the clothes I wore—that was not touched by Maggie. Eric would tease me that my music taste was stuck in the nineties, but that was because all my favorite songs were Maggie's first. I never picked out a piece of jewelry or a blouse or a pair of shoes I couldn't imagine Maggie wearing. A therapist once suggested that without my sister, without the person I've spent my life trying to emulate, I was left craving the experience of creating an identity for myself. Of being a person separate from the mythology I'd built around her. And while I'm not generally a fan of therapists, even I have to admit that one was pretty perceptive.

There's no way I'll get to work on time if I take the bus, so I take an Uber and slip in through the side entrance, a metal door halfway down a ripe, muggy alley lined on both sides by dumpsters. Already, I can feel the pulse of the music in my chest, even before I make it to the front of house. It's crowded—par for the course on a Saturday night—and Marco, one of the other two bartenders on shift, gives me a dirty look as I set up behind the bar. He's wearing a mesh shirt and a ton of eyeliner, to the point where he could just as easily be bartending at Hydrate up on Halsted as here.

"So I guess you're such hot shit now you can't be on time to work, huh?" he says as I pass behind him.

"That's a funny way of saying 'congratulations,'" I reply, taking the order of a girl with enough hardware in her nose to set off a metal detector. Marco raises a perfectly waxed eyebrow at me.

Marco is a poet—a good one, by all accounts—who got his MFA at one of those extremely refined liberal arts schools out east. No one quite understands why he's working here, especially since there's a rumor going around that he's actually a certified, Mensa-grade genius. One of the security guards claims he's heard that Marco speaks as many as six different languages. And while Marco complains constantly about the nonexistent earning potential of the modern poet, part of me suspects he works here because he enjoys it. Because he can't imagine himself in academic committee meetings, on the tenure track somewhere, wearing a tie and running an indie lit mag and holding office hours. It makes him seem like a kindred spirit, someone else who landed here because being upstanding and normal feels beyond their reach.

"You've changed, honey," he says, pursing his lips like a disappointed schoolteacher. "Acting like a prima donna now that the money people take you seriously."

"Please," I reply, mixing the girl's old-fashioned. "I was late to work even before I was winning awards."

"True," Marco replies, and he seems oddly cheered by the

reminder. He busies himself at the bar for a moment, and when he turns around, he has a shot in either hand. "To your award," he says, and hands one to me. We toast, and I down it so quickly I can't register what it is, until the burn has given way to a taste that is very much like sticking your head into a men's locker room and inhaling deeply. I gag a little.

"Jesus," I croak. "Was that Malört?"

Marco's smile is so devious that I know the answer even before he replies. "Malört for you. Koval for me."

"Dick," I say, and receive a cackle and a slap on the ass from Marco as we both go back to taking orders. The club is dark and thrumming and hot, and it isn't long before that thing takes over, that particular flow I get into when performing a mindless task over and over, under the neon lights of the bar. Wearing a mask of black makeup. Music pounding around me. The darkness hiding all but the most vividly painted features of the people in the crowd.

"You're gonna give me a heads-up before you quit, right?" Marco asks as he passes behind me, heading for the register.

"You can't get rid of me that easily," I reply over my shoulder. "It all depends on what we put together for next season."

"Better get to work on it, then," Marco says, tapping the nonexistent watch on his wrist with all the easy bravado of a twenty-six-year-old with a graduate degree. Someone who doesn't envy my position, coming up on thirty and suddenly faced with the need to take my career seriously. An age when aimlessness becomes a liability.

He's right, I realize. I need to get to work. I think of the call I got this morning. Someone with information on a case that might be connected to Maggie. I remember it, the voicemail on my phone.

"Hey, I said vodka." There's someone leaning over the bar. A dude with what looks to be a fake lip ring and a bouffant haircut. Probably a schoolteacher during the week, who loves to think of himself as hard-core for wearing a lip cuff and a black T-shirt to the club on the weekends. Who's had a subscription to Suicide-Girls since college and truly believes that jerking off to girls with nipple piercings makes him edgy. But I realize that I'm making his cocktail with cranberry juice and Jäger, which would have been an unpleasant surprise, had he not been paying more attention than me. Still, I glare at him for his tone as I restart his drink.

As soon as I get a break, I bang my way back out to the alley, beyond the reach of the music, and listen to the voicemail again. Ava Vreeland. She would like to meet, at my earliest convenience. I check the time; it's already after midnight. Too late for any reasonable person to call someone they don't know. Her phone is probably on Do Not Disturb anyway—she sounds like the business type, a person who keeps regular hours. I decide instead to send a text, assuming that the likelihood of her calling me from anything but a cell phone is basically insignificant in this day and age.

> **This is Marti Reese, returning your message. I would like to meet and discuss your case.**

I'm just about to turn my phone screen off and head back inside when three dots appear beneath my message. Then:

> **Where are you now?**

A small alarm triggers within me, a flash of red I can almost taste. Anyone could be on the other end of that phone. It's not out of the realm of possibility that this is some sort of scam. That it's actively dangerous, even. I think of the calls I've been getting. Silence on the other end of the line, someone content to call me and say nothing. Satisfied with making it known that he is aware of me. Thinking of me. That he has taken notice.

Still, I text back.

Club Rush. Working my night job. After all, how dangerous could it be to meet someone here, of all places? One look at security and this person could be out on their ass.

On Wolcott?

Yes.

I can be there in 20. Does that work?

Sure.

She doesn't reply after that. Immediately, I'm less certain this was the right move. After all, what sort of person drops everything on a weekend, after midnight, to go to a goth club and discuss a cold case with a bartender-slash-podcaster? A crazy person, that's who.

I half consider leaving right then and there. Faking sick for Marco, catching a cab home. Letting the night play out however it will for Ava, blocking her number, and forgetting about her. Still, my curiosity lingers. I want to know what sort of person she is. I want to hear what she has to say.

She arrives in fifteen minutes, not twenty. I spot her right

THE LOST GIRLS

away, because she's totally wrong for this crowd and still walks in like she owns the place. She's wearing a dark trench coat over a black suit dress, a cluster of thin gold chains hanging around her neck, and what appear to be Christian Louboutin heels. Her hair is dark and curly, cut in a loose bob at her chin. Her lips are so red they look waxy and black under the lights. She's beautiful, in an excessively well-tended sort of way. And of course, she notices me as immediately as I have her, glancing toward the bar and making eye contact before I can stop gaping at her. Suddenly, I feel like a clown, in my makeup and wig. My cheap lace dress. I'm a small, excessively painted child, caught playing dress-up.

She threads her way through the crowd, moving surprisingly quickly for how packed it is. People seem to make way for her, whether they realize it or not.

"Marti?" she asks when she reaches me. I nod and motion her to the one reliably open barstool in the place, because it's situated behind a large concrete pillar to the side of the bar, cut off from the rest of the dance floor. She slips out of her coat before she sits, and I see there is a name tag clipped to the pocket of her dress: "Advocate Health Care System. Ava Vreeland, MD." I wonder if she's left it there for my benefit. Because it might make me trust her, to know that she's a doctor. To be honest, it does. Her eyes follow my gaze.

"Oh," she says, pulling the tag from her pocket and stuffing it into her purse, which is understated in the most expensive way. Gucci, I think. Ten years out of Sutcliffe Heights, and I can still recognize designer threads when I see them. "I was just catching up on charts when you texted."

I turn back to my counterpart at the bar.

"Marco, I need another five," I say, and get a very exaggerated eye roll for my trouble, but he waves me off. Marco is in his element when he's busy enough to get pissy with the clientele. I turn back to Ava. "Want a drink?"

I watch as she glances behind the bar, taking in our fare. This is clearly not the sort of establishment in which she's used to drinking. She probably usually orders Negronis, if she ever has occasion to sit at a bar these days. Or maybe an Aperol spritz.

"How about a whiskey sour?" she asks, probably trying to remember what she drank in college. I mix it with Maker's and a heavy hand. She raises her eyebrows when she takes her first sip. "It's good." She folds her hands on the bar. We eye each other for a moment, clearly both unsure of how to start. "First off, congratulations on your award."

"Thank you."

"Are you guaranteed a second season now?"

"I guess it depends on the material," I reply. "We're exploring a few different angles at the moment."

"And I'm one of those angles?" she asks, revealing a narrow gap between her front teeth. The sort of imperfection that's charming in a face like hers. Still, she can't possibly come from money, despite how expensive she looks now. Not with that smile. Where I'm from, orthodontia is the gateway to cosmetic surgery. Not just straightening, but all manner of filing and reshaping and the whitest of veneers if nothing else can be done. And no pediatric dentist worth his referral fee would have let a gap like Ava's go, if her parents could afford to close it. Which means they likely couldn't.

"The podcast has generated a number of leads," I say. "We're trying to investigate the most credible ones."

"And you've probably googled me and consider a board-certified ER doctor to be credible enough?"

I haven't googled her. That's the problem with acting on impulse, texting her before thinking it through. But I play it off.

"I also like the angle," I reply. "Instead of looking into a theory about Maggie, looking at a connected case. A kidnapping?"

Ava shakes her head. "A killing."

There's a pinch in my stomach, as if I've swallowed a tiny flake of glass, though it's what I suspected. I've kept up with all the local disappearances within the past ten years. If any were at all similar to Maggie's, I would know about them.

"Who?" I ask, pulling my phone out of my pocket, ready to take notes.

"A woman named Sarah Ketchum. She was strangled to death seven years ago and buried in LaBagh Woods."

"On the North Side?" I ask, because those woods ring a bell. Ava nods. I seem to remember hearing about that, a few years back. But I never looked into it seriously and can't remember why. "So what makes you think I'd be interested?"

"Google her," Ava says. I do, though the Wi-Fi in the club really, really sucks. It takes a moment for her photo to appear on the screen of my phone. It's a yearbook photo. Sarah is button-nosed with wavy blond hair, large eyes, and a smile full of straight, polished-white teeth. Those veneers, probably.

She's the spitting image of Maggie.

"She was eighteen when she was killed," Ava continues as I consider the photograph.

"No offense, but if you throw a stone in the town I'm from, you'll hit a girl who looks like this," I reply. Even I looked like that once, before I cut off my hair, before I grew shadows beneath my eyes.

"Ten years ago, if you threw a stone in the town you're from, you might have hit Sarah Ketchum," Ava replies.

I shake my head. "No women under the age of twenty-five from Sutcliffe Heights have been killed in the past two decades." I know this, cold. I have made it my business to know this.

"That's because the police report said she lived in Palos Hills," Ava replies. "Southwest suburbs," she says, when I furrow my brow. "Because after her parents divorced, she lived there with her mother. Went to high school there. But she spent every other weekend and half the summer staying with her father."

"In Sutcliffe Heights?" I ask.

"On Galley Road," she replies.

My heart gives a strong judder beneath my breastbone, making me cough, momentarily breathless. "Galley Road."

"Forty-six oh three," she replies. I reach for the nearest bottle, which proves to be gin, and pour myself a shot. I take it quickly, in hopes that it will shock my brain back into functioning properly. Ava sips her whiskey sour through its tiny cocktail straw.

"Jesus," I say, and pour myself another shot. There are three balconies in my childhood home, all overlooking the back of our property, which is a full acre of woods and grass. If you stand on any one of those balconies and look northwest, past the Miller house and over the estates on Sullivan Way, you can glimpse the roofs of the houses on Galley Road through the trees. "Why haven't I heard about this?" I ask.

The girl would have been only four years younger than me. LaBagh Woods isn't exactly close to Sutcliffe Heights, but it's still on the North Side, so it should have hit my radar. The only reason I wouldn't have followed the case would be if it had already been solved.

"Wait, do they have her killer already?" I ask as a vague framework begins to take shape in my mind. I remember watching the news of the arrest from my dorm room at Northwestern.

"He was convicted of her murder and sentenced to life in prison without the possibility of parole," Ava replies.

"But he was a kid, wasn't he?" I ask, conjuring an image of the man being marched into the Cook County courthouse in handcuffs.

"Yes," Ava replies. "He just had his twenty-fifth birthday."

"So there's no way this case could be connected to Maggie, regardless of where Sarah Ketchum is from," I say, feeling the shard dissolve in my stomach. The man who killed Sarah Ketchum would have been four years old when Maggie disappeared. Disappointment follows, rather than relief. That's how it is for me, these swings between terrible excitement and desolation. Never solace. Never a warm, nourishing breath.

"That's what the police say as well," Ava replies.

"And what do you think?" I ask, because she is so impassive, she watches me with an almost theatrical calm. I can tell that part of her is enjoying this, this slow unveiling of facts, my reactions to each. Like the town gossip, reveling in every bit of shock and horror as she relays her stories to her neighbors.

"You didn't google me, did you?" Ava asks.

"No," I reply, because what does it matter? "I've been a little busy."

"Well, I think they have the wrong man," she replies, matter-of-fact. "I think whoever killed Sarah Ketchum is the same person responsible for your sister's disappearance. And I think he's still out there."

"That seems like a stretch," I say, but Ava is already shaking her head.

"Consider it. Two teenage girls, about the same age, the same physical type. Both of them taken by a man with a car. Both of whom lived, at least for a time, within a square mile of each other. What exactly are the odds of that?"

"Fourteen years apart?"

"There could be a dozen explanations for a gap like that," Ava replies. *A gap*, I think. A gap in a pattern of behavior. A killer with a pattern of behavior—the holy grail of every citizen sleuth on the true-crime forums I follow. Looking for order in the violent chaos around us. How seductive an idea.

"Hey." A voice behind me cuts between us. I turn to find Marco, glaring at me. "Are you ever getting back to work? Or do I need to call someone to cover your shift?"

"Fuck off, Marco," I say, but with no real malice. "Five more minutes. And I'll close by myself."

"Next Saturday too," he says.

"Fine," I reply, and with a triumphant grin, Marco goes back to the other end of the bar. Ava takes another sip of her drink.

"I know it sounds like a stretch," Ava says. "But if I'm right, it means that an innocent man is spending his life in prison, and that it's only a matter of time before another girl gets killed."

"Did you know her?" I ask. "Sarah Ketchum?"

"Not really."

"Not really? So then why do you know where she spent her summers?"

Ava toys with the cocktail straw in her drink, drawing it in lazy circles through the fast-melting slivers of ice in her glass.

"Because," she says, a sheen in her eyes catching the neon lights above the bar, a wash of green. "Because my baby brother is the one in prison for her murder."

FOUR

I wake to the alarm on my phone, which I can't remember setting. It's Sunday, so by all rights I should be sleeping in. Instead, a bright tone sizzles through the air by my left ear, and I have to stanch the impulse to throw the entire thing across the room to quiet it. This is the main problem with not having an actual alarm clock. There is no snooze button to bang on, only a lit pane of glass. The idea of a button. Not a sufficient place to put my rage at being awake at eight a.m. on a Sunday, when I went to bed after three. After I told Ava that I wasn't in the business of going out on a limb for men convicted of murdering women. After she left, and I spent the rest of the night alternating between mixing drinks and googling the case. After I closed the bar by myself, which took easily twice the time it would have if Marco had been helping. But now I remember, my presence is required in Sutcliffe Heights, at the quarterly luncheon for the Margaret Reese Foundation, the charity that has become my mother's sole purpose in life since Maggie's disappearance.

I try not to dwell on the woman my mother was before Maggie went missing. How graceful and warm she once was. How unprepared she'd been to learn that the world contained more than what she'd seen of it. That it was not a place of order and decorum. Or, that its order was that of a meat grinder, eating everything it was given and spitting out a bloody, crumbling mess. I was lucky to learn that lesson early. My mother had further to fall; the damage was arguably greater.

She grew up in Lake Forest, Illinois, where the oldest of the old Chicago money have their estates. When she married, she and my father—a physics professor at Northwestern—received her trust fund and bought our family home in Sutcliffe Heights. Our house was modest for the area—a mere $3.5 million, four-bedroom affair. Farther north on Lake Michigan's shore, our neighbors boasted estates that went for double or triple that. Maggie and I grew up assuming we were middle class, especially compared to our grandparents. As if anyone but a wealthy few in the entire state of Illinois lives just a short walk from a neighborhood beach. The third coast was ours, ours alone, because there was so little of it and our lives were so terribly charmed.

Still, Sutcliffe Heights's proximity to Chicago made all the difference when it came to the response to Maggie's disappearance. Everyone knew that merely a fifteen-minute ride on the Union Pacific Metra line could have deposited Maggie within the city limits. Half an hour and she could have gone all the way to Ogilvie station, in the living, breathing heart of the city, with its arterial Amtrak lines, which could have taken her anywhere. If she ran. If she'd chosen to disappear.

That was what the detectives from the Sutcliffe Heights PD thought, when they interviewed us in our living room the night Maggie disappeared. Already, they were more interested in Maggie's behavior—the chance that she was simply a runaway—than in the man I'd seen. Perhaps it wasn't a kidnapping at all; perhaps they could all just go home.

In that way, at least, the media was an ally. There was nothing more sordid or tantalizing than a rich white girl snatched from the woods near her family's home, so that was the narrative they ran with. There were already news vans outside our house, spotlights frosting our front windows, when the police interviewed us that night. Looking back, I know that none of it was luck. I know that the police and the media took Maggie's disappearance seriously because of who we were and where we were from and what she looked like. But still, it is difficult not to feel fortunate, after seeing two decades' worth of women disappear without even a ripple through the city's consciousness, that there was any response at all. Even if all the police wanted was to label her a runaway and move on with their lives.

"Does she have any friends in the city?" one of the detectives asked, writing in a narrow notepad. My mother shook her head. "Anyone that you may not know about? Did she ever take the train into the city by herself?"

"She's sixteen. She isn't allowed to take the train without one of us," my mother said, motioning to my father with a cigarette dangling between two of her fingers. I'd never seen my mother smoke inside the house before. It was unprecedented behavior, and it scared me, to the point where I considered narcing on my sister. About the times when she'd put on enough makeup to look eighteen, pulled on a Northwestern sweatshirt over her party clothes, and joined her friends in a lip-glossed pack for the quick Metra ride into the city. Admitting that she'd broken the most fundamental rule of our childhood—to never breach the borders of Sutcliffe Heights—seemed like the most complete betrayal I could imagine. But then, there was the man in the car. My sister letting go of my hand. Telling me to run.

"She does," I said, interrupting the adults in their conversation. "She goes into the city all the time."

I still remember the feeling as the words slipped from my mouth, even all these years later. The feeling that I was ruining Maggie, somehow, in the eyes of my parents. And they were so angry at her that they were even angrier at me, because she was gone and I was the one left who could be punished for her recklessness. It was the first taste I got—my mother shouting at me in front of those detectives, ash dropping from her cigarette onto our white carpet—of what life would really be with Maggie gone. It was the first glimpse I had of the woman my mother would become.

Now, six months after our latest screaming match, it seems almost silly that I'm still required to attend events for the foundation. Especially since the impetus of the argument—the podcast's popularity, my separation from Eric—has only magnified in the ensuing months. And because my mother responded by cutting me off from the family trust, since threats of grounding, sending me to my room, and military school were no longer viable options for a twenty-nine-year-old.

But still, even with no family money to lose, even with no careful détente with my mother to sustain, I'm not allowed to miss a family photo op. That would be the truly unforgivable offense, and I'm not quite prepared to torch what little remaining goodwill I have with the little family I have left. No matter how tempting a few more hours of sleep would be.

When I glance at the screen of my phone, there's a voicemail from a blocked number. A voicemail left at precisely three thirty a.m. The same time as the others.

I know, even before I listen to it, what it will be. A thick sort of silence. Menacing. The message is thirty seconds long. I delete it without listening to it.

I take a shower, trying to warm myself after the chilling effect of the voicemail, and then search through the family-approved side of my closet for something to wear. I sold most of my old clothes—all Reformation and Everlane and Anthropologie, the necessary wardrobe for the young wife of an investment banker from Kenilworth—to cover the security deposit on my apartment and the attorney's fees from my divorce. It was an outlay of cash that I had to fight Eric to keep him from paying himself, as there was no way I would allow him to pay for the divorce that I'd caused. Still, had he known I was paying with my own money and not my family's, he never would have made the concession.

I finally settle on slouchy tweed trousers, a sleeveless silk blouse, and ankle boots, though I'm not at all confident that this isn't the same outfit I wore to last quarter's luncheon as well. There's just something about the fact that both Maggie and I are wearing dresses in every photograph hanging in my mother's house that makes me desperate to wear pants.

I catch the Metra at Ravenswood, and the experience is as disorienting as ever, like retracing the steps of my adolescence, which was always moving in the opposite direction. Pulled into the city, not slipping away from it.

It's not a long journey, after all. Sutcliffe Heights is the first truly wealthy suburb north of Chicago. Of course there is Evanston, with its university and its beautiful old mansions, but Evanston is the sort of place where you still have to be careful when you walk alone at night. It's still a place where you can get a studio apartment for under a thousand bucks a month, where concrete underpasses are tagged with graffiti, where the people who live on your block could be any race, any creed, any religion. And it has not one but—horror of all horrors—seven L stops. Sutcliffe Heights is blessedly safe from all that *diversity*—a word as bad as a curse there, unless of course you are extolling the virtues of *diversity of thought*, which has become a popular sentiment among Chicago's country-club intelligentsia. Sutcliffe Heights is fenced in by money, beyond the reach of the CTA, made up of expensive houses separated by woods, lined up on the lakeshore. The only place the children of Sutcliffe Heights hear Arabic spoken is in the classrooms of their private school, where it is offered alongside Latin and Mandarin and French. It's a cesspool of wealth and privilege, and Maggie understood that at a much younger age than I did. It was why she loved Chicago the way she did.

She wasn't the only kid from Sutcliffe Heights who took the occasional joyride downtown. We were all latchkey kids, even though none of our mothers worked. My mother was never home, always had a charity event to plan, or a luncheon with friends, or a spa appointment. It was the nineties, after all, before it became a cardinal sin to leave your kids unattended during summer vacation. It wasn't only that the world felt bigger back then—before the internet and cell phones and social media shrank everything to a mere moment's availability. It felt looser. Before a text message could pin you down, hold meaning no matter if you chose to acknowledge or ignore it. Back when a ringing phone could be missed, and you would never, ever know who was calling. We told time by the sun, during those summers. If we forgot our wristwatches, sundown was dinnertime. As long as we showed up when the table was set, no one ever asked where we'd been.

Maggie started babysitting me when she was ten years old, and by the time she was sixteen, she was my tour guide into the vast urban sprawl of Chicago. I was her willing apprentice, in all things. She taught me the art of slipping away, and I made myself in her image. Six months before she disappeared, she led me onto the Metra and into one of its tepid bathrooms, sliding the door shut behind us and locking it. We waited five minutes in half-giggling silence until we reached the Davis stop, and then Maggie led me back out—unseen by the conductors—into the concrete and weather-beaten brick of Evanston, where she bought us L passes and took me downtown on the Purple Line.

We walked all the way to Navy Pier, where Maggie bought an ice cream for me and a pair of seashell earrings for herself, in the clot of vendors and tourists packed onto the long stretch of the pier. She smoked a cigarette as we watched seagulls circling, diving down to pick discarded French fries off the rocks. It was the most potent feeling of freedom I'd ever experienced in my short life. I looked at my sister and knew there was nowhere we couldn't go. I would follow her anywhere. That day is still my high-water mark, the measure against which I compare any happiness that may wash into my life. I do not expect that measure to ever be met.

Now, it takes no time at all for the low brick buildings of Rogers Park and Evanston to give way to the greenery of the North Shore. As if there is a line drawn between the two, where the concrete stops and the forest begins. And then the automated voice announces Sutcliffe Heights, and the train's double doors open to the breezy sunshine of the northern suburbs. I step off the train, and there is Wilson with the Mercedes, waiting to drive me home, despite the fact that I haven't called ahead to announce which train I'd be taking. He opens the door for me before I even reach the car.

"How long have you been waiting here?" I ask, slipping into the cool leather interior. The front seat, because Wilson knows I won't sit in the back, no matter how much he gently insists.

"Not long," he replies, an impassive, knowing smile on his face. Deep lines around his mouth, at the corners of his eyes. His nose spotted with the filaments of broken blood vessels. Somehow, I always remember his looking this old, this weathered.

"Hours?" I ask.

"Not hours," he says before he shuts me in, rounds the front of the car, and gets into the driver's seat.

"Liar," I reply, holding up the book sitting in the center console of the car. *David Copperfield*, its dog-eared page nearly halfway through the paperback.

"I started it a few days ago," he says as we pull out into the sparse Sunday traffic.

"Sure you did."

"Would you have preferred it if she left you to walk?"

"It's a ten-minute walk to the house. I think I could have managed."

"So you wouldn't have been angry at her for that too?" he asks. I scowl at him in response.

"You know, Carla and I listened to your podcast," he says. "We thought it was very well done."

"I'll make sure not to rat you out to Mom," I reply, though it's surprisingly good to hear praise coming from Wilson. He and his wife have been employed by our family since Maggie and I were kids. Carla was our cook, our sometimes-nanny, our housekeeper. Wilson drives and takes care of the grounds and takes care of Carla. So it's good to know that someone else who knew Maggie— someone else who loved her, and who felt her loss acutely— approves of my work.

"Don't be silly," he replies. "I told her the very same thing."

"You told my mom you listened to my podcast?" I ask.

"And that I thought it was very well done."

"You're braver than I am."

"She's the one who asked me to listen," he says, and the sentiment is almost funny, it's so jarring. I turn in my seat so I'm facing him.

"My mother told you to listen? My mother. Samantha Reese. Blond, about five foot eight, posture like she's having an affair with her chiropractor?"

"The very same," Wilson replies. "She asked me to listen, and to let her know if there was anything on it potentially compromising about the family."

"Ah, I see," I say. "I guess she doesn't have time in her schedule for things like that. Protecting the family honor from her traitorous daughter."

"You're too hard on her," Wilson says. It's a familiar refrain, as if he's waiting for me to finally reach the age where I forget all the ways in which my mother made my childhood difficult. "She was afraid it would be too upsetting for her, to listen herself," he continues.

"She didn't have to live it in real time," I say. "She didn't have to talk to the person who found the body. She didn't have to give her DNA." Most days, I try not to think of that morning, the backs of my legs sweating against the plastic chairs at the Twenty-Fourth District police station. Trying to puzzle through the tangle of what to pray for, waiting to give DNA that might match the Jane Doe's body.

I was certain that praying for my sister to be dead, just so I would finally have an answer, was likely something God would disapprove of. I could pray for forgiveness, for spending so many years trying to forget my sister, trying to forget the questions that remained unanswered as I went to wine tastings with Eric and trained at the gym and watched Netflix with Andrea.

It finally came to me when Detective Olsen knelt before me, his tie loose and shirt unbuttoned at his throat, his eyes already apologetic as he peeled open the packaging of the DNA test. An impulse rang out in me like the shuddering peal of a bell. The desire to be comforted by men. The comfort I could only draw from dancing at the edge of the abyss I feared the most: being defenseless, daring them to hurt me. The pleasure so much more acute when they did not.

"We'll have the results in a few days," he said. "I'll call you. You don't have to come back down."

I nodded, unable to talk.

"Hang in there, okay?" he said, a hand on my shoulder. Eyes concerned, as if he could guess all the things I was about to do. Like that very night, unable to sleep, when I would go for a run and end up in the back storeroom of Mathilde's bar, having sex with a man who was not Eric for the first time since I was twenty. Or a few weeks later, when I would be pressed against a sink by one of Coleman's caterers. Or all the others who would follow.

But in that first moment with Detective Olsen, in that clarity of wanting, I remembered what to ask for. *Give me another chance*, I prayed to whoever would listen. *Give me another chance, I won't forget her again.*

"You think your mother wouldn't have done those things if they'd asked her?" Wilson says, turning down the long, tree-lined street that leads to our house. I try to imagine Wilson driving my mother into Rogers Park, waiting with her in those plastic chairs for Detective Olsen and his DNA test.

"I think there's a reason I got that call," I reply, remembering all the times I took the receptionist from the medical examiner's office to breakfast in the past ten years. To keep Maggie fresh in her mind. To make sure she had my number when she needed it. "It's because I was the only one still looking for her."

Wilson is silent for a moment. And I think I've won this round, until he continues, softly. "She looks, in her own way."

"Right, by hosting five-hundred-dollar-a-plate lunches for Maggie's foundation."

"And inviting that reporter from the *Tribune*," he counters.

"Who writes for the style section. But Mom wasn't too keen when the podcast got three column inches on the front page."

Wilson's silvery brow twitches. This has clearly been a topic of conversation in the house, though I can't tell what side he's taken or who he's been arguing with.

"Your mother would prefer if you didn't investigate so . . . publicly."

"She would prefer if I didn't share details about Maggie publicly. Like the fact that she might have had sex. With another girl."

"It's not that," he says. "The thing that keeps her up at night now is you living alone in that city. Knowing the man who took your sister might also be there."

This, too, is a familiar worry. Of my mother's. Of Andrea's. Of mine. The more I become a public figure, the more likely it is that whoever took Maggie will notice me. I think again of the calls. This morning's voicemail makes five of them in the past month alone.

"So why did she cut me off?" I ask, to deflect the fact that this line of reasoning sharpens the pulse in my throat. "Because I'll tell you, I could be living in a place with much better locks right now."

"She was hoping you would come home," Wilson replies as we turn off the main road and pull down the tree-lined driveway of my childhood home. "I think she's still hoping that."

"Well, someone is going to have to disabuse her of that notion." I raise my eyebrows at him theatrically until he notices.

"Don't look at me," he says, a hint of a laugh in his voice.

THE EVENT IS already under way as I step inside, the smell of perfume and fresh flowers thick in the air. Lilies, my mother's favorite. Funeral flowers, my sister would have joked. I'm barely in the front door when Jasper, my grandmother's Pomeranian, skitters up to greet me. I scoop him up and let him lick my chin as I tuck him under my arm, navigating around the groups of women in designer suits chatting in the living room, searching for my grandmother. She's easier to spot now, in her wheelchair, sitting on the back deck. And I'm prepared for it, when she turns and catches sight of me, that moment of disappointment that's always there. That the granddaughter who has crept up behind her, the one Jasper leapt from her lap to greet, is not Maggie. I don't bother to remind her that Jasper never met Maggie, that it was Pepper we used to play with as little girls. I've learned the lesson well by now, that there will never be a time when my grandmother is entirely happy to see me.

"You look like that girl. The one whose husband tricked her into giving birth to the antichrist," she says, eyeing my hair as I lean down and kiss her powdery cheek, depositing Jasper back in her lap.

"Mia Farrow?"

"That's the one."

"Well, good," I reply. "Feel free to spread that rumor when people ask why I'm getting divorced." I don't tell her the truth, that all my life I kept my hair long because Maggie's was always long. That I never wanted to be anything but beautiful in the way my sister was. Until I could no longer stand it, being a living memorial to her.

"Can you imagine? Your mother would be scandalized." She gives a small chuckle, amused by her own wickedness. After all, this is not her crowd. While my mother's family has always been wealthy, my grandmother was a postal worker who raised my father mostly by herself. She received her money, her family connections, and her status in much the same way my father did, through his marriage to my mother. It has always been a point of affinity between the two of us—while my father took to his marital wealth as if it were a birthright, my grandmother has always been uncomfortable in these circles, just like I have.

"Not as much as if you offered to do readings for them," I reply, though I know I'm poking the bear a little.

"This crowd?" my grandmother asks. "It would be like squeezing water from a rock. What am I going to do, give them stock tips?"

My grandmother is aware that I don't much believe in that sort of thing, tarot or tea leaves or my grandmother's brand of magic, which is much more the daytime TV variety. I once found a newspaper article from the eighties that mentioned her being brought on as an investigative consultant with the CPD on the case of a missing five-year-old. The boy had been found alive two days later, though the article didn't go so far as attributing that result directly to my grandmother.

And I still remember running home the night Maggie disappeared and finding my grandmother already at our house—an aberration, especially on a weeknight. Already asking, when I was barely through the door, still catching my breath and choking back tears, what had happened to Maggie. Before my parents even realized anything was wrong, my grandmother already seemed to understand. But I have no interest in hearing what she has to say about Maggie anymore. Because whatever peculiar talents she might have, they've never done us any good in finding my sister.

"Where's Mom?" I ask, glancing back through the French doors and into the open-concept kitchen. Everything is pristine, white tile and granite countertops and cream-colored cabinets paned with glass. Because the caterers are undoubtedly prepping the food downstairs in the basement's wet bar, hauling trays up and down the narrow back staircase to the dining room.

"She breezed by about a half hour ago. Asked if I wanted a drink. Actually laughed at me when I suggested she should bring me a gin rickey, and now I haven't seen her since."

"You're not supposed to be drinking, Grandma," I chide. My grandmother has been in a wheelchair since she had a minor stroke about a year ago, which left her on a perpetual course of blood thinners. Since she could no longer manage the staircase in her Jefferson Park two-flat, she's moved into my mother's first-floor guest room, and the two of them have been at each other's throats ever since. I actually feel a little bad for Mom, considering my grandmother is much friendlier when she has a couple drinks in her, and her medication has kept her sober for the better part of the last year.

"Please, you think a doctor knows more about what's going to happen to me than I do? Believe me, honey. When I go, it's not going to be because I got a little too tipsy over lunch."

"I'd prefer not to think about it," I say, giving Jasper's head another scratch and squeezing my grandmother's shoulder. But she catches my wrist as I straighten up.

"You'll find her, you know," she says, her voice low, her eyes intent on mine.

I don't want to talk about this, about Maggie, about any of it. I don't want to ask her the question I'm desperate to answer: Alive, or dead? So I just nod.

"I know," I reply, giving her arm a squeeze. My grandmother waves me off, and I slip back inside, nearly colliding with a wide-eyed caterer as I head for the back stairs. I make my way up without turning on a light, though the staircase has always been dim, relying only on the ambient light from the kitchen and the upstairs hallway if the chandelier suspended above the steps is switched off. Still, an entire childhood sneaking up and down those steps after dark has left me with the ability to climb them blindfolded if necessary.

The upstairs is quiet, despite the running current of conversation downstairs. The door to the master suite is open, so I kick off my shoes and pad across my mother's pristine white rug, passing her perfectly made bed and its four hundred pillows—compliments of Carla's morning sweep—to the balcony at the back of the house. I step out onto the sun-warmed concrete, peering at the map of Galley Road I pulled up on my phone. From where I stand, I can see a line of three houses, one off-white, one slate gray, and one pale yellow, through the break in the trees behind our house. But 4603 is blue, just too far to the west of the yellow house to see from here. I find I'm disappointed, though really, the proximity is all that matters. That Sarah Ketchum lived so close to the house where Maggie and I grew up. That two girls who lived within blocks of each other would both be plucked out of their lives, would both have met violent ends. It strained plausibility to imagine it could be coincidence.

The truth is, I've been thinking about Sarah Ketchum all morning. Despite the fact that I told Ava I wasn't interested in her story. Despite the fact that I told her I didn't care about her brother and wasn't interested in turning my podcast into a second-rate knockoff—just another true-crime dive into the case of an innocent man behind bars, as if the murdered girl were nothing but a set piece in the larger story of *his* wrongful conviction. As if Sarah were simply an inconvenience in his life, and the injustice of his story should supersede the injustice of hers. After all, there has to be someone in the world who cares only for the girls, who has no interest in solving their cases to the satisfaction of the courts but wants only to know what happened. To finish their stories, instead of simply tacking them on to the fates of the men who may or may not have killed them.

Still, I cannot deny the bigger picture here. If Ava's brother did not kill Sarah Ketchum, it means that Sarah Ketchum's murder might be linked to Maggie's disappearance through more than coincidence. So taking up Ava's case, working to exonerate her brother, could be a means to my own ends. Of figuring out who took Maggie from us. Of figuring out what really happened to Sarah.

My eyes adjust slowly as I go back inside; everything around me is foggy with the shadow images the sunlight has burned onto my retinas. I step into the hallway and peer at Maggie's bedroom, its door always closed. My room, on the opposite side of the hall, is empty of belongings. Only a bed, a dresser with some old spare clothes inside, and a desk against the window remain. But Maggie's room still holds every possession she owned. It is still full of all the things that made up her life. Every secret she ever had is hidden there. So I go inside. Now, and every time I come home, though I know my mom doesn't like it. She doesn't even like when Carla dusts in there. Still, I feel as much right to claim the space as my mother, and so I've been systematically going through Maggie's belongings for the past ten years. Through everything, again and again, until my mind has become a map of her space, an index of all the things she bought and collected and saved.

I sit on her bed and gaze at the mobile of polished seashells hanging over her window. At the photographs stuck in the frame of the mirror over her dresser. At her easel, splattered with paint, the source of so much mess, my mother insisted she only paint outside on her balcony. At the landscapes tacked to her closet doors, studies of our yard in summer and autumn and even winter, when she sat outside wearing fingerless gloves, warmed by an electric heater my dad set up for her. I see it first, in the winter study, with its trees bare of leaves. But then, when I rise from the bed and look at autumn, at spring, at summer, it's still there. The scrap of blue sending me rushing out onto her balcony, squinting at the horizon. From this angle, the gap in the trees has shifted just enough to reveal a slice of that blue house. An upstairs window. It's 4603 Galley Road, Sarah Ketchum's house. My pulse beats heavily in my hands, throbbing at the base of my tongue. If Sarah Ketchum ever stood at that window as a child, she might have seen Maggie painting on her balcony. Or—I can barely let myself imagine it—whoever lived in any one of those houses might have seen Maggie, might have been aware of both girls. Might have watched them. Might have waited for the right moment to strike.

"What are you doing?"

I turn and see my mother standing in the doorway to Maggie's room. She's in her late fifties, though she could pass for forty-five, because she's got an excellent colorist and has always been very careful about the sun. She's started in with the fillers too, though she's always been very canny about how much work is too much. She's leaning against the doorframe, which means she's at least one drink deep. This is a woman who can hold her liquor, but there's a certain slackening of the body that occurs after a drink or two.

"Just, you know. Visiting," I say.

"And here I was thinking you came to visit the people in your family who are still around," my mother replies.

"Grandma said you were busy."

"You could have at least said hello," she says.

She comes into the room and opens her arms for a hug. She's wearing a cashmere wrap over her Givenchy dress, and the fabric is so absurdly soft that I almost want to put my head on her shoulder, to stay there. Tell her all the secrets I've kept to myself. Tell her the ways I've spared her. But I don't. Because that would be yet another victory for her, in our years-long competition over which of us can need the other less.

"I didn't know if you were talking to me again," I say as she releases me.

"Don't be silly," my mother says, taking my hand and leading me out of Maggie's room. As if I've conjured up the rift with my mother entirely from my own imagination.

"Silly," I say, as if I'm unsure of the definition of the word.

"I mean, can you blame me for being upset?" she asks. "Eric's been like a son to me."

"Well then, maybe you should have invited him today instead," I reply.

"Have you heard from him?" she asks, ignoring me, leading me down the grand front staircase Maggie and I used to pretend was the drawbridge of our imaginary upstairs castle.

"He called a few days ago."

"And did you clear the air at all?"

"It was a voicemail. I haven't talked to him yet."

"You haven't called him back?" The skin between my mother's eyebrows creases as much as the Botox will allow. It's one of the chief annoyances of my life that, without any supporting information at all, my mother has correctly assessed that my divorce is entirely my fault. And she's also deluded herself into believing that reconciliation is only one good conversation away.

"I've been a little busy this week," I reply. "We're starting to plan for a second season, now that we won the APA award."

"Not still about Maggie?" she asks, a hand at her throat.

"No," I reply, hedging. "A different case." I watch the relief pass through her. That I will not continue my public discussion of her elder daughter, that I will not further damage the image she's cultivated for Maggie over the years. Of the perfect girl, the perfect victim.

"I wish you would just stop with this," she says, shaking her silver-blond bob.

"With trying to find out what happened to her?" I ask.

"With trying to make every little thing public," she replies. "It's unseemly, this need for attention."

"Maybe it has to do with how little attention I got as a kid," I reply under my breath, but I know she hears me. She just chooses to ignore me.

"You tell the whole world everything there is to know about your sister. This family. But I'm not allowed to know why you're divorcing my son-in-law? Even when it's like losing another of my children?"

"Jesus, Mom. You really don't pull any punches, do you?" I ask. But this shouldn't be a surprise—my mother has a particular talent for making everything about herself. About the toll Maggie's disappearance has taken on her. As if nobody on earth has ever suffered more than she has.

"I want you to make this right, between you and Eric," she says, like I'm an unruly teenager still, and marriage is a test I've failed, a dent I left in a neighbor's car. Quitting a summer job without notice. "You need to make this right."

Involuntarily, my mind conjures an image of Eric sitting

before me, his fists clenched, his eyes squeezed shut, as I beg him to tell me what to do.

"I can't," I reply, my voice flat. Because I don't want to admit that if I could have saved my marriage, I would have a hundred times by now. I don't want to explain to her that she's right. It's my fault, all of it. My mother, who has never tolerated even a chipped manicure in her entire life. She could never understand how deeply the impulse to ruin my own life took hold.

She clears her throat, a dry sound. A kind of tic she's developed, now that she's past the point of tears. A way of showing displeasure. Because that's the thing about my mother—for all the satisfaction she gains from displays of her own suffering, I haven't seen her cry in years. I wonder if she's even capable of it anymore, or if she's had to sever completely the part of her that feels.

"Well. There are a few people I want you to meet," she says, her tone suddenly false and sunny.

"Okay," I reply. She doesn't look at me. I know her well enough to know that she probably won't look at me for the rest of the afternoon.

"A couple of VIP donors, and a reporter from the *Trib*."

"Sure. What do you have to drink at this thing?"

"The usual. Mimosas. And a very nice sauvignon blanc," she replies, as if she's been giving this spiel all morning. She leads me toward the living room, which is still crowded with her guests.

"Grandma said something about gin."

"Your grandmother knows that I don't serve spirits before cocktail hour," my mother says, leading me into the crowd. "And that she can't have any, regardless."

* . * . *

IT'S JUST AS miserable as any other fund-raising lunch for Maggie's foundation, with its weak cocktails and its waterlogged, underripe plates of roasted vegetables and rubbery chicken. Overly painted women who press my hand as they shake it, their eyes inquisitive. As if they might be able to see evidence of the things they've heard about me, if they peer intently enough. There is a subtle difference this year too, and it takes me a moment to recognize it. It has to do with the way my mother introduces me around. In previous years, she'd introduce me as her younger daughter and segue into status updates about my marriage to Eric. *Have I seen you since the reception? Oh, of course, and now they've got the most beautiful three-bedroom in Wicker Park! Completely rehabbed, of course, but still full of that vintage charm.* Everything was always described as beautiful. Everything about my life a resounding success.

This year, when she introduces me, it's as Maggie's sister. As if I'm not her actual daughter, but rather some distant cousin, related to her only incidentally. Or worse, a stepchild. I can't help but be stung by her inattention, no matter how her bragging of the previous years might have rankled me. Here I am, forever the second child, always the sister of a missing girl. Always suffering from my mother's attention as well as her inattention.

As soon as the lunch plates are cleared from the table, I slip away. Out the front door and down the drive, heading north when it meets the road. Because there's no way I can be this close and not investigate.

Forty-six oh three Galley Road is very much like the other faux-Victorians in Sutcliffe Heights, a two-story blue house, attempting quaintness beneath its wallpapering of money. Harkening back to a time when a house like this might have been owned by a schoolteacher or an electrician, instead of an investment banker. I ring the bell and play the game I always played as a kid, growing up in this place. Trying to guess whether a family member or a member of the household staff will answer the door.

It's a middle-aged woman, and immediately I clock her manicure, her Eileen Fisher tunic, the pool of placid skin between her eyebrows—more Botox, surely—and recognize the lady of the house. But she's opening her own door, so I've scaled the first hurdle of investigation—going straight to the source.

"Hi," I say, giving her a self-conscious little smile. "My name is Martha Reese, and I was wondering if I could talk to you quickly about your house."

"Oh," the woman says, "we're not looking to sell, if that's what you're asking."

"Oh no," I reply. "I was wondering if you knew anything about the people who lived here before you." I've looked up the sale history of the place, and the people who live in it now bought it five years ago. Already after Sarah's murder.

"I'm sorry," the woman says. "Who are you?"

"I'm researching a podcast," I say, trying to figure out what tactic to use here. Andrea usually does the talking in these situations, so I'm a little at sea. "I'm looking into the history of Sutcliffe Heights. Some of the major events that happened here, that would have made national news."

"I see," the woman says, her face relaxing a little. "A podcast? That's like a TED Talk, right?"

"It's like a radio show that you can listen to on the internet," I reply.

"Well," she says, "my husband and I have only lived here for five years. I must have the seller's information somewhere." I can see her internal calculus running again as she pauses, and I've never been more relieved to have worn a luncheon-approved outfit. She seems to come to the conclusion that I'm too well-dressed to be up to anything nefarious. After all, money recognizes money. "Would you like to come in?" she asks.

I SIT IN her living room, drinking iced tea as she looks through a box of records she's recovered from her home office. A couple greyhounds lounge on the couch opposite us, watching me with tired wariness. I'm clearly a break in their daily routine. Interrupting their afternoon nap, probably.

"What are their names?" I ask, motioning to the dogs.

"Charles and Diana," she replies. "My sister breeds them, so she's in charge of the naming. You'd think that there's never been a significant world event since the eighties. My last two were Sonny and Cher."

"That's sweet," I say as she fishes a sheet of paper out of the box, holding her cheaters a little away from her eyes as she considers it.

"Here we are," she says. "Abigail Woods was the previous owner."

"Abigail Woods?" This is a strange turn, if Ava has her facts right. "No one named Ketchum?" I ask.

The woman shakes her head. "No, I don't think so."

"Oh," I say, and perhaps the woman can see that I'm a bit deflated by the news, because she pulls her reading glasses off and points them at me.

"You know, I think this was the seller's second residence. I seem to remember she lived in New York most of the year."

"Do you know if she had a renter or if someone else lived here?" I ask.

"Her brother had lived here for a while, did some work on it, I think. The Realtor said he was a contractor in the area, that he'd done all the improvements himself. But the house was vacant already when we bought it."

"And she never gave a reason for why she wanted to sell?" I ask.

"The typical reasons," the woman said. "The upkeep on a second residence was too much; you know, that sort."

"Do you remember hearing about a girl who lived here once?" I ask. "A teenager who was killed?"

The woman seems to blanch a bit. "Killed here in the house?" she asks. "Oh no, I think they have to report that before they're allowed to sell."

"No," I say quickly. "Not in the house. The information I have is that her father lived here, and she would have spent time here as a teenager. She died later, once she moved into her own apartment."

"You know, I do seem to remember something like that," she replies, sitting down next to me on the couch, the veins in her feet blue and puffy beneath the ankle strap of her sandals. "She went missing, right?"

"Yeah, she disappeared while walking to meet her friends one night. Her body was found in LaBagh Woods two days later."

"Right." The woman nods. "So terrible. I do remember some of the women in my book club talking about that, when we read *The Virgin Suicides.*"

"But you didn't know she lived here?" I ask.

"I had no idea. I just knew she was a local girl. I wonder if my husband knew about it," she says. "You know, if you need to interview either of us for your radio cast, we'd be happy to help." She scratches her number beneath Abigail Woods's contact information on a piece of paper and hands it to me.

"Thanks," I say, setting my glass down and getting up. "I'll be in touch if I have any follow-up questions."

"Of course," she says, also rising. And then she makes a motion with her arms, a waving that looks more akin to someone who has just been dropped into cold water. "Oh, I remember!" she says. "Her name was Maggie something, wasn't it?"

"Maggie?" I repeat, and then press my back teeth together until my temples ache.

"Yes," she says, picking up steam. "Now I remember, they were saying she went missing and was found in the woods. Maggie something-or-other. A local girl. Does that help?"

I want to tell her that Maggie isn't the girl who was found in the woods. That she was never found. That this woman should tell her goddamn book club to stop gossiping about my sister. But instead, I force a smile.

"Yes," I reply. "That's very helpful."

FIVE

As soon as I let her know that I want to discuss Sarah's case, Ava invites me to dinner at her apartment that Friday.

The rare weekend off for me, she says in her text. **So we can get to know each other a little.** The address Ava gives me turns out to be new construction in Wicker Park, one of those modern affairs where the front is all windows, two floors of green glass reflecting the sky and the street behind me. I ring the bell and watch Ava approach through the frosted panel in the front door, her figure swaying slightly as she descends the stairs from the second floor, a curl of smoke behind the glass.

"Hey," she says when she opens the door, ushering me inside. "I barely recognized you without the goth outfit." I raise a hand to my hair, remembering the dark wig I was wearing the night we met, feeling heat crawl up my neck.

"Yeah, it's all a bit much, isn't it?" I ask. I can hear something that sounds like "Chain of Fools" playing from the landing above. Ava's curly dark hair is clipped back, away from her face, and she's barefoot, holding a round globe of red wine in one hand. She looks almost impossibly young for a doctor, except her lips are red with lipstick, and I'm pretty sure the loose blue wrap dress she's wearing is Ralph Lauren. And the condo, on first glance, probably cost as much as my mother's house.

"I thought it was amazing," she replies.

"This is for you," I say, offering the bottle of wine I've brought, because it was on sale at Mariano's, marked down to $15 from $25. I know just enough about wine to know that it's not a great label. After all, Eric and I once joked about having a house wine at our old place, because we bought rioja by the case at Liquor Park. Nowadays, when I'm not swilling vodka, I consider a $6 bottle at Trader Joe's to be treating myself.

"Oh, lovely," Ava says, as if she's genuinely delighted by my meager offering. "Beaujolais is Ted's favorite."

I follow her up the front stairs and onto the apartment's main floor, which is a high-ceilinged living room in front and a kitchen that looks like something out of *The Jetsons* in the back. A man stands with a dish towel thrown over his shoulder at the kitchen island chopping greens. The room smells of dill and browned garlic and roasted nuts.

"Marti, this is Ted," Ava says.

"Welcome," Ted says, flashing uncannily white teeth as he waves the blade of the knife in greeting. Ted is tall and strapping, a guy who might have modeled for Abercrombie & Fitch in high school. His sandy hair is parted and slicked to the side, like he's the sort to keep a black fine-toothed comb in his front pocket. "Can I get you something to drink?"

"Marti brought Beaujolais," Ava whispers as she passes behind him, as if it's a delightful secret. She grabs another large wineglass off a hook beneath their cabinet.

"Brilliant," Ted replies, and it strikes me as something my father used to say. Ted is Yacht Club Ken, in every way. But there's also something endearing about him, the charm of a golden retriever puppy who thinks the world is a marvelous place because people have always been so enamored of him. Not the sort of guy you'd guess would have a brother-in-law in prison for murder.

"This place is amazing," I say, gazing around, from the giant windows framing the setting sun, to the fireplace in the living room, to the glass partition where a metal staircase climbs to the third story.

"Ted's in real estate," Ava explains, pouring a glass from the wine decanter on the counter and handing it to me.

"Commercial now," he says, going back to his chopping. "But I still have a knack for the residential, when the need arises."

"We've been here two years, and sometimes it still feels like we're just getting settled in," Ava says.

"That's because she sleeps at the hospital as much as she sleeps here," Ted replies, as if he and I are coconspirators. "*I'm* settled in just fine."

Ava gives him a flick on the shoulder. Admonishing and playful at once.

"C'mon," she says, grabbing the decanter and motioning for me to follow. "Let's go out back."

Out back is a large patio on the roof of the garage, surrounded by greenery, overlooked by a third-story balcony. Ava curls up on one of the lounge chairs, and I follow suit. Around us, windows from taller buildings are lit from within, and I catch glimpses of movement here and there.

"Ted seems great," I say. "He cooks."

"Ted's all right," she says, demurring in a way that makes it clear she enjoys the compliment. "Sometimes I feel bad for the poor guy. He had no idea what he was getting with my family. I'm pretty sure if I hadn't proposed, he would have eventually come to his senses and bailed."

"You proposed?" I ask.

"In the car one day. I think we were actually driving to one of Colin's court dates. I just up and asked him, and he nearly ran a red light, he was so flummoxed." It's the first time she's mentioned her brother by name, I realize. Colin. Her brother, the convicted girlfriend-killer.

"Where are you from originally?" I ask, though I already know the answer.

"I grew up in Albany Park," she replies. "Mom worked in the office at a high school, Dad was . . . well, I guess Dad was a lot of things over the years." I let this drop, mostly because it feels like she wants me to ask her about it. It's a trick I picked up from watching Andrea interview people for the podcast. Never let the other person direct the conversation.

"Do you get up there much anymore?" I ask.

"Not recently," she says. "Plus, we moved between rentals a lot. Any type of visit would be more like a bar crawl around the neighborhood. Colin used to spend time up there, but I never really went back once I was out."

The irony is, she and I grew up only a few miles apart. But from what I've gathered in the week I've spent googling Colin's case, her upbringing was quite different from mine. Blue-collar, for starters. And then there was the violence. First, their father's— the kind that landed Ava's mother in the ER every few months for the better part of ten years. And then there was Colin's record. A bar fight that ended with charges of assault and battery, resulting in a hundred hours of community service.

Her brother's attorney presented evidence of their father's abusiveness at his murder trial, perhaps as an attempt at mitigation for Colin's criminal record. It backfired, of course. It made Colin look like just another link in the family's chain of male violence. The sort that was learned by example, a power that could be gained only through the ability to hurt another person more. Unlike my family, who traded power by proving we could need each other less and less. Until any need at all became a weakness.

Still, sitting on the deck and watching the lights in the buildings around us flicker on one by one, I can't help but imagine the ways in which Ava and I have traded places. She, who started with such difficulty, whose talent and intelligence have bought her a rightful place in Chicago's young and mighty upper crust. And I, who was gifted a place in old Chicago money as a birthright but threaded trip wires through the rooms of my own home. Found a perverse relief in the wrong step that brought it all down.

"So I assume you've looked into the case by now?" Ava says.

"Just what I can find online," I reply. "It'll take a Freedom of Information Act request to get copies of the police and medical examiner's records."

Ava nods.

"Let me know if you need me to have my attorney put some pressure on them," she says, and it surprises me a bit, that she wouldn't have her own copies. "I know, on first glance, the case against him looks pretty good," she continues. "Not like the cops or the prosecutor railroaded him. Like they did their jobs. Looked at the boyfriend, found he had a prior assault charge. His DNA was a match to what they found on her. He even admitted he was at the apartment when she went to meet her friends."

"So what do I tell my producer when she says the same thing?"

"Tell her that the evidence also fits his version of the story. He was there that afternoon. They had sex. She left to go meet her friends at the bar, and he slept for a while, took a shower, left, locked the door behind him. Met me and Ted at Au Cheval for our grandmother's birthday dinner."

Ava pulls a thin black vape pen out of the pocket of her dress and offers it to me. I decline. I feel like I should keep my head as straight as possible for this conversation. She takes a long pull, the end of the pen lighting up blue.

"Sleeping at her apartment doesn't look like a great alibi."

"It isn't. Unfortunately, he wasn't operating as if he'd need an alibi that night. He didn't know she was gone until the next morning. Her friends just thought she flaked. They didn't report her missing until she didn't show up to work."

"So tell me why I should believe he's innocent," I say, and Ava smiles. She seems to enjoy my incredulity, the skeptic in me.

"All the evidence they have against Colin is circumstantial. He was the boyfriend, he was the last one to see her, he was the last person she had sex with. He had a prior arrest."

"Right," I say, sipping my wine, which is diminishing quickly.

"Look at the things that don't fit. She went missing from Rogers Park but was found in LaBagh Woods. Which means she was transported by car, and Colin didn't have a car. He didn't even have access to one," she says. I get the feeling that this is not the first, or even the twentieth, time she's made this particular case to a third party. "Add to that the timeline. We know she was taken between six and six forty-five in the evening, and Colin showed up for dinner in the West Loop for our seven thirty reservation. That doesn't leave enough time to drive her to the woods, half-bury her body, and get to the West Loop in the dregs of rush-hour traffic, freshly showered. Even if he did have a car."

"He could have killed her earlier in the evening. The timeline is based on when he claimed she left to meet her friends, right?" I ask. Because, in spite of myself, I'm hoping Ava has an answer. And she does.

"One of her friends called her at five fifty-three, asking Sarah to bring a necklace she wanted to borrow. She talked to her."

"Did Sarah have the necklace on her when she was found?" I ask.

"In her back pocket."

I hear someone climbing the stairs behind me, and we both turn to find Ted on the landing.

"Dinner's ready," he says, "whenever you two are."

"Thanks, sweetie," Ava says, though clearly we're not finished yet, because Ted turns and heads back downstairs. I'm trying my best to think of ways in which Colin might be guilty. Working backward, away from the police's line of reasoning, trying to find holes in her story.

"So he stashed her body somewhere," I say, "went to dinner, and came back to dump her afterward."

"Stashed her body where?" Ava asks. "Her roommate came home at eight. He says the apartment was empty."

"Her roommate's a guy?" I ask.

Ava nods. "Dylan. A friend of hers from art school. Not a fan of Colin, unfortunately."

"And Dylan's got an alibi?"

"Airtight," Ava replies. "But he helps to establish the timeline that night. So the question becomes, how is Colin transporting Sarah's body to wherever he stashed it, and then from there to LaBagh Woods? And why?" I can see a bright flicker in her eyes, flint sending off sparks. She knows she has me. "Why would he go to the trouble of dumping her in those woods when he has no easy means of moving her?"

"It was familiar," I reply, remembering the accounts of the trial I read online. "That's what the prosecution argued, right? It was close to where you two grew up, so he knew where to hide a body that wouldn't be readily found."

"Colin isn't that stupid," Ava replies. "To take that risk, of moving the body to a place that might link him to the murder. And still, that doesn't answer the 'how' of it."

"No," I say. "It doesn't." I'm grasping now, trying to remember all the reasons I was initially against this. Trying to remember why everyone was so sure Colin was guilty.

"It's a circumstantial case," Ava says, something like victory in her expression. "It shouldn't have been enough to convict him. But you know this city. You know that nothing ever works out the way it's supposed to here." She knows she's winning me over, except she isn't smug about it. She's not battle-weary in the way I would expect for someone who has spent the past seven years fighting in Chicago's court system. Instead, she's alight with something, the promise of victory, even a small one. The prospect of convincing me of her brother's innocence.

And that's when I realize it. She needs me. This whole evening is designed to impress me, because I have somehow become the person who can help these people most. Rich and sophisticated and influential as they are, they need me.

Ava stands, offering a hand to pull me up.

"Let's go get some dinner," she says. And as I take her hand, I know what I'm doing. I'm agreeing to it, to take the case, to help Colin. And I can't stop myself from being a little thrilled at the prospect.

DINNER TURNS OUT to be pasta with garlic and fried hazelnuts, a roasted cauliflower side with capers and dill tahini, and brown bread with a marmalade that tastes of both oranges and mustard seeds. In short, it's the best meal I've had in recent memory. We wash it down first with my Beaujolais—which is rich and smells a bit of decaying violets—and then with some sort of fizzy gin cocktail that Ava expertly mixes at the bar cart by their fireplace.

The music has changed to chill and chic, a mix of Billie Holiday and Ani DiFranco and David Bowie and the Volcano Choir. Ted talks for a long while about his plan for growing tomatoes this summer, the varieties and growth medium and potential uses he's considering. Salsa and canning and methods for sun-drying. It's all extremely civilized, the sort of hobby a man adopts when he realizes it's easier to buy beer than to brew his own. And then he makes a detour into the kitchen and pulls something out of the freezer, setting it on the counter.

"Dessert," he says when he sees me watching.

"Oh lord, I don't think I could possibly eat any more," Ava says, padding over to examine the pint of ice cream he's pulled out. "Except for Jeni's, of course," she quickly adds when she sees the label. "I'll always have room for that."

There's a moment, when the two of them look at each other, and there is such fondness in their eyes that I find it almost poignant. It seems fragile, for two people to love each other so genuinely, as if the world is simply waiting to do something to ruin them. It's the way my parents looked at each other, once upon a time.

I think of Eric, of course. Of the way we were in college, in the first years of our marriage. How we were still each other's greatest source of solace, greatest source of joy, back then. Eric, the youngest of four boys from a Kenilworth family even wealthier than mine, though not without its own tragedy. He'd lost a childhood friend in a skiing accident when he was in high school and described her much in the way that I described Maggie to him: As young and fierce and beautiful. Full of promise. The way everyone talks of girls who are disappeared from the world at that age, as if sixteen is the mighty pinnacle of a girl's worldly luck and potential. No matter how they go.

The way he talked about her, I think Eric might have been in love with her. It was the classic story—a house full of boys, the girl next door. The tagalong, tomboyish and bratty and beloved by all of them, though none more than Eric. The sort of childhood friendship that begins with a shared disgust for all the adult amusement at your pairing and then shifts the moment that puberty sends your body haywire. She had been his first, he told me one night, early on in our relationship. The first everything, he said. And all I could think was, *Christ, how could I possibly compare?*

But there was a strange symmetry to it, Eric's history and mine—when we met. I knew that if his friend had still been alive, that bright girl, bright in all the ways that mattered, he would not have been with me. And I think he suspected that if Maggie was not gone, I would have lived an entirely different life, one that would not have brought me to him. He once described me as being the sort more likely to eschew college altogether, to travel through Europe and Southeast Asia and Central America, uncaring of my parents' disapproval. Learning how to sketch and to surf, reading all the local poets. Living the sort of young adulthood only ever afforded to women of means with an undaunted certainty of their own freedom. I don't know if he's right, if I would have gone off into the world fearlessly had Maggie not gone missing.

But there was a balance in our relationship, at first. He knew what it was to mourn someone lost too soon. So he gave me as much latitude with my own grief as I needed. When we were in college, Eric seemed to want nothing more than to hold me in his dorm's twin bed, an arm locked around my chest, and listen as my secrets came pouring out of me. I told him all of it, about Maggie and my family and the reckless things I'd done as a teenager to try to fix it all, and the more reckless things I'd done when it would not be fixed. The drugs. The boys. The places I went, because I heard that they were places where lost girls might turn up. Flophouses. Strip clubs. Bus stations. I turned over my secrets before him like tarot cards, from a deck stacked with Death, its specter appearing again and again. That I was damaged made me fascinating to boys, I knew that much. And I loved fascinating Eric. He became the golden center of our life, and I was a tiny planet that circled him in an unsteady orbit. Always half swallowed by the absence of his light. Always half in love with the dark.

Now, as I watch Ava and Ted, I wonder if Ted ever hates Ava, secretly. If there is a part of him that cannot stand her devotion to her brother, a frailty in him waiting to be pressed. I wonder if Ava realizes that she'll have to change, eventually, to keep him. I learned that the hard way with Eric, that in marrying me he'd cordoned off his grief for the girl he once loved. Eventually, Eric lost patience for comforting me, because I was incapable of shutting out Maggie. Because the truth was, no matter how I tried to forget her, she lived in my life as an active presence; she would not allow herself to be ignored.

"Marti," Ted calls. "Ice cream?"

I give him an exuberant nod. And maybe it's the wine or the gin or the music, but I suddenly remember that I have not yet met everyone I will love in my life. That I may still find more people to love. It seems eminently possible, tonight.

WE'RE HALFWAY THROUGH our ice cream when the topic shifts back to Colin. To the night Sarah Ketchum was murdered.

"I like to think I'm good at reading people," Ted says, eating out of the pint, while Ava and I use bowls. *Like civilized people*, Ava said when she spooned out our portions. "I make these deals all the time with people, and I can always see it, you know? If they're holding something back, or if they have more room to move with the financials than they're claiming. And I'll tell you, Colin showed up to the restaurant that night, and not a blip on my radar. Nothing out of the ordinary with him."

Ava nods. "One of the things I kept coming back to at first was that I knew I would have been able to tell that night, if he'd just done something so horrific."

"Tell me about the assault charge," I say, because I'm drunk enough now that I have no hesitation with demanding information.

Ava lets out a long breath.

"Well, it's not good," she says, already regretful. "He was in college. His first year at UIC. And you have to understand, our old neighborhood? He ran with a pretty unrelenting crowd. So he was out at this bar with a couple of his friends, and there's some sort of disagreement with this other group of guys about who had the next game on the pool table."

Ted makes a show of sucking his front teeth, his lip curling.

"I know," Ava says. "I know. But you have to think about it in context, you know. He was a stupid kid, he was drunk, one of the other men called him a"—she stumbles a bit over the word, wincing as she finally says it—"a *faggot,* and Colin broke a pool cue across his back."

She shakes her head, and I notice how her hair is escaping its clip, floating down around her face in dark curls.

"It would have been one stupid arrest in college, if he'd never met Sarah. Something to report on his bar application one day, if he made it through law school."

"Was that where he was headed?" I ask. "Law school?"

"We were encouraging it," Ted replies, exchanging a look with Ava. I see the instinct of a big brother in Ted. Trying to be upstanding, a good example for his brother-in-law. Maybe a streak of hard-ass in him as well. "He's such a smart kid. He just couldn't ever get out of his own way."

"It's not like he could have prevented what happened," Ava says.

"I know," Ted replies. "I just mean, it was always something. If it wasn't this . . ."

"What, a murder charge?" There's a current of tension in Ava's voice now. One that I knew had to be there, somewhere under

the surface. Because no couple is this happy. The light trill of Ava's phone ringing cuts through the moment of unease.

"Excuse me," she says, getting up and moving to the opposite end of the kitchen to take the call.

"She knows what I mean," Ted says as soon as she's preoccupied with her call. Perhaps more to himself than to me. He pauses, his eyes meeting mine in a way that feels weighty, in a way that makes me almost uncomfortable, with Ava out of the room. "Ava told me about your sister," he says. "I'm sorry."

"Thanks," I say, flatly, because this is not my usual script, alone with a man, talking about my sister. This is usually the point in the conversation when someone makes a move, after I describe my childhood trauma, and the man who's listening decides that he knows exactly the method with which to fix me. And it's generally an enjoyable enough game, letting them try. Ted seems like he'd be up for the challenge, at least for a little while. But it's a thought I don't allow to linger.

"It's Colin," he says, motioning toward Ava, who is speaking so quickly into the phone that it's difficult to even catch a word of the conversation floating across the large kitchen.

"How do you know?" I ask.

"She's speaking Portuguese," he replies. "They both speak it, so they could talk to their maternal grandmother as kids. She was fresh off the boat, and married into a family of micks." He shows me the claddagh ring on his left hand, as evidence. I've seen a matching one on Ava's as well. "Now they use it to avoid eavesdropping while he's in prison. If that's not the American dream, I don't know what is."

"It looks like she did all right, at least," I say, motioning to the expensive trappings around us.

"She's like her mother. Too smart to keep her IQ a secret, not smart enough to jettison the men in that family before they drag her down." He smiles bitterly, and it's still a charmed expression on that face of his. "Do you think there's a connection between your sister's kidnapping and Sarah Ketchum's murder?" he asks.

"I don't know yet," I reply. "There are certainly similarities. The geography is compelling. But that's a lot of time to lapse in between the two."

"Yeah, Ava told me about that too," Ted replies. "I gotta say, I'm not sold on it. At least, not in the way she is." I'm about to ask him why, but then Ava is strolling back from the kitchen, plopping down on the couch next to Ted, and pulling his arm around her shoulders.

"So," she says, with a look between the two of us that's almost wary, "what have you two been talking about?"

SIX

I haven't been to the Twenty-Fourth District police station in Rogers Park in over a year, since the morning I gave the DNA sample that proved Jane Doe was not my sister. It looks the same as it always has. The same as it did the first time I came here, on the night of Maggie's disappearance. After a report came in of a blond teenager seen getting out of a silver sedan near the Rogers Park Red Line station. That tip was why her case was active both in the Sutcliffe Heights Police Department and in Rogers Park, why I spent four hours that night sitting in that station looking through thick, greasy books of mug shots, trying to recognize the man in the car. But today is different—I'm not coming here to inquire about Maggie. After my dinner with Ava and Ted last night, I've decided it's best to get some information from a third-party source. So as Ava suggested, I'm on the hunt for Sarah Ketchum's case file.

I also haven't been back to this—or any—police station since the podcast became a minor sensation, both in Chicago and across the country. And I'm not sure its content will particularly endear me to Chicago's finest. Partially because they're not huge fans of citizen crime-solvers trying to step all over their territory, but also because I wasn't entirely complimentary of their handling of Maggie's case. I'm not sure I won many friends in the CPD with the podcast's release, but now I just hope I haven't lost any.

Silvia sits at the front desk now, because it's Saturday, and she works the weekend shift when her ex has her daughter. She lights up when she sees me walk in, though I know deep down that it has more to do with the caramel Frappuccino I'm carrying than with me. I've brought one for myself too. Another trick. So it doesn't feel so much like a bribe as an excuse to do something bad with someone else. A shared guilty pleasure.

"How's Maya?" I ask, forgoing pleasantries as I hand her the drink.

"Taller than me, the rascal," Silvia replies, taking the straw between fingers tipped with pink acrylic nails and sipping from it.

"Junior high?"

"Freshman in high school," she says, as if such things should not be allowed, her daughter advancing beyond elementary school.

"Jesus," I say, because I remember playing with Maya on the linoleum floor of the police station, when I was eighteen and she was only three.

"So what can I do for you, honey?" Silvia asks.

I grin, because I know how transparent I am. And Silvia doesn't suffer fools; she knows ours is a collegiality born of necessity.

"I'm looking into a case that might be connected to Maggie," I reply. "Sarah Ketchum. I've got her case number."

Silvia sits back in her seat. "This for the podcast?"

I make a quick determination that lying is not the way to go here. Odds are, Silvia will hear about it if anything she gives me makes it into season two. And this isn't a bridge I want to burn.

"Potentially," I say, and watch Silvia's eyebrow twitch. People in her position are only successful when they're good at keeping information away from those who might make it public.

"You know, there are official ways to get that sort of thing."

"I'm trying, believe me," I say. "But the central office is dragging its feet on my FOIA request. They're saying it could take four to six weeks to get a copy of her records." It's not quite the truth, though that's what the CPD website does say. If I were honest, I'd admit that I haven't put in a FOIA request yet. I don't much want to tip off the brass that this case might be getting a bit of publicity sometime soon. My name is bound to raise some red flags in the central office these days.

"And you're hoping that I can grease the wheels?"

"I'm hoping you might have access to a copier," I reply. "You know . . . make an extra copy of the redacted file, toss it out. You can't be held responsible for things people steal out of your garbage." It's not the first time we've pulled this particular trick. Except back then, I was the sister of a missing teenager, an unsolved case allowed to go cold. A feral, desperate little thing. Silvia was more than willing to color outside the lines for me then. She must have understood the brutality of growing up how I did, always looking. Back when nothing was ever enough. Now, however, she's a bit more reticent.

"I'm sorry, honey," Silvia says. "Giving records to you, that's like leaking to a reporter now."

"You're right." I know I'm asking too much. If I hope to ever get Silvia's help again, it's time to start backpedaling. "Maybe just point me in the right direction, then? Do you know who I could talk to about the case?"

"The only one here today is Detective Olsen."

"Of course," I mutter. I remember Detective Olsen, how he looked at me the day of the DNA test. Like he could see all the furious girls inside me. The guilty, neglected child. The wicked teenager, her every pose and motion vengeful. The woman who knew better than to hope. "He's here now?" I ask, reticent.

Silvia motions behind her. "In the bullpen," she says, a flicker of amusement crossing her face. Like she's considering making popcorn to watch what's about to go down. "Back right."

I pause for a moment.

"What's his deal?" I ask. "Is he a Boy Scout or a tough guy or what?" Even from our brief meeting the year before, I could tell he wasn't like Detective Richards, who used to call me on Maggie's birthday and always sent handwritten Christmas cards to my parents. But still, there was something decent in Olsen, behind the scrim of professionalism. Something that was not merely pity.

"A marine," she replies. "Little of both."

"Great," I reply as I pass her desk, heading back into the bullpen. Pairs of desks are checkered throughout the room, with offices on its perimeter. Down a narrow hallway on the south side of the building, I know, are the interview rooms. The first is where I sat the night Maggie went missing, looking through the mug shots of violent offenders in the area. Hundreds of them.

Becky, the woman at the front desk back then, made me cup after Styrofoam cup of Swiss Miss cocoa as I tried to remember what the man in the car looked like, his face blurring with all the blank, dead-eyed faces of the men in the mug shots. And then, when I couldn't find him after four hours, my dad took me home and I threw up all that cocoa into the toilet in the upstairs bathroom, while my parents shouted at each other in the kitchen. Because my parents always turned to anger when things were out of control. And things never really ever got back under control after that.

I spot Olsen sitting at a desk toward the back of the room. I've grown accustomed, over the years, to dealing with the old guard of Chicago's finest when it comes to my sister's case. The weathered, oft-mustachioed men at least twice my age, or the capable, compassionate women who are always good for a little bit of feminine solidarity. So Detective Olsen—hawkish and fair, more handsome than he has any right to be—caught me off guard last year. Still catches me off guard now, if I'm honest.

"Detective Olsen?" I ask as I approach.

"Yeah?" He glances up, but his face betrays no recognition. My hair is different, after all. And our interaction was brief, just long enough to collect some cells from the inside of my cheek. I was the one brimming with anticipation that day, already edged with despair. I was the one who remembered everything, who felt every moment as if I'd been stripped of my skin. His unbuttoned collar remained with me for days.

I decide the fact that he has forgotten me is an opportunity.

"I was wondering if you could help me find some information," I say, my voice a half octave higher than usual, turning back to my old strategy. The young damsel, in need of saving. Because if men are going to insist on being macho this far into the twenty-first century, it's fair game to use it against them.

He shuts the file he had open in front of him. There's a toothpick tucked into the corner of his mouth. I wonder if he's recently quit smoking.

"What is it that you need?" His voice softer than I expected, its slight rasp another clue.

"I was hoping to get some information on a case," I reply, handing him the sheet of paper with Sarah Ketchum's case number on it. "I'm studying the sociology of violent crime against women on the North Side of Chicago." He considers the case number.

I know enough by now to know not to lie to a cop. So instead I've learned to be vague and to let them draw their own conclusions. You don't say you're a student, but you imply you are when you use the word "studying." Technically, I am studying two cases of violent crime against women on the North Side of Chicago. Plus, when I was still a sociology major at Northwestern, I wrote a paper on that very topic. If he asks follow-up questions, at least I'll be ready with semicompetent answers.

"Is it an active case?" he asks.

"No, it was closed about seven years ago."

"You're going to have to put in a Freedom of Information Act request with the CPD's central office."

"The woman at the front desk told me that I might be able to talk to a detective about it. On a more unofficial basis."

"Silvia let you in here?" he asks, glancing toward the front of the station. "How did you manage that?"

"What do you mean?"

"She usually rivals the city's best bouncers."

"I told her I needed help," I reply, trying to look innocent. Confused. The sort of girl someone might take pity on.

"I wish I could," he says, offering the paper back to me, "but you're going to have to go through the proper channels."

"Okay," I say, taking the paper. He goes back to his computer screen, while I linger for a moment. Hoping the possibility of helping someone in distress will supersede his marine's dedication to protocol. I remember the evenness of his voice as he explained the process of the DNA test a year ago, as I bit off what little was left of my fingernails. He's a man who knows how to speak with someone having the worst day of her life. I wait, until his fingers pause and he glances back up at me.

"Is there something else?" he asks.

"I'm sorry," I say, and conjure a sheen of tears. Unlike my mother, I'm capable of crying on command. "It's just that I'm not sure I can wait to get the file through a FOIA request. I'm behind where I should be on this, and I was just hoping you'd be willing to cut me a break."

He sits back in his chair, considers me. *There it is*, I think. The look he gave me when we first met, when he knelt in front of where I sat. An unexpected kindness from someone who did not need to be kind.

"What's your name?" he asks.

"Martha," I reply. I have to actively stop myself from saying "Maggie." It's a habit I've developed, to answer that way when men ask my name.

"Martha," he repeats, and reaches again for the slip of paper, which I hand to him, and then I wait with my arms crossed as he looks it up on his computer.

"The Ketchum murder," he says, extracting the toothpick

from the corner of his mouth, tossing it into the trash can beneath his desk. This is clearly serious business.

"Are you familiar with it?" I ask.

"Pretty familiar," he replies. "I knew the guy who worked it, before he retired."

"Detective Richards?" I ask, because Richards is the only detective in the unit to retire in the past five years.

"How did you know that?"

"Newspaper article," I reply. "He gave a statement; it came up in my research." It's not quite a coincidence that the same detective would have investigated Sarah's case and Maggie's. After all, Detective Richards transferred from Missing Persons to Homicide a few years after Maggie disappeared, and he had a knack for handling high-profile cases that the top brass seemed to appreciate. It's not a huge surprise that he'd be assigned to the murder of a teenage girl. But it's close enough to a coincidence to get my blood up. Still, I can tell I've lost some ground here with Olsen, so I shift gears.

"I understand if you can't help me with the file. But could you tell me anything about the case? Just for context?" I pull my little Moleskine journal from my pocket and prepare to write.

"If you want a statement on the case, you really should contact our press office," he says, almost regretfully. Almost.

"I'm not a journalist," I say, and as soon as the words are out of my mouth, I begin to realize all the ways in which they're not quite true. "I'm just . . . looking to get a sense of the case, to fill in the blanks until I can get the file. Anything you can remember from what Detective Richards said."

He lets out a sigh, considering me with pursed lips.

"The boyfriend killed her," he says finally. "Strangled her in her apartment, and then half-buried her body in LaBagh Woods. They found his DNA on her and in her apartment. And he didn't have an alibi for the time of the murder."

I know what he's doing, even as he pauses, watching me scratch notes down in my journal. He's giving me what an internet search would reveal. What was widely reported on during the investigation and the trial.

"And the boyfriend was the only suspect the CPD investigated?"

"He was the primary suspect," he replies, watching me cannily, in a way that makes me slightly nervous. As if he's figuring me out, though I'm the one asking the questions.

"Did they ever find the car he used to dump the body?" I ask, giving it a shot. And immediately I know it's a step too far, using one of the tactics Colin's defense attorney used at trial. The question of the car, how he could have moved her body such a distance without one. Because whatever openness there was in Olsen's expression snaps shut.

"They didn't need the car to get the conviction," he replies, folding his arms over his chest. "What school did you say you go to?" he asks.

"Northwestern," I reply, shutting my notebook. Great, now I'm actively lying to a police detective.

"What program?"

"Sociology," I say.

"And you're focusing on violence against women on the North Side of Chicago?" he asks. "Seems to me there's a lot of violence on the South and West Sides that is in desperate need of some study. Especially from someone at Northwestern."

I know this argument. It's a good one; it's one I grappled with in the first season of the podcast. It's one that I know still weighs heavily on Andrea as well. The ways in which Maggie's case got media attention because she was young and white and from a wealthy area. She went to a good school. She had parents with the resources to force a protracted, thorough search for her. I watched as a seventeen-year-old Black girl from Woodlawn went missing the following summer and only got a day or two of media coverage, versus the weeks the local papers and TV stations afforded to Maggie. And the wash of guilt surges up inside me, because there is so much I have not been able to do, with my vision tunneled to a pinprick, with my sister squarely in the middle. There is so much else I should be doing. *The weight of them could drag a fleet of ships to the ocean floor.* I hear my own voice echoed back at me, as it was played over the loudspeaker at the awards ceremony. My own acknowledgment of all the other women I'm failing by looking only for my sister. But of course, anger follows closely on the heels of despair.

"It would be nice if all your colleagues shared your concern," I reply. Because even the handling of Maggie's case came with a healthy dose of institutional misogyny from the Chicago Police Department. Questions about whether Maggie was sexually active, for instance. Whether she had more than one boyfriend. Whether she drank alcohol, did drugs. Whether she could have been pregnant. Whether she was rebellious, engaged in risky behavior. Whether she *knew better than to put herself in danger*, as one cop had put it. As if she were responsible for preventing her own kidnapping. I can only imagine the sort of assumptions the CPD must make about girls from the South or West Side. But I can tell that Detective Olsen doesn't appreciate the comment, so I decide an exit strategy is my best bet. "Anyway, thanks so much for your time, Detective Olsen," I say. "I think I have everything I need."

"You don't need the case file anymore?" he asks, stopping me as I turn to go.

"I thought I had to go through the proper channels for that."

"Well, I could bend the rules a little bit," he says, and his friendliness is as flat as the papers before him. "If you feel like telling me what you really want with it."

"What do you mean?"

"I mean, unless you've got a Northwestern ID in your purse, I'm going to assume you're not a student there."

I swallow, trying to keep my composure. I'm not good at this, being put at a disadvantage. Having to show my hand to a stranger.

"I'm trying to see if Sarah Ketchum's case might be in some way related to another case in the same area."

"What other case?" he asks. His tone suggests that his patience is wearing thin.

"Maggie Reese," I reply.

"Shit," he says, revelation easing some of the rigidity from his posture. "You're her sister."

"I was wondering if you'd recognize me." I think of the last time he saw me. Long-haired and twitchy, sick with grief. A conflict-free diamond on my left hand. I don't blame him. Sometimes I don't even recognize myself anymore.

"And you have a radio show?"

"It's a podcast," I reply.

"I thought you said you weren't a journalist," he says, his mouth tight, teeth suddenly sharp.

"I'm not," I reply. "I'm a victims' advocate. I just . . . contribute to a podcast."

"And why exactly do you think they're related?"

"The cases? I don't know if they are," I say quickly. "But they were similar ages. Similar physical types. Sarah's father lived close to where Maggie and I grew up—"

"Her murder was over a decade later," Olsen cuts in. "Do you know how many disappearances and killings there were in Chicago between these two cases?"

"They were physically similar. They both disappeared at the same time of day." I tick my points off on my fingers as I speak. "They were both transported by car. Colin didn't have a car. He didn't have access to one. So who took Sarah from Rogers Park to LaBagh Woods?"

"*Colin* didn't have a car," he repeats. "What, you're on a first-name basis with Colin McCarty now?"

"I know his sister," I reply.

He lets out a breath and presses both of his hands together, as if he's praying, his fingertips resting against his mouth for a moment. "Look, I can't imagine how difficult it was for you to lose your sister that way," he begins, and my anger flares again. Anger at every cop who ever gave my family their opinion about our situation. The runaway theory. The pregnancy theory. The idea that Maggie disappeared of her own volition, or because she'd dared to have sex, dared to go into the city without my parents. As if the whole Chicago Police Department could close up shop and go home if young girls would just learn to behave and follow the rules.

Well, I have news for all of them. I've broken every rule in the book, and somehow I'm still here.

"Don't patronize me," I snap at him. "Did anyone here ever consider anyone else for Sarah's murder? Did you even think that it might have been someone else?"

"No," he says, and his eyes are on mine. Stripped of artifice.

Unnerving in their directness. "Listen to me on this, okay?" His voice unwavering, so sure that it's easy to be swept up in his certainty. "He did it. Colin McCarty killed that girl. We never had to look for anyone else. Because sometimes, in cases like that, you just know it cold."

"Well, I'm not so sure," I reply. He shakes his head, scratching out something onto a piece of notepaper and handing it to me. It's a name and phone number, with a Chicago area code.

"What's this?" I ask.

"It's the name of a guy who works for the *Sun-Times*," Olsen replies. "He covered the Ketchum case. He was a real thorn in the CPD's side at the time, but he'll have a copy of the case file."

"Why would you help me?" I ask, a little bewildered that it's that simple. To actually walk away with what I came here for.

"I think you need to see what's in there," he replies. "Because it's not pretty."

IT TURNS OUT, Olsen is right. The *Sun-Times* reporter is more than happy to email me a copy of Sarah Ketchum's case file when I call and tell him about the podcast.

"They railroaded the kid," he says, his voice a loud buzz of indignation over the phone. "I don't think they even looked at anyone else at the time. Having someone else dig into the case is probably the best thing that could happen right now."

I print out the file at the FedEx on Clark Street, hovering over the printer as it churns out pages, for fear that someone else will pick the stack up by mistake and see the grisly typewritten descriptions of Sarah's body. I can't help but feel protective of her, this girl who looked like Maggie, who only made it a few years further in her life than Maggie did. I don't want some stranger seeing the inventory of her clothing, the list of her injuries, the evidence that was collected from her. When I have the whole file, I stuff it into my backpack and bike home, already feeling a creeping sense of horror at what the pages may contain.

When I open the door to my apartment, I kick a manila envelope that has been slipped beneath it. Acid wells in my throat when I pick it up and find Eric's precise script on the note inside.

Marti—my attorney sent these over. Just a draft. Have yours take a look. I was hoping to give them to you in person, but I guess this is the best I could do. Don't hesitate to call if you have any questions. Be safe.

Eric

There is a little mark on the paper before his signature, where it looks like he began to write "Love" but then thought better of it. The envelope contains our divorce papers. This is not exactly a time for affection.

It would be easy to be cut by the formality of his note, something that could have been a polite message to a colleague. But I know Eric well enough to know that he must have agonized over it, scribbling it in the hallway outside my door, with its burned-out fixtures and its moldering carpet. That's the problem with having such a collegial divorce. There's so much more pain in its niceties.

I pull out my phone and track him, watch the blue dot that is his phone move southward on Milwaukee Avenue. I wonder what he's doing. Try to imagine him, the angles of his face, whether he's as lonely as I am. I'm waiting for the day he remembers that we can still track each other. Every time I open the app, I steel myself against the possibility that this will be the time when my access to his phone is denied. But each time, the blue dot is still there. And I wonder if he's forgotten, or if he's doing the same thing I am. Keeping tabs on me. Wondering what I'm thinking.

All of this would be so much easier, in some ways, if Eric was angry with me. That's the other problem with having a traumatic childhood. The people who love you always give you a pass on your bad behavior. If a body shows up in the morgue that could be your sister, and if you spend the next year coming undone in ways that make it impossible for your life not to crumble around you, the people who love you will still love you, even after all that's left of your life is rubble. Even if they can't stay married to you. Even if they were hurt, perhaps irreparably, when the walls came down. And their forgiveness just seems to make everything worse.

Sometimes I wonder if our marriage might have been saved if Jane Doe had never arrived at the morgue. If I'd taken Eric's advice and pursued a master's in criminology, or volunteered for a women's shelter, or gone back to therapy. Even in hindsight, it seems impossible. Because without Maggie, my life is like a chipped teacup, always an imitation of the perfect thing it once might have been, sharp along one edge, dangerous in a way it was not before. Useless and too full of memory to be discarded.

I comb through Sarah Ketchum's police file in the few hours I have before I have to get ready for work, eating frozen pizza and drinking vodka with olive juice, since I haven't replenished my stock of vermouth since last week. The case file contains the incident report from the discovery of Sarah's body and the medical examiner's report. It contains a list of evidence collected from the woods where Sarah was found and from her apartment. In the crime scene photographs, her apartment appears both bare and cluttered, all its furniture of the threadbare and pressed-wood variety—a futon, a papasan chair, an IKEA coffee table—and its walls covered with music posters. Florence + the Machine. The Lumineers. Arcade Fire. The Black Keys. The once-ubiquitous poster of six naked backs painted like Pink Floyd album covers, thrown in for good measure. Stacks of DVDs in a wire rack against one wall of the living room, stacks of fashion magazines next to her bed. Audrey Hepburn smiling down from above the desk, diamonds at her throat, a long cigarette holder in her black-gloved hand.

"You have to decide," Maggie instructed me once, as she sketched my portrait on her bedroom floor, "whether you're an Audrey or a Marilyn." At seven years old, I had no idea who she was talking about. But, like always, I was an eager student, unwilling to show my ignorance for fear of losing her attention.

"Which are you?" I asked, determined to be whomever she was.

Maggie gave me that sly, amused smile of hers. "I'm an Edie Sedgwick," she said, and I nodded. As if, yes, this was exactly right.

I pull my hand through my own shorn blond hair as I page through the report. The records reference photographs of the body as well, which are mercifully not included. A lot of the personal information has also been redacted—sanitized for public consumption.

Still, there are plenty of horrors here. Sarah was found facedown and partially buried in the underbrush of LaBagh Woods thirty-six hours after her roommate reported her missing. The report notes rain the previous night, and the only footprints found near her body belonged to the men who found her. She was wearing a T-shirt, jeans, and sandals. The cause of death is listed as strangulation. Her hyoid bone was broken, and there were pete-chiae in her eyes, both consistent with the finding. Skin was found under the ring fingernail of her right hand. Semen was found inside her.

Reading the file makes my whole body ache, from the base of my skull to deep in my hipbones. I close the file, toss it into the cluttered mess that is my coffee table. Suddenly exhausted, and a little too drunk.

I draw a bath in my dingy little bathroom. Hot enough that the window above the tub begins to cloud with steam. I look into the eyes of my reflection in the mirrored medicine cabinet; I look older than twenty-nine, my blond hair lank, my eyes deep-set with shadows. I feel about a hundred years old as I step into the filling tub, the water so hot I have to grit my teeth until I grow used to it, my skin flushing where it's submerged.

I cannot help but think of Maggie, as the water reaches my waist, my breasts, my shoulders, my throat. I think what a blessing it is, to never have seen a report like this on my sister, an inventory of her body and its injuries, an accounting of the manner of her death. There is never the knowledge of these things without the horror, and perhaps that horror is too great a price to pay, after all. I hold the thought, like a pearl between my teeth, as I sink below the surface of the water. Letting the heat burn every other thought away, my hair floating around me like a halo of golden, dead leaves.

SEVEN

Ava and I go to visit the prison the next morning. It's a three-hour drive, made slightly longer by the fact that we stop for coffee before heading out of town, and then again at a rural McDonald's to use the bathroom and buy some hash browns. Ava drives, because I haven't driven a car in about twelve years. Plus her ancient-looking VW Cabrio has a manual transmission, and I never learned to drive stick. The late-nineties convertible gave me pause when she first pulled up to the curb. But Ava only shrugged at my surprise.

"Ted thinks I'm crazy too. But they used 'Pink Moon' in the commercial for it," she says. "And ever since then, it was the only car I've ever really wanted."

It's one of the things I'm beginning to realize about Ava. Beyond the designer clothes and the beautiful house and the Adonis husband, there's a girl in there who might love something, even if it's wrong in all the ways that matter. Even though Ava could likely afford a car that costs fifty times what the Cabrio is worth. Even though she's the only woman in that McDonald's wearing Louboutins. She still drives this boxy little car, because she doesn't care how gauche it might be to love it because of a commercial. She still gets two orders of hash browns.

"How did you get the warden to agree to this?" I ask, polishing off the last of my coffee, which tastes burnt and acrid in its Styrofoam cup. "My partner said it's nearly impossible for podcasters to get approval to record interviews in prison."

"Ted called in a favor," Ava replies. "He's part of this big development deal on the North Side. Had an alderman reach out on our behalf."

"Lucky he has friends in high places."

"Lucky now," Ava says, correcting me. "Seven years ago, when Colin was first convicted, the two of us had so little money we could barely get him a lawyer."

"Really?" I ask.

"I was in med school, up to my eyeballs in debt," Ava says. "He'd just gotten his license. And Ted's parents weren't about to foot the bill for his girlfriend's brother's murder trial." The bitter note in her voice betrays the resentment that must exist between Ava and her in-laws. Perhaps between her and Ted, even. Another live wire, stripped bare between them.

"Now I never know what I'm going to find on these visits," she says, turning the radio down a bit. It's summer hits of the nineties, more millennials-on-a-road-trip music than driving-to-prison music. Though perhaps the more times you've been down this particular road, the less it seems like a somber, momentous occasion and the more it seems like just another long drive.

"I think in some ways, prison is having a deadening effect on him," Ava says. "Like the more time he's there, the less he can imagine getting out. When he was first convicted, I really thought I'd have him out in a year. I think I had him convinced too. So each year that goes by and he's still there, he gets angrier. Gets into more fights, puts himself in danger. It's like I've made it worse by keeping his hope alive."

"Hope is . . . ," I say, trying to find the right way to describe the thing I handle like a shard of glass. Delicate, brilliant, likely to cut if held too tightly. "Tricky."

"You know better than most," Ava replies. "It can turn against you quickly." She knows it too, I think. It's clear in the way she says it. She understands the thing that most people don't realize about hope: that too much of it can ruin you.

Outside the car window, buildings give way to soybean fields. The day is overcast. Cows dot the landscape. Raindrops occasionally fleck the windshield, chased away by the fast swings of the wipers. Everything is shades of gray and damp, loamy green. In the distance, the hidden sun curls threads of milky yellow through the clouds.

"I spoke to one of the cops in Rogers Park," I say. "He seemed pretty certain they have their man."

"Yeah, they've all been certain, since day one," Ava replies. "No matter what we put in front of them, alternative theories or different evidence or issues with their case, they never wavered from Colin. They were never anything but completely sure."

"He helped me get a copy of the case file," I say.

"Did you bring it with you?" she asks. I nod. It's in my bag, along with a mic and a handheld recorder Andrea bought for me.

"The detective seemed to think it would be convincing."

"Was it?" she asks.

"I don't know," I reply. "She's got his DNA on her. Under her fingernail. And . . ." I hesitate at using the word "semen," when it's Ava's brother we're talking about.

"He admits they had sex that afternoon," Ava replies, seeming to understand the source of my hesitation. "It accounts for a lot of the evidence they used against him at trial."

"But we're just supposed to take his word for it?" I ask, trying not to sound as incredulous as I feel. There's something about reading the case file that centered my focus back to where it should be: on Sarah. My agenda is not freeing Colin. I'm here to find out what happened to her, the story that lives beyond the edges of what can and can't be proven in a courtroom. It's a good thing to be reminded of from time to time.

"Go into my bag," she says, motioning to the Burberry tote on the back seat. "There are some papers in there you should see."

I lean back and grab the bag, its velvety leather heavier than I expected. I pull a packet of papers from it and look them over. It's an unredacted version of the case file. I compare it to my copy, where the personal information has been blacked out.

"So?" I say. "They're basically the same."

"But not exactly the same," she says. "Look at the evidence page."

I compare the two. The one in Ava's is a photocopy, complete with shadowy edges and flecks of dust. Mine looks like a scan, all black and white, a PDF with all the gray noise removed. But the information is the same.

That is, until I look closer. Nearly lost in the photocopy is a faint notation under "Evidence collected from victim's apartment," a marking that looks like it's been eclipsed with Wite-Out.

"What does that say?" I ask, squinting at the muddy reproduction.

"That's a third hair sample," Ava replies. "It was taken off the initial evidence list before it was released in discovery."

"Seriously?"

"They were afraid it might put someone else in Sarah's apartment around the time of the murder," Ava says. "Dylan's bathroom was off the living room. But Sarah had the master. You had to go through her bedroom to get to hers. So the police thought it would create reasonable doubt in the trial."

"But couldn't it have been from a houseguest, or from someone who lived there before?"

Ava shakes her head. "She had one of those mesh drain covers. The hair was caught in it. So it had to have been recent. And her roommate said that nobody but Colin had visited the apartment in the past few weeks."

"So someone was in her apartment, and she was hiding him from her roommate."

"Showering in her apartment," Ava says.

"You think Sarah was seeing someone else? Cheating on Colin?" I ask, and Ava lets the question hang.

"Do you have any doubt as to why the police are so convinced they've got their guy?" Ava asks. "It's because they ignored the possibility it was someone else. It's called pitting evidence. They remove anything that might threaten their case. We only found out about it after his conviction. Someone in the SA's office leaked it to our defense team. We still don't know who."

She's speaking in the plural, when she talks about the police. But of course, it wasn't the Chicago Police Department, writ

THE LOST GIRLS

large, who would have decided to hide the evidence in Colin's case. It would have been Detective Richards. The man who sat next to me for hours the night Maggie went missing, watching as I thumbed my way through the heavy books of mug shots stacked before me. Who told me that I'd been very helpful, even when I couldn't recognize a single one. *One of the good ones,* I always thought when faced with reports of CPD misconduct. Its racism and brutality. News stories of unlawful detainment and CIA-style black sites. *At least one of the good ones was assigned to my sister's case.* Now, however, I'm not so sure.

"But isn't this already enough to get him a new trial?" I ask.

"Not according to the appellate court of Illinois," Ava replies. "They said that simply the presence of another hair in the shower drain wouldn't have been enough to establish reasonable doubt for the defense."

"Did they ever test the DNA?"

"During the appeal," Ava replies. "But it didn't match anyone involved with the case, and it didn't match with anyone in the criminal database. So it's a dead end."

"Jesus," I reply, thinking again of Detective Olsen. How willing he was to help me get the redacted case file, the one that didn't contain the hair sample from Sarah's shower. His certainty that Colin killed Sarah Ketchum. An idea based on nothing, slipping away as easily as water cupped between hands. "What about the second appeal?"

"Ineffective assistance of counsel," Ava replies. "Three years after the conviction, Colin's attorney died of a Vicodin overdose. It turned out he'd been addicted for years, and there was evidence that he was high for most of Colin's trial."

"And that wasn't enough, either?" I ask.

"Marti, a few years ago the court denied the appeal of a man whose defense attorney literally fell asleep during his cross-examination of a witness," Ava replies. "My advice? Don't get convicted of murder in the first place."

"Not bad advice," I reply, beginning to understand Colin's anger. I think of all the years that have passed since Maggie disappeared. Maybe losing hope is simply the pragmatic choice, at some point.

IT'S LATE MORNING when we reach the prison. Ava has already taken me through what happens next, so I'm prepared for the metal detectors, the visitor release form, the pat-down by a bored-looking female guard wearing blue latex gloves. The guards seem particularly suspicious of Ava, in her suit dress and her stiletto heels, and of me by extension. Because we don't seem to belong here, among the other visitors. She asks Ava twice if she's counsel, and twice Ava shakes her head. They look even more wary when she produces a printout of the email from the prison's warden, stating that we should be allowed to bring recording equipment with us into the visitation room. They make us wait twenty minutes while the guards get the warden on the phone so he can confirm his permission.

It's not like I expect, though. Not like you see in the movies, a line of chairs on either side of a counter, separated by a Plexiglas partition. No, we're ushered into an open room with a scattering of green plastic tables, most already taken up with groups of people. Couples. Families. Some have little children with them. And the inmates are not wearing orange, like on TV. They're dressed in gray.

We take a seat at an empty table, and I pull the recorder out of my bag, plugging in an external mic and setting both out on the table between us.

"Colin's going to be okay with this?" I ask, motioning toward it.

Ava nods. "It's pretty much the point, isn't it?"

I don't have a chance to respond, because there's a flash of red hair in my peripheral vision, and I turn to watch Colin McCarty walk into the room. His skin is sallow, almost jaundiced, beneath the copper of his hair, and the patchy facial hair growing around his mouth reminds me of how young he is. Twenty-five years old. But his eyes are the same as Ava's, large and blue, though his stand out beneath pale eyelashes like drops of cerulean paint. His mouth has an almost feline curl at its edges, and his arms are wiry and heavily veined. He moves like he's imitating a boxer in his approach to the ring, all overblown swagger.

"Sis," he says when he reaches Ava, one arm looping around her shoulders in an embrace that seems false in its casualness. As if they're meeting at a backyard barbecue, instead of in a prison visitors' room.

"This is Marti," Ava says, turning to me. Colin looks me up and down in a way I don't appreciate and then glances at the recorder on the table. He says something, his mouth full of small, square teeth that make him look younger still. I don't catch the words, though it sounds a bit like Spanish. Portuguese, I remember, from my conversation with Ted.

"What?" I ask.

"Ignore him," she says to me, before clapping him on the shoulder, the reprimand of a weary schoolteacher, looking him in the eyes. "She's here to help you. How about you sit and answer some of her questions?"

"Sure," he says, giving me a Cheshire smile. His voice is higher pitched than I would have expected. "It's nice to meet you."

"I wish it could be under better circumstances," I say, though I'm only being polite. I seem to have already developed a healthy dislike of Colin. I know his type. His swagger, his brutishness— it's a combination that makes me certain that he's exactly the sort of guy who'd break a pool cue over another's back for being called a gay slur. No wonder a jury didn't believe his story.

"What, no Ted this time?" Colin says, straddling one of the plastic benches as Ava and I sit across from him.

"Not this weekend," Ava replies, and Colin gives a little snicker.

"Ted doesn't like me," Colin says to me, as if it's a point of pride. He seems entirely pleased with himself, actually, which is a strange posture to take when you're serving a life sentence. As if this is exactly where he wants to be.

"That's not true," Ava says, but it's a weak effort, we both can tell.

"What happened to your hand?" I ask, motioning to his left. Three of his fingers are splinted, and the back of his hand shows dark bruises.

"I got into a disagreement with one of the other residents here. Certainly not the first time," he replies, pulling his hand quickly away from Ava as she reaches for his wrist.

"Just let me take a look," she says.

"You know, they do employ actual doctors here," he says. "They gave me an X-ray and everything. Real twentieth-century medicine."

"What was the fight about this time?" Ava asks.

"Nothing important," Colin replies. "You know what happened here last weekend?" He motions around to the visitors' room. "Guy's brother got married in here. They did the whole ceremony right over there, vows and everything, so my buddy could be there for it. Let me tell you, there wasn't a dry eye in the whole place."

"What's your point, Colin?" Ava replies, her tone so flat the question seems hypothetical.

"I'm just saying, it would have been nice to be invited to your wedding," Colin says, turning again to me, his mouth seeming perpetually wet. "They got married at the Drake hotel instead. Would have cost less to do it here."

"Well, kid," Ava replies, "you get convicted of murder, you're going to miss a few family events." She says this like a parent admonishing their child that there will be no dessert because his homework isn't finished. Colin lets out a hearty laugh, and it's the first glimpse of him that doesn't feel like tough-guy posturing. The edge of a charm that probably once existed in him. Enough to draw a girl like Sarah Ketchum, once upon a time. A girl taught to look for something deeper, a bad boy with a secret vulnerability, waiting for excavation.

"So what's your story, Marti?" he asks.

"I thought I was here to interview you," I reply, a bit surprised that Ava hasn't explained my story to him already.

"Right to business," he says. "I like it. Okay, well, what do you want to know?"

"I guess," I say, caught a bit off guard by the abruptness, "I guess, tell me your memories of the night Sarah went missing."

He inhales slowly at the question, through his nose. Then he shrugs.

"It's funny," he says. "It's to the point now where I've thought so much about that night that I can't remember what are actual memories and what I've sort of cooked up myself since, you know?"

"I'm not sure I do," I reply.

"Like, everything is hazy. We were high, and I wasn't paying attention, you know? It's not like I knew it would be the last time I saw her. When I try to remember, I get things wrong. Like, I could have sworn she was wearing this pink dress when she left," Colin says. "She wore it all the time, because it was really short, and she had great legs. But then, it turns out, no. She was wearing jeans that night, and this white T-shirt, when she was found. So I must have been imagining a different night when she wore that dress."

"It's called a false memory," Ava interjects. "Our brains create memories that we never actually experienced sometimes, sort of filling in the blanks with inaccurate information. It's one of the big problems with eyewitness testimony, actually. You see what you want to see, a lot of the time."

Like a car that shifts from blue to gray to silver in my memory, I think. *Like a man's face I've never been able to recognize.* These ideas that haunt me, made of nothing. As insubstantial as vapor. I wonder if I've conjured them up all on my own, if the man and the car might dissolve with the lightest breath of air.

"But I mean, it was a regular day," Colin says. "I had class in the morning, and then I went over to her place after."

"Was she in school?" I ask.

He shakes his head. "She'd gone to art school for a semester or two but then dropped out and moved in with a friend of hers. They were both working for the same temp agency."

"Dylan Jacobs, right?" I ask, trying to fill in the details. Dylan's name came up a lot in the police report, first as the person who reported Sarah's disappearance, then as a possible suspect. Until the cops focused on Colin, that is. The other man in Sarah's life.

"Right. Dylan. He was a real . . ." Colin's eyes alight on the digital face of the recorder. "Well, he was always giving Sarah his opinions on the people in her life."

"People like you?" I ask.

"Dude seemed to think Sarah should be with someone more like him," Colin said, sitting back and crossing his arms, a pose of calm assurance that strikes me as either completely fake or completely natural. "Turns out, she wasn't into the sensitive types."

"He's got an alibi, right?" I ask.

"He was working at a call center that week." It's Ava who replies. "They record all of the calls their employees make. He's on tape through the whole period of time when Sarah was likely taken."

"Plus, I mean, you should have seen the guy," Colin replied. "I don't think he saw the inside of a gym in his life. Sarah could have taken him, if it came down to it."

"He's a sweet guy," Ava replies, a corrective. Probably for my benefit. "He threw her a surprise party for her birthday, invited all of us, stuff like that. He called me a couple times after Sarah disappeared. I got the sense that he didn't have anyone else to talk to about her."

"He threw that party to make me look bad," Colin replies. "To make it look like he'd had the idea and planned the whole thing. Like I wouldn't have thrown her a surprise party on my own."

"Honey, come on, you wouldn't have. You have a lot of exceptional qualities, but planning really isn't one of them." She says it with just enough sarcasm that it's clear she doesn't think many of Colin's qualities could be considered exceptional.

"Whatever, can I tell her the story now?" Colin says, as if this little detour has been entirely Ava's fault. She waves her hand, offering him the floor. "So," Colin says. "Dickhead had a job that week, but Sarah had the day off in between gigs. So I meet her at her place after class, and we just kind of hang out. We smoke a little, we hook up, we make some chicken salad and watch a movie. Then she's gotta go meet her friends, so I crash in her room while she gets ready."

"Why didn't you go with her?" I ask. "To meet her friends?"

"I was not their favorite person," Colin replies, his smile all mischief, like when he mentioned Ted. "It's tough to imagine, I know. But she still ran with her art school pals, and I think they all assumed that I was the reason she dropped out."

"Were you?" I ask, and Colin levels me with a dead-eyed stare.

"No." The simple word unsettles me, though I can't quite pinpoint why.

"Did she say goodbye before she left?" I ask, trying to smooth over what was clearly a question too far. Trying to get him back to talking.

"Yeah. She wakes me up, tells me to lock up when I head out."

"Did you have a key to her place?"

"No," he replies. "There was a lock in the door handle, you know? So you can just turn it and pull it closed." He's quiet for a moment, chewing absentmindedly on his lower lip. "Sometimes I think I dreamed that part. Her waking me up, giving me a kiss. Because I could have sworn she was wearing that dress when she left."

He looks almost wistful then. And suddenly there's a gentleness to him, an unexpected flash of nakedness beneath his haughty, rough veneer. Still so much a boy, beneath it all.

"What happened then?" I ask, if only because I want to pry at this glimpse of him, wedge something into the space he created between who he is and who he might have been. I want to keep him talking.

"I sleep for a little longer," he says. "Get up, shower, head to my grandma's birthday."

"How did you get there?" I ask.

"Cab," he replies.

"That was verified by the police," Ava interjects. "They found the driver, he's part of the established timeline. He remembers Colin being quiet, and his hair being wet. Nothing incriminating."

"Grandma's dead now," Colin says, and sniffs. "Passed right after the trial. That was the last time I ever got to celebrate her birthday."

This is a familiar lament, this idea of time lost behind bars. Of years being stolen and people slipping away. But part of me is still Maggie Reese's sister, and that part pulls against any burgeoning pity for Colin. After all, he is still here. So is his sister. They can still make each other laugh. His loss doesn't compare to the loss the Ketchum family has suffered. Time is nothing. I have had a lifetime of this already.

"So tell me about Sarah." Sarah, the reason I'm here. Not for Colin. Not even for Ava. I want to understand who Sarah Ketchum was, so her story will not be diminished to the reverberations of her murder. So she will not be just a dead girl.

And I want to see Colin's face as he describes her to me. Because deep down, I really do think I'll be able to see it, if he killed her.

"Well," he says, turning his hands palms-up on the table, like he's praying. "She was smart." He enunciates the word to give it emphasis, as if saying all of its consonants will demonstrate the scope of Sarah's intelligence. "She should never have been working at a fucking temp agency, that's for sure."

"So why was she?" I ask.

"She was also kinda fucked up," he says. "Not in like a bipolar way, but more in like an 'I'm not taking any of Daddy's fucking money' way. I guess her dad up and left her mom when Sarah was still in diapers. He had all this family money, and he still fought her mom for every cent of support. She said one winter they were living in a rental where the hot water kept going out, and her dad wouldn't give them an advance on the next support payment so they could move." His face twitches, like a wince of anger. "He was the one paying for her college, but he hated the fact that she was studying fashion design. Kept threatening to cut her off if she didn't change majors. So she took his fucking power away from him and dropped out. Just like Sarah; she'd rather quit school than let someone else make her choices for her."

"Was her dad pissed?" I ask.

"Oh my god, you should have heard him screaming at her over the phone," he said. "I was across the room and I could hear it. You know, she's stupid and impulsive, just like her mother, or no daughter of his was going to be a fucking dropout. Really cruel stuff, actually."

I glance at Ava, but she's already shaking her head. As if she can read my mind. As if this affinity between the two of us already lends itself to telepathy.

"Dad's got an alibi too," she says. "On a golf trip with some guys from his office."

"Plus, no one gets that angry at his kid if he doesn't love her, you know?" Colin says. *The sentiment of a kid whose father used to beat the hell out of him,* I think. But then there's my family, their indifference a different brand of that same kind of cruelty. How nothing I did could ever draw their focus from my sister's disappearing act.

I begin to notice a shifting at the tables around us, a sort of simultaneous gathering of belongings. I glance again at Ava.

"Time's almost up," she says. It feels impossible, even though I check my watch and realize she's right. We've been here for almost an hour.

"Will you come back?" Colin asks, and I can't tell if he's directing the question toward me or Ava, though she's the one who answers.

"Of course," she replies, while I remain quiet.

WE HEAD BACK to Ava's car in silence, the feeling of walking to the parking lot from the prison something like an escape. I only realize now how claustrophobic it was, inside those walls. The constant surveillance of the cameras, the constant presence of the guards. I imagine living my life like that, never being able to walk more than a hundred yards in any direction, and can't stop the rush of pity I feel for Colin then, no matter how misguided.

"So," Ava says when she unlocks the car. "What do you think?"

I get in, sitting heavily in the passenger seat. I play it all back in my head, trying to parse the conversation, trying to remember every word.

"What did he say to you when he came in?" I ask.

"Oh," she says, rolling her eyes a little. "It was Portuguese. It's sort of a family thing, we drop into it sometimes."

"I know, Ted told me," I reply, noting her attempt at deflection. "So what did he say?"

"He made a joke that if I was going to start bringing him women, he'd prefer ones with bigger breasts," she replies, wincing a little. But it makes me trust her, somehow, the fact that she tells me what he said. She's being honest, despite her own embarrassment. Despite the fact that it might offend me. It's as if Colin is just another one of those things she loves despite knowing better. And that devotion is enough to make up my mind.

"Look," she says. "He's a pig. Admittedly. But I swear to you, he's not a killer."

"Yeah," I reply as she starts the car and throws it into reverse. "I know."

EIGHT

Two days later, Andrea and I sit at opposite mics in her little bedroom studio, the conflicting case files open between us. It's just like Andrea to want to record this conversation. Just like she did when Jane Doe was found, turning the recorder on before I'd even gotten back to our table in the little bistro in Lakeview. Already recording, even though she didn't know what had happened yet.

"So," she says now. "From the beginning. Convince me."

Convince her, I think. But of what? Should I try to outline the ways in which Sarah's murder might be linked to Maggie's disappearance? Make the case that Colin McCarty may be innocent? Or simply pitch the whole story as interesting enough to carry our second season, even without any certainty of either the former or the latter?

I know how to begin, at least. I've been in the podcasting game just long enough to know that everything is a narrative. That Andrea means it when she says to start at the beginning. Not of Colin's case, but of my story. I have a part to play in this, whatever it will be. And I am the one our listeners trust, whether or not I'm truly worthy of it. The Virgil in this particular hell.

"So, this was the morning after the APA awards," I say into the mic, and Andrea gives a tiny nod. This is what she wants. I launch into the story, recounting the mysterious phone call from Ava, my first impression of her when she walked into the bar, when I discovered how close the house on Galley was to my childhood home, how Ava convinced me to review Colin's case.

"And she's right," I continue. "There's a discrepancy in the case file. Whatever did happen in that apartment, it's not as airtight as the state's attorney wants you to believe."

"So, you think this single blond hair in Sarah Ketchum's shower drain is enough to create reasonable doubt?" Andrea asks, clearly elated at being able to play the prosecutor here, though she's good at hiding it. Andrea, who probably would have been sucked into the legal world if journalism hadn't gotten her first.

"Alone? Probably not," I say. "But when you take into consideration the other problems of the case—like, how does Colin move the body within the CPD's established time frame?—suddenly it all seems very thin. And when you take into consideration the similarities between Sarah and Maggie, as well as the geographical proximity between the two . . ." I trail off, because this is the most tenuous of all my arguments. I can't appear to want too badly for the cases to be connected. I cannot demonstrate my own hunger for answers. Dispassion is what our critics will demand. I try to choose my words carefully.

"Look, it's true that these cases happened many years apart. But if they hadn't, if they'd been even a couple of years closer together, as soon as Sarah was reported missing, the similarities would have been more obvious. There are only two factors here that argue against a linkage: time, and the fact that Colin McCarty was convicted of Sarah's murder. But if the CPD hadn't focused only on Colin, you'd have two unsolved crimes involving teenage girls with similar physical descriptions, both of whom lived within view of each other for a period of time, transported by a man in a car at about the same time of day. So, I think it's worth investigating. I think there's more here than is apparent on first glance."

"Okay, so assuming that all of that is true . . . ," Andrea says, but I can already see that I have her. Her knee is hopping beneath the table. Pent-up energy, waiting to be unleashed in the right direction. "Where do you think we should start? The case is already seven years old, and Colin has already lost two appeals."

"I think we have an advantage, because we have a case to compare this one against. If we're operating under the assumption that Sarah and Maggie were linked in some way, we should start there. Try to find out as much about Sarah Ketchum as possible, and see how much crossover between them there actually is."

"Okay," Andrea replies. "So, here we go, I guess." She hits a button on the keyboard, ending the recording. She pulls off her headphones, and I follow suit.

"What do you think?" I ask, as if I haven't been talking to Andrea for the past hour. As if only now I'll get the real version of her.

"How much coffee have you had?" she asks.

"Why, do I sound manic?" I ask. The answer is three cups already, but I don't tell her that.

"Not quite, but I don't want it to sound like you're too invested in this."

"Speak for yourself," I reply, motioning toward her bouncing knee. It immediately stops. Still, Andrea is full of tells. The minute she tries to tamp one down, another surfaces. It'll be a few minutes, tops, and she'll be picking her cuticles or playing with the zipper on her hoodie.

"You know," she says, and then pauses, as if reconsidering what she was about to say.

"What?" I ask.

"Nothing," she says. And then, "Eric called me."

"My Eric?" I ask, though even as I say it, I admonish myself. He's not mine anymore.

"Yes," Andrea replies, kindly I think. "He said he hasn't heard from you in a while."

"Well, we're getting divorced," I reply. "I'm not sure this is really the time to be keeping in touch."

"I think a proof-of-life here and there would be appreciated."

I roll my eyes. "I'll try to be more regular with my Instagram posts."

"I wasn't sure whether I should take his call, to be honest," she says then. "I mean, should I be freezing him out? You haven't been very specific about how angry I should be with him."

"Not angry," I reply, though the idea of Andrea's righteous anger being deployed on my behalf is seductive. But Eric doesn't deserve it. "It wasn't his fault."

"I'm married, honey," she replies. "So I find that hard to believe. Plus, everyone always says infidelity is just a symptom of a larger problem."

A symptom of a larger problem, I think. Or a thousand tiny problems, every truth I kept from him, all those years.

"Of course it was," I reply.

THAT'S THE DIFFERENCE between Andrea and me; I have good control over my tells. When one of mine breaks the surface, it's because it's become tectonic. Built up so much power the whole world shifts.

It wasn't Eric's fault that I hid it all from him for so long. That he came into my life just as I was trying to figure out who I wanted to be, outside of Sutcliffe Heights and away from the people who knew me only as Maggie Reese's sister. Eric, at twenty-one, was delightfully serious. An economics major at Northwestern, like a middle-aged man trapped in the beautiful body of a high school lacrosse player.

And I was a puzzle to him, which I adored. His ordered mind seemed to have trouble teasing me out; his brow furrowed at my brashness and my sarcasm and at the fact that I kissed him in the middle of our second date, instead of waiting to be kissed after he walked me home. I loved the experience of being confounding, away from all the people who knew me so well. I loved being the focus of his gaze, after spending so much of my short life failing to draw the attention of my parents. So it also wasn't his fault that I decided—without consciously realizing it—to become the girl he wanted. Whomever she was. I wanted to be her.

I moved into his off-campus apartment at the end of my junior year, when I grew tired of the dorms, tired of my roommates. Eric was sweet, and reasonable, and he cooked and never let the trash get too full before taking it out. I wanted to be out in the world with him. And it was so easy, to love a life that was simple and clean and orderly and thrillingly adult. It was easy to love Eric, too, for all those same reasons.

We were married the year after I graduated. We bought our three-bedroom condo, with the backyard where we planted tomatoes in the spring. And in those first years, I made myself believe I could be normal. I could make Maggie small, a footnote only, like Eric's lost childhood sweetheart. After all, there was so much to lose in the life we shared. We were the sort to buy secondhand records and make reservations at Alinea when it wasn't an occasion. *Wednesday is reason enough, for us.* We went to dinner parties and dazzled Eric's coworkers—that couple, the one that seems especially charmed because they have survived something, my story the stuff of cocktail-party lore. We got season passes to Ravinia and went to every show, from the Chicago Symphony to the seventies cover bands that cycled through every year, sitting on the lawn and drinking cheap wine amid the tang of citronella candles. Eric introduced Andrea to an old ex-girlfriend–turned–friend—a thoroughly lovely designer named Trish—and the two of them were living together by that same time the next year. Eric dropped hints about children, and I pretended to be content.

It took effort, keeping my sister from my thoughts, in those years. Physical effort. I frayed at the edges. Picked the skin from my thumbs and developed stress fractures from overtraining and drugged myself to sleep at night, afraid of the nightmares that never seemed to stop. I smiled wide when his coworkers asked me what I did for a living, as if all my pretending was not work enough. Trying to hide the fact that beneath the woman Eric had married was a humming shell of bone, a woman with unblinking eyes, fixed on a single moment in the past. Unable to sleep, unable to settle. And all it took was a body in the morgue to summon her out.

ANDREA AND I arrive at the hospital at dusk, just as the sodium-vapor glow of the streetlights flickers on around us. Illinois Masonic Medical Center, its imposing brick structure overseen by the platforms of the Wellington L station. The same hospital where Jane Doe's body was left, outside the ambulance bay, her veins full of heroin and antifreeze. On a night not unlike this one, I imagine. The moment that began my undoing.

We ask for Ava at the reception desk, and a bored-looking security guard emerges from a pair of double doors to lead us inside to a small staff lounge, just a couple of couches, a table, a little kitchenette with industrial coffeemakers on its counter, and a flickering pair of vending machines. Ava rises from one of the couches when we enter, and I introduce the two of them.

"Feel free to set up here," Ava says, motioning to the couch and the coffee table. "I'm just keeping an eye on things until the night shift comes on."

"Thank you for letting us interrupt you at work," Andrea says.

I watch Andrea carefully as the two of them size each other up. I know what Andrea sees: Ava's perfect manicure, the expertly applied makeup—its effect making Ava look both glowing and barefaced. An ingenue in a movie, waking with perfect skin and lush eyelashes in the soft morning-after light. But there are also the scrubs, the white coat, the sneakers gone beige and soft from wear. The practical digital watch on one wrist, its screen scraped and nicked. And I know Andrea, her practicality. I know she will only hold Ava's beauty against her until she realizes how unfair it is to do so. After all, despite their differences, it's only a matter of time until the two of them recognize each other for what they both are: overly bright girls, finally grown old enough to be seen as savvy and capable instead of simply precocious.

"You're sure you don't mind us holding you up after your shift?" Andrea asks, setting her recorder between us on the table, quickly unfurling a mic and plugging it in.

"Whatever I can do to help," Ava replies. "I'd probably stay late anyway sending emails. Since it's a little late in the evening to be calling congressional offices."

"And that's what you'd generally be doing?" Andrea asks, turning on the recorder and checking the audio levels, before turning her attention back to Ava. "Spending your free time reaching out to members of Congress?"

"There have been four high-profile convictions in the past twenty years that have been overturned after a senator called for a review," Ava replies, all business. It's difficult not to be impressed with her, as if she instinctually knows that Andrea will appreciate this approach. Speaking in a way that will make the interview easy to cut together. "It's one avenue I'm exploring right now."

"And the others?"

"In the absence of grounds for another legal appeal, I've been trying to get the Innocence Project and other criminal justice–reform organizations to review his case. And lobbying the governor for a pardon."

"And you're doing all this in addition to twelve-hour shifts in the ER," Andrea says, less of a question and more of a way to state facts for the podcast's audience.

"Yeah," Ava replies. "My husband hates it. He thinks I'm going to burn out. He hates all the night shifts especially. Being apart, me coming home in the morning and just sleeping all day. I think he assumed this situation would be a lot more temporary than it has been."

"Colin's case?" I ask.

"And the job," she replies. "Like, once our fifth anniversary rolled around, I think he expected me to be downshifting. Getting ready to have kids, all that. But we're in this constant state of limbo, with Colin's case the way it is. I feel like I can't do anything that would shift my priorities right now, or take away from the little energy I have to put into his case."

I think of the way Colin joked in the prison visitation room, about missing Ava's wedding. And I know how Ava must be feeling, to perpetually delay life events in hopes that Colin will not miss many more. It's why I skipped both my high school and college graduations. It's why I convinced Eric to get married at city hall, with only his best friend and Andrea as witnesses. Despite the fact that he was just Catholic enough to feel guilty for not getting married in a church, and my mother was just pushy enough to insist on throwing us a reception after the fact. I'd finally had to tell him the truth to convince him to elope: I didn't want to have a wedding without Maggie there. I did not want to walk across a stage and get a diploma, because Maggie should have gotten hers first.

So I understand Ava's single-mindedness. Her obsession. By the end of my marriage, Maggie was like a poltergeist in our house, rattling dishes in their cabinets and making lights flicker in the night. I could no longer sit still; I could no longer sleep.

Suddenly I was back to the habits I'd had as a teenager. Walking through bus stations and strip clubs and shelters, showing Maggie's picture to anyone who would talk to me. Spending sleepless nights on crime-solver forums online. Scrolling through Facebook, the profiles of anyone who had ever reported living in Sutcliffe Heights, searching their pictures for the man in the car. The Jane Doe had been a reminder, in the placid adult life I'd crafted, that my sister was still out there somewhere. Maybe in the ground, rotting. Maybe alive and suffering. And I could not be allowed to be comfortable, I could not allow myself the possibility of happiness, after that.

But the hellish truth of it is that you simply can't delay your future forever. Or you end up like me. Nearly thirty, with nothing but ruins of the half-lived life I tore down before it could become any more real. A monument I'd built to my own selfishness.

I glance up from the recorder churning away between us, picking up the hum of our silence. Meet Ava's eyes. There's a recognition there, between Ava and me. The things we can see, just by looking at each other—the things our listeners will never know.

"So why emergency medicine, then?" Andrea asks. "Wouldn't another specialty have you home in time for dinner most nights? Give you more time to work on Colin's case?"

"Am I an adrenaline junkie, you mean?" Ava replies. "My husband certainly seems to think so. But honestly? I think it has more to do with Sarah. I'd gotten to know her pretty well, in the year she and Colin were dating. And seeing what happened to her . . ." Ava swallows. "I think I wanted to be in a position where I could fix some of the horrible things that people do to each other. Balance the scales of violence a bit, for women like her."

I watch as Ava picks at a small chip in her nail polish with her thumbnail, worrying at the small, imperceptible defect. Making it bigger because she can't leave it alone.

"Or maybe it's just because we spent a lot of time in emergency rooms when we were kids." She says it offhand, a note of black humor in her voice. "So I just . . . I never wanted to be anything more than I wanted to be an ER doctor."

"That's quite the dream," Andrea says.

"Yeah," Ava replies, motioning to the room around her. "And the hell of it is, I can't feel it. After everything, after all the work it took to get through college, med school, the loans and the studying and the crazy hours during residency, I still can't let myself feel like I've achieved it. Not with Colin in prison. I can't let myself feel like I have the thing I've always wanted. Even if it's true."

I watch Ava, transfixed. By her honesty, the way in which she articulates the thing I've always felt. The splinter inside me that is Maggie, the sharp thing that will not let me rest without a bit of pain. I look at Ava. It's a moment before I realize that Andrea's gaze is fixed on me instead.

"It's like," Ava says, "I'm not allowed to dream for myself anymore. Not until I fix this."

WE SPEND THE next hour sporadically recording in between Ava's last few patients, weaving from topic to topic so Andrea will have plenty to cut together as she edits. Ava's background in medicine. Context about her childhood in Albany Park. What Colin was like as a kid. It's ostensibly a slow night, but that doesn't stop her from being paged or summoned by a nurse every five or ten minutes, usually just as we're getting somewhere. Still, I can tell it's going a long way for Andrea, to see Ava in this environment. To see how capable she is, how competent. After all, could someone like this—someone who rattles medication dosages off the top of her head for the nurses and stitches up the split fingertip of a three-year-old across the hall—really misjudge her brother so egregiously? It seems impossible that Ava could be trusted to treat illness, to evaluate pain and resuscitate the dying, and not be trusted to be a reasonable arbiter of her brother's innocence or guilt.

The night shift is coming on when we finally pack up our things. Ava offers to buy us dinner, but I am bone-weary from my last shift at Club Rush and Andrea has to get home in time for Olive's next feeding.

"It's the one flaw in the two-mommy plan," Andrea says, pulling the milk she pumped earlier out of the lounge's refrigerator and tucking it next to the recording equipment in her bag. "I'll tell you, if I could draft Trish into taking a nursing shift, it would make all the difference."

"Are you two thinking of having more kids?" Ava asks, eating a fluorescent-red potato chip out of the bag she bought from one of the vending machines. Barbecue. I remember again how Ava loves the strangest things.

"That was always the plan," Andrea replies. "We'd switch off. I'd go first, then a couple years later she'd take a turn. But it feels sort of up in the air now, you know? Like, Olive is such a good baby, and it's still so fricking hard. Sometimes I think we'd be nuts to introduce more chaos into our family right now."

"Well, I was going to say that if Trish has a baby quickly enough, you could still be nursing in time to help out with the next one."

Andrea lets out a hearty laugh, and I know my plan has

worked. No matter her reservations about Colin, at the very least Andrea has developed a fondness for Ava.

"No way," she says. "If I had to go it alone this time, it's all up to Trish next time. Fair is fricking fair."

I DON'T SLEEP when I return home from the hospital, despite how tired I am. My apartment is hot and my skin feels sticky, buzzing with awareness against the muggy air of my bedroom. I don't open my windows, even for the breeze. Too many girls have gone missing from bedrooms with open windows.

Instead, I pour myself a drink and try to see what I can find on Facebook. In the past seven years, Sarah's profile has taken on a shrinelike function, like the profiles of so many deceased millennials. Friends post messages and memories and links to songs that remind them of her, creating a sort of hazy shadow image of the girl Sarah was. The sort who, according to her friends, loved Florence + the Machine and Prince and—to the explicit dismay of a particular friend named Rick—Justin Timberlake. The sort who scored a bunch of *Twilight* posters from her local movie theater and took to hiding them in her friends' apartments—in the bottoms of drawers, taped to the inside of a shower curtain. Once, brilliantly, beneath another poster hanging on a wall, which was finally found a year after her death, when her friend was packing up to move out of his apartment. He posted it to Facebook when he found it, a photograph of the smoldering eyes of Robert Pattinson tacked to his wall. *"You still have me laughing, even after you're gone,"* the caption reads.

Dylan Jacobs, Sarah's roommate, was also a frequent flier on Sarah's Facebook wall. Particularly right after her death, when

Dylan was trying his best—in those early days of social media—
to crowdsource information about her murder. Had anyone in
the vicinity of Greenview and Touhy seen Sarah leave her apartment? Had anyone seen a car parked at the entrance to LaBagh
Woods after sundown on the nineteenth? The family was offering a $20,000 reward for any information that would lead to an
arrest.

This was before Colin was implicated, of course. Based on the
loose timeline I'm putting together, Colin was questioned the day
after Sarah disappeared but wasn't arrested until the following
Saturday. After her body was found half-buried in LaBagh Woods.
After the requisite time for them to get the DNA match, I assume. As soon as the CPD had that, they had their man.

The tenor of Dylan's posts changed after Colin's arrest. Suddenly, it was all about bringing the person who killed Sarah to
justice. It was all about keeping her memory alive. I envied the
shift. What a luxury, to find a place to put your fury. What a relief, to believe that justice is possible.

I comb through the comments, read every word of every post.
This was 2012, after all. Back before the adult world believed that
social media actually made much of a difference in anything,
back before crowdfunding and doxxing and Russian bots and in-
fluencers were making the news. I doubt law enforcement spent
much time here, if any at all. So I doubt they saw the commenter
who said they saw a girl matching Sarah's description at a bar,
looking for her friends. Or the one saying they saw a girl a few
blocks from Sarah's apartment, except she was wearing a dress
and not jeans. Or the account of a silver sedan that pulled off Foster Avenue and turned into LaBagh Woods, despite the fact that
the woods weren't a place most people would go after dark. I

chew on nothing as I read them, all of them, drinking a screw-driver on my living room floor. My teeth hurt. My jaw aches. Has the CPD seen any of these? Do they even know these leads exist?

And then a new possibility occurs to me—Dylan Jacobs might not even know about the hair in Sarah's shower drain. That evidence was only uncovered after Colin's conviction, and it's possible that nobody ever questioned Dylan about who might have been showering in Sarah Ketchum's apartment that week. Sarah's roommate might be the key to this whole thing, and he might not even know it.

Dylan isn't hard to find. Though his Facebook and Instagram accounts are set to private, his LinkedIn fills in the blanks. He went to law school at Chicago-Kent after Sarah's death, purportedly to become a prosecutor, according to a post on Sarah's Facebook wall when he got his acceptance. Telling her that all he wanted was to protect the next vulnerable girl, put criminals behind bars. It makes me think of Ava, actually. The reason she chose emergency medicine when a different path might have been easier, or at least made Ted happier. How experiencing that kind of violence—the kind that happened to Sarah—can slip inside someone's DNA. How it can be the seed of something else, an entirely different kind of life. I wonder if that's what Ava and I recognize in each other. The dark blooms that have flowered within us, from coming so close to that kind of violence and escaping. Alive, if not unscathed.

Dylan's virtuous thinking apparently didn't last past his 2L year, though. Because according to his LinkedIn, he ended up at Waller Goodman, a Milwaukee litigation firm, after graduation. I find his email address on the firm's website and start composing a note. Standard stuff, really, saying that I'm a victims' advocate,

working on a podcast about violence against women on the
North Side of Chicago. Asking if I can speak with him about
Sarah. Within minutes of sending it off, I have a reply.

"Thank you for your email. This mailbox is no longer in use.
For general inquiries, please contact milwaukeeoffice@waller
goodman.com. If you are reaching out regarding an ongoing legal
matter, please reach out to grego@wallergoodman.com."

I hesitate only a moment before I forward the email on to whomever "Grego" is, asking if I might have Dylan's forwarding address or current contact information. After all, this is an ongoing
legal matter, of a sort. My head is starting to cloud with the
vodka, my thoughts turning like leaves caught in a swirl of wind.

My phone lights up the haze of my living room, making me
jump. I almost decline the call without looking at it, because the
only person I can think of who would call me this late is the man
who's been leaving me long, silent voicemails, content for me to
listen to him breathe on the other end of the line, as if he wants
nothing but to hear my voicemail recording. But no, there's a picture attached to the name on my screen. Me and Eric, taking a
selfie on the Michigan Avenue bridge, the pink flicker of sunset
lighting up the buildings behind us.

I know I shouldn't answer. Because the fucking divorce papers
are sitting on my kitchen counter, and no, I haven't looked at
them yet. Because I'm in no condition to talk to Eric right now,
well after midnight and well into my third drink. But there's
something about sitting alone on my living room floor, drinking
vodka, reading the comments on a dead girl's Facebook page,
that makes me want to talk to him. Because I have not yet learned
to break the habit of wanting Eric when I'm lonely. I tap answer
before the call goes to voicemail.

"Hey."

I can hear a subtle shifting on the other end of the line, as if he's straightening up. I can tell he didn't expect to reach me.

"Hi," he says. "Sorry, I thought I'd get your voicemail."

"Yeah?" I ask. "Well, is it something you can tell me?" I don't know what is allowed anymore. I don't know who we are, like this. People who used to know each other, to *know* each other, who are now on different sides of a line that's been carved deep into the sand between them. So deep, any step toward each other might cause a slide, might open a chasm. Might turn the ground beneath us into air.

He's silent for a moment, and immediately I think of the blocked number, the voicemails full of dead air. But no, Eric would know how that would scare me. And as much as I've hurt him, Eric would never be so cruel.

"I'm not sure I even know," he says. He's been drinking. I can hear it, in the looseness of his speech. I wonder if he can hear the same in mine. "I spoke to Andrea the other day."

"Yeah," I say, quickly, because I feel the need to claim Andrea's loyalty, to prove she does not share confidences with Eric that she doesn't also share with me. "She told me you called."

"She was telling me about the next season of your podcast."

He's fishing for something; I can tell by the way he keeps making statements and letting them hang as if they were questions. It's a habit he picked up as our marriage dissolved, often repeating things I'd say back to me, as if the words had lost all their meaning. Like: *"You're six weeks late."* And: *"You don't think it's mine."*

"Yeah," I reply, less concerned with taking up the space of silence between us now. There was a time when I could not bear it, could not stand even ten seconds of Eric's wordlessness. I remember begging him, actually begging, to tell me what he was thinking. To tell me what he wanted me to do.

"Do you think it's a good idea?" he asks. "Continuing this? I mean, I know how successful the first season was. But I also know . . ." He trails off, but it doesn't matter. I know what he was going to say. That he knows what it cost.

"Isn't this what you always wanted me to do?" I ask. "Find an outlet for my grief? Use what happened to Maggie to fuel something productive?"

"Yeah, like volunteer work. Your mother's foundation. A PhD. Something like that," he says. "Not . . . citizen crime-solving."

"It's not about solving the crimes, Eric," I say. "It's about telling their stories. The girls. The families."

"And you think you're the best person to be doing that?" he asks.

"Maybe not," I reply. "But it's what I've got right now."

It's a trap that I've set, and he knows it. Because he won't ask me to come back. To be his wife again. He finally knows me too well to want me back.

"I saw Coleman the other day at the gym," I say, to break the silence. "He said you're going to be his kid's godfather."

"Yeah," Eric says. "He's over the moon." He lets it hang. The eternal comparative, someone else's happiness, the sort that so easily could have been ours. "He didn't mention that he saw you."

"I get the impression that he's not my biggest fan."

"He wasn't an asshole to you, was he?" Eric asks. Still the white knight. Still wanting to protect me. I think of Coleman's cocktail party last summer, emerging from the upstairs bathroom with sweat at my hairline, my eyeliner smudged, my hands shaky. Like an addict, trying to mask the satisfied mania of a fix. Willing to do absolutely anything to prevent myself from coming down again. How I blamed Eric for not recognizing the change in me, blamed him for making me go to his friend's stupid cocktail party in the first place. How horrible I was then. Sometimes I think the price of it—losing Eric, our marriage, my home, my family—was not nearly enough. Sometimes I think a bigger penance is still waiting for me out there.

"No," I say. "He was a perfect gentleman." Because Coleman is right to hate me for what I've done. And sometimes I wish Eric would hate me for it too.

It's only after we hang up that I see the date on the screen of my phone. It's after midnight, but still. Yesterday was our sixth wedding anniversary.

NINE

Club Rush is particularly busy when I arrive, despite the fact that it's a Wednesday night. I was planning on doing a full Elvira tonight, with my waist-length black wig, but after the call with Eric and the sleepless night that followed, I don't have the time or the energy to make the effort. Instead, I use red lipstick to draw a line across my face at eye level and smudge it around my eyes like a mask, spiking my hair with some mousse my stylist gave me as a sample last time I was in. A silver choker collar is enough to make my black tank top and jeans look punk.

Marco gives me a high five when I arrive, and it can only mean one thing: he's rolling.

"Are you holding out on me?" I ask, and he laughs heartily, in a way only a twentysomething on drugs can.

"You look ah-maz-ing," he says, making the word its own

three-act story. He loops an arm over my shoulder so we may speak conspiratorially. "So, admittedly, yes, I might have borrowed some of my friend Bobby's pharmacopeia on the way here, but if memory serves I think I might have given the last of it to my Uber driver as a tip."

He must notice my disappointment, because his dark-lined eyes go wide.

"Not to worry!" he says, as if I'm a child who has spilled my milk and he is Mary Poppins. He actually cups my cheek. "I'm never without my own supplies. I left a little present for you in the loo."

"Is it your friend Bobby?" I ask, because I've met Marco's cohort of friends, and every one of them could be a Gucci model.

"Better," Marco says, grinning.

WHEN I STEP into the employee bathroom behind the bar, I'm elated to find that Marco has left me two perfect lines of coke on top of the toilet paper dispenser. Bless him. I snort them tightly and immediately promise myself that I will make good choices tonight, because it bears repeating now that I've stacked the deck against it.

The elation comes on fast, with a hard edge to it, as I slide into the rhythm of taking orders and mixing drinks. I remember how good this feels. To not think about dead girls. To let the Siouxsie and the Banshees song careening from the sound system batter me into a thoughtless daze. To not remember the things I have done, to Eric, to myself. The next time Marco crosses my path, I give him a giant smacking kiss on the cheek.

A face at the bar catches my attention, and the person gives me a little wave, though I can't place him. Except to note that he doesn't fit in this crowd, in his polo shirt and slacks. He looks like he belongs in a gastropub in Fulton Market, not here.

"Hi," I say, because, while I'm definitely firing on all cylinders, it's not really helping my cognitive function at the moment.

"Hey," he replies, half-shouting over the music, giving me a perfect old-Hollywood smile. Fuck, he's handsome.

"How are you?" I say, and he squints at me, as if he's unsuccessfully trying to wink. But no, he's assessing me, seeing what my game is. This is not the reaction he was expecting. Oh god, did I fuck this guy at some point? He's wearing a wedding ring. Shit.

"I'm good," he says, playing along. "I came to talk to you."

"Okay," I reply, unable to muster anything else.

He gives a little exaggerated laugh. "Can we go somewhere quieter?" He motions to the ceiling, clearly indicating the thrash of music that has us nearly hollering at each other.

But a silent alarm goes off within me, even despite the elation in my drug-addled system. It's the sense I've honed over years of encountering men and evaluating how dangerous they are, beneath the surface. And I'm not sure I should go anywhere with this man. I'm not sure I should be alone with him.

"I don't have a break for a while," I say, but a bit too quietly, because he leans forward, so close I can smell the cool brightness of his aftershave. Something expensive.

"What?" he says. And then I remember him. Ted. Of course. Ava probably told him where to find me. Ava, who will be on shift at the hospital tonight. Relief heightens my euphoria, and suddenly tonight has that magic sheen, like the whirling skin of a soap bubble. Like anything might happen.

"Okay! One sec," I shout back, and motion to Marco that I'm

taking five. He gives me two big thumbs up. Whatever he took must be really excellent shit, because he's clearly out of his mind. The bar is packed, and on any other night, he would happily skin me alive rather than let me take a break. But I know better than to ask twice, and motion Ted toward the back exit.

I lead him out to the alley, which is quiet as soon as the metal door slams shut behind us. It's raining lightly outside, with a bit of chill in the air. But not enough to drive us back into the noise inside.

"So what's up?" I ask, leaning against the brick wall, ignoring the proximity of the dumpsters, which are probably crawling with rats.

"I wanted to come see you on neutral ground, without Ava," he says, crossing his arms, as if touching anything in the alley will contaminate him. "And I'd appreciate it if you didn't mention this to her, either."

I can feel my heartbeat in my hands, in my tongue. Faster than a moment ago. What is this man after?

"Okay," I reply. "Sure."

"I hear you two went to see Colin," Ted says. "What did you think of him?"

"Well, he's not my type," I say, even before I realize how it sounds. Like I'm flirting, unabashedly.

Ted's teeth flash, in what could be a grin or a well-controlled grimace. "Ava seems to think his case is locked in for your second season."

"We started recording last night," I reply, trying somehow to reel back into my most professional persona. I stand up straight. Stop scratching at the skin of my wrist, which is my habit when

I'm keyed up. Already, the skin there is raw. *Wake up*, I think. *Be normal.*

"I think you should reconsider," Ted replies, unfolding his arms and shoving his hands into the pockets of his slacks. He's uncomfortable; I can see it in the way he holds himself. This is a betrayal. I recognize it from the men who were married, back in the day. Back when I was married too.

"Why?"

"Because you don't know Colin," he replies. "If you did, you'd know that killing that girl—"

"Sarah," I say, cutting in.

"Right," he says carefully. "If you knew Colin, you'd know that killing Sarah was something he was . . . capable of, I guess."

"What makes you say that?" I ask.

"That bar fight?" he says. "His prior arrest? It wasn't the first time he got violent over nothing. You should have seen him, even with Ava sometimes. And she loves him more than anyone in the world."

"He hurt Ava?" I ask, the heat going out of me, icy sparks of rain on my skin.

"No, nothing like that," Ted says quickly. "But, just his temper. It was out of hand. And their father was a bastard. Neither of them will really go into it, but he was really violent with Colin when he was a kid."

"So why does Ava disagree with you about Colin?" I ask.

"Because she's his sister. She loves him; she can't see him the way other people can," he replies.

"Or maybe she sees him better than other people," I counter. After all, I'm willing to consider Ava's point of view. I'm not sure if I trust Ted's yet. "Look, what's the worst that can happen? If he's guilty, we won't find anything, and he'll stay in prison. If he's not, maybe we can help with his next appeal."

"I don't want Ava getting more invested in the possibility of his innocence than she already is. It's already sucked up enough of her time and our life as it is," he says, and I can hear the simmering resentment in his tone. I think of what Ava said at the hospital, of the years she's waited to begin their life together, numbing herself with work and exhaustion and the minutiae of Colin's case. The years she's made Ted wait.

"And anyway, you know how these things go," he continues. "All you have to do is ask the question, make an argument. If enough people are listening, no matter what you find, it'll never be over."

"Colin said that you don't like him," I reply, though it's a cheap argument. I can see it now, though. How troublesome it must have been to Ted, to have such an unruly brother-in-law. To have Ava's attention divided, drawn away from him. After all, Eric already knew my whole story when he married me. Ava was someone else back when she met Ted. Tragedy came for her later.

"I was always the bad guy, for him. Just because I wanted him to take some fucking responsibility for his life," he says. "And now look where we are."

"I'm sorry," I say, though I'm not. It just seems like the sort of thing you say to someone like Ted, someone who is bemoaning the single flaw in his perfect, placid existence. The good job. The beautiful house. The beautiful wife. "But I gotta say, I understand where Ava is better than most people. And even if nobody in the world agreed with her, I don't think she'd ever stop trying to get him out." It is a similarity between me and Ava. Both of us, with our lost siblings. How neither of us will ever stop until the world gives them back to us. One way or another.

"I have to go back in," I say, and reach for the handle on the door.

"Wait." He moves fast, his hand around my forearm, stopping me from opening it. It's an electric feeling, the way he grabs me, and my brain's response is a rush of something that is both fear and excitement. I have to focus on not reacting, not letting the muscle memory of a hundred fights kick in, the instinct that wants to step forward and snap my hand toward my head to break his grip. Instead, I let his hand remain on my arm. Every part of me still awash with the drug, every hair on my body standing on end, until he realizes how close he is to me. Or perhaps he realizes that I've stopped breathing.

He releases my arm, but he doesn't step away. He's close enough that I must tip my head back to look him in the eyes.

"I'm asking," he says, "please reconsider. This is not a family you want to get wrapped up in."

"I'm sorry," I say again. It's all I can manage. I do not trust any of my instincts in this moment. I've learned that I cannot always recognize when I'm putting myself in danger.

"I don't think you are," he says, and the flash of those teeth might be fury or the tease of pleasure. I can't tell, with him.

"We should go inside." The rain is picking up now.

When he shakes his head, a droplet of water falls just below my right eye. But then he steps back, holds up both of his hands, as if he's pleading innocence.

"Fine," he says, and walks down the alley to the street, leaving me there, breathless, at the back door. When I touch my face, brushing away the droplet clinging to my lower lashes, my fingers come away red.

"THAT'S KIND OF fucked," Andrea says, not even trying to edit herself, which is how I know she's a bit too shaken by my story.

We're having breakfast in the same bistro in Lakeview where I got the call about the Jane Doe all those months ago. I wonder if Andrea remembers that this was the place, or if the memory has faded enough that this is just another café in her rotation, a place to meet and discuss business matters over a latte and a scone. There's a strange symmetry to it though, as I look around at its mosaic tabletops and its gleaming copper espresso machine and the leggy ivy plants hanging from the ceiling. The last time I sat in this bistro I was married, and owned a home, and was engaging in extended negotiations with my husband about the prospect of children. Now I'm fighting the cocaine blues, the drumbeat of a headache behind my eyes, and all that is lost.

"I mean, admittedly I was . . . altered," I say, reaching for a word that doesn't sound as childishly irresponsible as "high." I know Andrea considers my conduct in the wake of my divorce to be something of a second adolescence, or at least a second bout of undergraduate abandon. I've done what I can to dispel the impression of immaturity—that cardinal sin—now that I'm one half of a podcasting enterprise and she's the other. But it's not so easy when I spend my evening doing lines in the employee bathroom.

"I might be making more of it than there actually was." I don't tell her that I can't quite remember how hard he grabbed me, that I woke this morning half expecting to see a line of shadowy finger marks inside my forearm. That there was one false note of disappointment ringing in my chest when I found nothing. Because the sort of mature, professional persona everyone expects from Andrea and me, in the wake of our success, is not very compatible with the part of me that thrills at balancing on a sharp edge between irresponsibility and true danger.

Andrea glances at her bag, which hangs off the back of the chair beside her. I know what she's thinking—that we should be recording this. I shake my head when she catches my gaze.

"It's not relevant," I say.

"It feels relevant," she replies.

"What am I going to do?" I ask. "Admit that I was high? And that he asked me to back off the case?"

"Threatened you," Andrea retorts.

"He didn't," I say, and then replay the whole exchange again in my head, just to be sure.

"But he thinks Colin has the potential to be a killer," she says. "That is relevant."

"Look, if I talk about it on the podcast, it fucks us. I lose credibility because of the coke, and it puts us in a tough spot because it makes Colin look guilty. There's a good chance Ava will cut us loose for publicly questioning her brother's innocence. And Ted will definitely stop talking to me if we make the conversation public, especially after he asked me to keep it from Ava."

"Okay," Andrea says, holding up a hand. "Okay, but will you do me a favor and at least take some contemporaneous notes about how the conversation went? Just so, if it needs to come up later, we can be on a little bit of stable ground?"

"Sure," I reply as one of the baristas drops off our breakfasts. A slim glass layered with Greek yogurt parfait for Andrea, and avocado toast with poached eggs for me. She looks at my plate wantonly as I cut into one of the eggs, orange yolk spilling over the bread. "Want some?" I ask.

"God no," she says. "I would one day like to fit into something that's not overalls or elastic-waist pants."

"Please," I reply, because Andrea is one of those women who gained so little weight while pregnant that, up until her third trimester, you could tell she was pregnant only when you saw her from the side.

I remember how excited Eric was when Andrea and Trish announced that their withdrawal from the sperm bank seemed to have done the trick. I think he imagined it would end our years-long uneasy truce in the matter of reproduction and finally convince me it was time for us to start trying. But that was the thing about Eric. He saw his own desire as a kiln, a place of creation. And if he wanted something badly enough, the heat of his wanting could make it so. It was as if he'd already forgotten his childhood. That when his friend had died, all the wanting in the world would not conjure her back up.

He did, however, manage to convince me to go off the pill for a few months. It's a concession I'll never stop regretting.

"You want to keep playing this out, don't you?" Andrea asks, her gaze darkening. "This thing with Ted."

"Maybe," I say, though she knows me better than to believe my feigned casualness. "The way I see it, Ted doesn't want Ava to find out he talked to me. Or that he thinks Colin is guilty. So that might be useful down the line, if we need his help."

"The word you're searching for is 'blackmail,'" Andrea says.

"I'm not suggesting that I extort him for information," I reply. "I'm saying there might be a benefit to maintaining this dynamic with him. Where he needs something from me."

"The one where he corners you in dark alleys and tells you that you don't want to get wrapped up in his family business?"

"Yeah," I say, finishing off my coffee in one gulp, just a touch vindictive. Andrea only drinks seltzer these days, and I know how she misses caffeine.

"Do you think Colin might be guilty?" Andrea asks, and it's the question I've been waiting for, because it's the one I've been tumbling around in my mind all morning. Smoothing its edges, a stone against sand. Turning it, again and again, until I can only see my reflection when I look at it.

"I think it's possible," I reply, knowing that this is not the answer Andrea wants. "But I don't think that should stop us."

"You want to waste the goodwill of our audience on a guy who might be guilty?" Andrea asks.

"I want to find out what happened to Sarah Ketchum," I say. "If that means we prove a guy like Colin is innocent, fine. But she's the one I care about here."

It takes only a moment for Andrea to nod.

"Okay," she says, convinced. "Just don't let Ava and Ted make you forget that."

"I won't," I reply, hoping she can't hear the catch of resentment in my voice. Because this is what I've been doing my whole life, chasing the ghosts of girls who never grew up. Who were never given the chance. It'll take more than Ava and Ted to distract me from that.

TEN

The first time I cheated on Eric was at Mathilde's, a dive bar in Wicker Park. Our local, mine and Eric's. A place where we knew the bartenders, where we had nightcaps after dinners out, and where we pregamed before parties. Where one of the bartenders had lit a match for me to blow out on my birthday, made the whole bar sing to me.

It happened the day I gave the DNA test to Detective Olsen. Four days after that call at the bistro, four days into recording the first season of the podcast with Andrea. Just as things were beginning to tilt out of my control. Giving my DNA was the thing that finally did it, made the possibility real. That my sister was dead. That I could have an answer.

I was supposed to be on a run. I'd been tossing and turning in bed for an hour before Eric suggested I take my nervous energy outside, put it to good use. Still, I shut my phone off a block away from home, so Eric couldn't track my location. I think I knew, as soon as I got out into the night air, that it wasn't a run I needed.

Carey, the man-bunned weeknight bartender at Mathilde's, asked me if I wanted water as I sat down, motioning at my moisture-wicking tee and skintight running shorts.

"God no," I replied. "The outfit is just a pretense." He poured me whiskey, a double, and I spent the next hour searching #bluelizard on Instagram, imagining the tattoo on Jane Doe's leg. Carey refilled my glass twice as I scrolled through hundreds of photos, finally pausing on a photograph of a woman's thigh. Posted by a tattoo artist in Bucktown, in 2015. In the photograph, a freshly inked blue iguana tattoo, with a halo of pink inflammation around it, shined in the light of the flash.

It was almost a perfect match for the tattoo on my side. The same shade of blue, even, a deep cerulean with orange detailing around its edges. Just like the stuffed animal Maggie had as a child. I wondered if it was the same tattoo on Jane Doe's leg, where she lay in a refrigerated drawer in the city morgue.

Carey rested his arms on the bar in front of me, drawing my eyes away from the phone.

"Last call. Want another?" I glanced around. The bar had emptied out, leaving the two of us alone.

"No, I should probably go," I said, quickly sending the artist a direct message on Instagram—asking for information on that particular tattoo—and dropping some cash on the bar. I didn't want to wait around for too long. Not with three drinks roiling in my empty stomach, not with the possibility of my big sister on a slab.

"You sure?" Carey asked. "On the house. If you keep me company while I close."

Go home, whispered the voice in my head. *Go home, go home.* Like the mantra I used in the middle of a nightmare. *Wake up, wake up, wake up.*

I RETURNED HOME two hours later. Stumbled in on unsteady legs, still shaking. I kicked off my running shoes and headed straight for the bathroom, hoping I wouldn't wake Eric as I crept in stocking feet across the bedroom floor. If he was awake, he didn't give any indication as I eased the door shut between us.

I tried not to think about the storeroom behind the bar, with its plastic crates and its black rubber floor mats and the neon light of the jukebox outside its door, turning Carey's skin from green to blue to orange. The way I'd been nearly nauseated with lust, flushed and shivering in the tiny space, laughing drunkenly into the frayed collar of Carey's T-shirt.

Without turning on the bathroom light, I peeled off my running clothes, my skin sticky with sweat, and turned the shower on, stepping into the cold stream before it even had the chance to warm. Lathering my hair with shampoo, taking handfuls of body wash to my skin. Rinsing my mouth, spitting into the drain. Turning the dials to keep the bracing cold. The memory of my college dorm rising in the dark. Of living without air-conditioning, the way cold showers would chase the heat from my skin for the briefest of moments, only until I would step back into the muggy heat, return to the close air of my tiny shared room. That was how it felt that night. Like even the gooseflesh on my skin would be short-lived, like I would only have to step back out into the dark, let my mind wander for a moment, and I would again be consumed with heat.

* * *

NOW, AS SOON as I step inside McGinty's, which Silvia promises is Detective Olsen's after-shift watering hole, I think of that night. Something about the smell of the taps and the blare of the TVs brings it all back. Makes me miss it, that old bar. The life I had before.

I glance up and find that it's still the top of the ninth of the evening's Cubs game. I was hoping they would have finished up losing by now, but it seems they're stretching out the torture a bit, so I take a seat at the corner of the bar and order an Old Style. McGinty's is your typical neighborhood dive bar, sandwiched in between a Mexican restaurant and a liquor store, narrow enough to accommodate only the bar and a few small tables in front, plus a dartboard and an ancient-looking pinball machine next to the bathrooms in the back.

I recognize Detective Olsen right away. He's sitting with a few other guys at a table toward the back of the place, and while he and his buddies are all in plain clothes, they're all clearly cops. I'm not sure if he notices me at the bar, but I can almost feel it when one of his buddies does. It's that sixth sense again, the one my friends in college would tease me about. Born from a lifetime of wariness, of watching the men around me more carefully than any adolescent girl necessarily should. Looking for a face I'll recognize. Waiting to see if I'm in danger. I can always tell when a man has noticed me, when I'm being followed.

So I'm not at all surprised when Olsen's buddy takes the seat next to me at the bar.

"Hey, John, can I get another?" he says to the bartender, laying it on a bit thick with his extremely misplaced Chicago accent, which should instead have landed him on the South Side rooting for an entirely different baseball team. But, like everywhere else in this city, the accent is shorthand for social status. And this guy is a cop, pure working class, and proud of it, even if he's off the beat and in plain clothes tonight.

"You want another whiskey?" the bartender asks.

"Nah, I'll have whatever she's having." He motions to my glass. I wonder if he knows he's a good ten years too old for me. He looks like he's within a stone's throw of fifty, with the beginnings of jowls and the slicked-back hair of a Donnie Brasco wannabe. Even on my worst day, I don't think this man would have made the cut.

"What are you having?" he asks.

"Old Style," I reply. I pull out my phone and pretend to be reading my texts. On one of the TVs mounted above the bar, the Cubs' pitcher hits the batter on the leg. A chorus of groans and curses swells around me.

"I told you this guy can't fucking close," the cop next to me says over his shoulder, in the direction of his buddies. "You watching this?" he asks me, motioning to the screen. He's drunk, I can tell.

"I'm waiting for a friend," I reply, my phone still open in front of me.

"Not a Cubs fan?"

"Not really." My voice is quiet. I'm wearing a denim jacket over a jersey sundress, and I make a show of pulling my jacket tighter around me. Hoping one of the cops at the table will notice my discomfort and come collect their friend. Hoping it will draw Olsen's attention enough that he'll recognize me.

"So where's this friend of yours? Making you wait," the cop says. The bartender sets his beer down on the bar in front of him.

"He's on his way," I reply.

"Oh, *he*," the cop says. "Your boyfriend?"

"No," I say, quieter still. There's always been something about meekness that attracts this sort of man. The kind who thinks he can badger his way into a woman's good graces, or at least into her bed.

"No? You don't have a boyfriend?" He's got his hand on the back of my chair now, a far more intimate pose than the situation warrants. He smells sharply of sweet cologne and sweat. I hear one of his buddies call to him from the table.

"I'm sorry," I say, motioning to my phone. "I kind of want to be by myself."

The cop leans back a bit, letting out a huff.

"Oh, I see," he says.

"No offense," I say quickly, because I know my indifference will only hurt his ego further.

"No, of course not," he says, his tone full of sarcasm. I can tell he's about to explain a few things to me. "You know, this is a neighborhood place. People generally come here to be friendly. To be social with their neighbors."

"I'm just here to meet someone," I say. I can feel the bartender watching us now, keeping tabs. He's a nice-looking middle-aged man, the kind of guy who lasts at a place like this because everyone likes him.

"Yeah, well, is it too much to ask for you to be a little friendly in the meantime?" the cop asks, and then the hand is back on my chair. "Here, how about I buy you a drink?"

"I don't want a drink," I say, a bit more forcefully. This has gone on long enough.

"Wow, okay," the cop says, louder still. "You are some piece of work, aren't you? A guy tries to be friendly, and you treat him like he's a regular fucking creep, huh?"

Out of my peripheral vision, I see the bartender motion to someone at the table behind us. And then Detective Olsen is suddenly between me and his friend, a hand on his friend's shoulder.

"Hey, Jimmy, how about you come back and watch the rest of the game with us?" Olsen says.

"Oh, now I'm the asshole here?" the cop says, clearly not so drunk that he can't tell he's being handled. "I'm just making conversation. Friendly conversation. And she acts like I'm assaulting her or something. Girls today—you can't even talk to them without being accused of something."

"Come on," Olsen says to the cop, and glances at me, perhaps for the first time. This time, I can feel that pulse of recognition when he looks at me. Like static in the air. "Come on, man. I'll settle up your tab." It's clear from his tone that he's not asking. It's a relief when the older cop relents, shoving away from the bar and trudging back into the surly embrace of the rest of his friends. I wonder why exactly Detective Olsen inspires this sort of deference from a guy who has clearly been on the job much longer. Though, when I glance between Olsen and the rest of the cops at the table, Olsen's the one I'd bet on in a fight. The others look like they're in various stages of middle-aged decline. Up close, Olsen's leanness betrays wiry muscle. The look of a fighter, the promise of tightly coiled power.

"Thank you," I say, letting the self-conscious hunch in my shoulders relax. Because, no matter how good I've become at defending myself, I'll admit it's still not a great idea to bait a drunk guy at a bar when he's got friends. You never know whether the man who appears at his shoulder will be there to try to calm him down or to back him up.

Detective Olsen is quiet, signaling the bartender.

"I'm closing out for Jimmy," he says when the bartender approaches. He hands over a small stack of bills.

"Can I close out too?" I ask.

"I've got you covered," Olsen says, motioning to the bartender, who gives a little nod.

"Oh, you don't have to do that," I say, but the older man is already heading to the register on the other side of the bar.

"Old Style here is two fifty. It's the very least I can do." His words are friendly but his tone is flat. I know his type, calm and militaristic. Handsome enough to be noticed, even if he says nothing. His silence its own kind of control. Without even a glance, he drops a few bucks on the bar and returns to his friends.

His indifference stings a little, actually. And my aim for the night—talking to Olsen about Sarah's case file—seems to have already failed. I do want another drink, but I'd feel silly staying here now that he's paid my tab. So I head to the bathroom, pee, and splash water on my face, trying to kill the last of my buzz before my bike ride home.

It's when I come out of the bathroom, pass the table of cops, that I feel it. A hand—a paw, really—grabs the left cheek of my ass and gives it a good squeeze, shocking me through the thin fabric of my dress. I go blank with heat. A rush of rage. A hum in my ears.

I move without thinking. Well, mostly without thinking. There's a voice in the back of my head shouting, *Cop! Table of cops!*, which is basically all that stops me from grabbing the nearest beer bottle and breaking it over his head. Instead I turn on him, grabbing his arm and putting my weight into his shoulder, tipping him off his barstool. He goes down like a bag of cement, wholly unready for a fight, connecting hard with the sticky floor of the bar. The impact knocks the breath out of him and I can hear the wheeze of air escape his gullet. He gasps as I pin his wrist and plant a knee in his stomach.

There's shouting around me. The cops are on their feet, and the bartender looks like he's considering an ill-advised vault over the bar. I sense one of the other cops moving for me on my right, a bald man who probably outweighs me by a hundred pounds, and mentally prepare myself to get slammed up against the bar's brick wall and handcuffed. But Olsen intervenes, blocking his friend's path, a hand on his chest.

"You are committing a felony right now," Jimmy's would-be savior is shouting.

"Easy," Olsen says, shoving the other cop back. "Everybody just calm the fuck down, okay?"

Another of the cops is gleefully holding out his phone, filming the whole thing. Olsen turns to me, one hand still outstretched to the cop he was holding back, who fumes red down to his collar.

"Would you mind getting off my friend there?" Olsen asks, as if I've accidentally stepped on Jimmy's foot instead of putting him on the ground. But there's something endearing in Olsen's politeness, so I give Jimmy a little extra jab with my knee and then let go of his arm.

"Were you just going to let him grab me like that?" I ask as I straighten up.

"I wasn't planning on it," Olsen replies. "Want to file a report?"

"No," I say. The last thing I need is a police report with my name on it, to be involved in an internal investigation of a CPD officer for a bar fight. "But maybe you should keep a tighter leash on your friends." Olsen gives one grim nod of acknowledgment as the other cop brushes past him and begins trying to haul Jimmy off the floor. You'd think I kneecapped the guy, for the fuss he makes getting up.

"Bro," says the guy who's filming, to Jimmy. "How does it feel to be taken down by Tinker Bell?"

"Fucking bitch," Jimmy says, straightening up, he and his counterpart both glowering at me.

"Do you want me to let her kick the shit out of you?" Olsen asks. He grabs Jimmy's jacket off the back of his chair and throws it at him, hard. "Go home, Jim."

"Who made you king shit, Olsen?" Jimmy's buddy says. All righteous bravado, the kind I've seen before a hundred times. Full of the misplaced certainty of a man who believes he's never wrong because he carries a badge. "She's lucky she's not in handcuffs right now."

"Sure," Olsen says. "Three drunk cops arresting a girl for acting in self-defense. I'm sure your captain would be thrilled at that, especially when she gets a lawyer and sues the department for sexual battery."

"Her word against ours," Jimmy says, crossing his overly tanned arms, clearly bolstered by his friend's confidence. A macho contact high.

"Until they find out who she is," Olsen replies.

"What?" Jimmy's friend says. "Who the fuck is she?"

"She's Maggie Reese's little sister," he replies. The name is enough. Between the notoriety of the case and my mother's continued philanthropic efforts, Maggie is still well-known in

Chicago's criminal justice circles. And now, because of the podcast, so am I.

"Fuck, are you serious?" Jimmy's friend says under his breath,
turning wary eyes toward me. I raise one eyebrow, a challenge.
"All right, all right," he says. "Fine. We're going." He herds Jimmy
out of the bar, under the disapproving gaze of the bartender. I
know what they must be thinking. If I get a lawyer, or go to the
press, or even just post about this on Facebook, I have enough of
a platform right now to ruin Jimmy's career. All of their careers,
maybe. I'm almost angry enough to do it.

But picking a fight with the CPD, no matter how sleazy some
of the men in their ranks prove to be, does me no good in my investigation. No matter how the echo of his hand through my
dress sends a surge of disgust into me, makes me bite hard on my
tongue to focus the new tide of rage. Honestly, I'm a little afraid
I'll cry if I remain here any longer. It's the part of me that is always eight years old, always wants to kick and sob whenever I'm
hurt. So I turn and grab my jacket, ready to head for the door, and
then Olsen is at my side.

"Hold up a sec," he says.

"What, am I under arrest?" The words come out like a challenge, but my eyes are wet, adrenaline receding. Opening a pit,
shame washing in. I blink fast, trying to hide it.

"No," Olsen replies. "I was hoping I could buy you another
drink. Make up for Jimmy being a bastard. Again."

"I'm not sure a drink is going to cut it," I reply.

"So what would?" Olsen asks. It's strange, to feel the sudden
pull of his attention, to be the object of his interest, when only a
few minutes ago I held none of it.

"Answer some questions about the Ketchum case," I say. "We'll call it even."

He smiles, shaking his head. A genuine smile, the first I've ever seen from him. "You never stop, do you?" he asks. *Stupid girl*, I think. Because there's no way I'm leaving now.

"No," I reply, and wonder what I'm getting into when he motions for another round from the bartender.

"HOW OLD WERE you in 1998, Detective?" I ask as I finish my first glass of whiskey.

"Twelve years old," Olsen replies. "Junior high."

"Let me guess," I say. "Spent the summer playing Little League in some suburb?"

"Not quite. More like setting my parents' garage on fire in Canaryville." Olsen is actually not bad company, now that he's speaking in complete sentences. The change is stark, when just a few minutes ago I was doing my best to get his attention, all meek and grateful in my lip gloss and floral dress. Batting my eyelashes, waiting to be saved. Eric's girl, all over again. But it seems I've underestimated Olsen as much as he's underestimated me. Because here I am now, suddenly sharp edged and formidable. A girl capable of anything. And now I have his attention.

"That doesn't sound very upstanding," I reply.

"Well, I took the long road to upstanding."

"So what are you doing watching a Cubs game if you're from Canaryville?"

"Rooting for them to lose, of course," he says. "Living on the North Side is good practice for being undercover."

"Is that something you have to do a lot in Rogers Park?" I ask, needling him a bit as I sip my drink.

"Not lately. But before I was here, I was on a joint task force with the FBI. Working on a white nationalist group downstate."

"Oh, so actually undercover?" I imagine it. Living as someone else, completely, even for a little while. The small measures I take—giving men Maggie's name, dressing up as a goth at Club Rush—are nothing compared to the immersion of being undercover. It seems a dangerous thing to think about for too long.

"Nothing as salacious as the stuff on TV," he replies. "I didn't develop a meth habit or anything. Mostly, I worked construction with these guys, hung out with them on weekends. The FBI wanted someone local—you say the right things about the old neighborhood, and suddenly you're in the fold."

"Did they make you shave your head?" I ask.

"Different kind of group," he replies, rolling up the sleeve on his right arm, just to the elbow. "They were more into ink." He has a large dark stain on the inside of his arm, a tattoo that's been blacked out.

"Jesus," I reply. "What was it?"

"Eighty-eight," he replies.

"Eighty-eight?"

"The eighth letter of the alphabet, H. Meaning . . ."

"Heil Hitler?" I ask, whispering to keep the bartender from hearing. Though somehow as I do it, whispering it seems even worse.

He gives one solemn nod.

"That's intense."

"Did you hear about that synagogue in Skokie that was firebombed last year?"

"No."

"So, there you go," he says, rolling his sleeve back down.

"They were planning to firebomb a synagogue?" I ask. But I can see it now, in the way he carries himself, something that could be a simmering viciousness beneath the surface. I can see the way he must have behaved while he was undercover, so potentially dangerous he would be seen as a trusted comrade to the sorts of people who firebombed houses of worship. I wonder how much of it is authentic and how much of it is lingering habit.

"Among other things," he replies.

"So was it hard to go back to your normal life after that?" I ask.

"I don't know," Olsen replies. "I'll let you know when it happens."

The bartender brings us two more whiskeys, collecting our empty glasses. He gives me a wise smile, as if he's somehow orchestrated this, a matchmaker proud of his work.

"So what about you?" Olsen asks. "Where exactly did you learn to flatten a guy twice your size?"

I give a demure little shrug. "Well, Detective, I heard about child sex trafficking at a pretty young age. You grow up with that in the back of your mind, you develop some interesting hobbies."

"Krav Maga?" he asks.

"Brazilian jiu-jitsu," I reply.

"Not easy."

"No." I shake my head. "It's kind of a ballast, I guess. To make me feel like I have some control, out in the world."

"How long have you been doing it?"

"I took a self-defense course in college that kind of kicked it off. But honestly, I should have started a lot sooner. I put myself in a lot of dangerous situations as a kid, after Maggie. I think I probably used up all my luck back then."

"Like what?" Olsen asks.

I try not to think much about my teenage years. Made up of typical rebellions—drugs and boys and skipping school. And then the atypical. Stealing into Chicago and walking through its back alleys. Its bus stations and motels. Looking at the faces of the women I found there, trying to recognize my sister. I think of it now and can't imagine how I came through it unscathed.

"Like trying to find my sister," I say, unsure of how much I should reveal to this man. The feeling of stepping out onto ice, slowly. As if I can force gravity to ease its hold, if I'm careful enough. "Or trying to prove that it wasn't Maggie's fault that she went missing."

"Why did you think it was her fault?" Olsen asks, chewing a shard of ice from his glass. I watch the muscles of his jaw work, the shadow of stubble there.

"I'm not sure the police ever really believed me, that a man took her. It seemed like they were looking for something she did wrong. A reason she'd leave. Or a reason she'd be taken, instead of all the other girls. Instead of me."

"If it means anything, Detective Richards believed you," Olsen replies.

"Really?"

Olsen nods. "He gave me his notes on the case when he retired. He seemed to think you were their best lead."

"Well, the cops from Sutcliffe Heights made it seem like the only reason a girl from our town would go missing was if she deserved it, somehow."

"How old were you?" he asks.

"Eight."

I think I see something, like a wince maybe, under his eyes.

"And I worshipped my sister," I say. "I thought she was perfect.

So I spent a lot of years trying to do all the things that would prove them wrong. Like, if I could be reckless and still be here, then it meant it couldn't have been her fault."

"So how long did it take to finally prove them wrong?" Olsen asks.

I think of last summer. The men I followed into hotel rooms, into the bathrooms at bars, into their apartments. No matter that I was married, that the crucible of my wild days should already have ended.

"I'll let you know when it happens," I reply.

WE'RE ON OUR third round when I show him the page from the case file Ava gave me. The one with the Wite-Out in place of the third hair found at the scene. His brow furrows as he examines it, an unguarded moment, and suddenly I can see the boy he once was, large eyed and inquisitive, the sort of boy who only grew angry when the world would not tolerate his earnestness.

"What is it?" he asks. "I can't quite make it out."

"It's a third hair that they found at the scene. They took it off the evidence report so it wouldn't be used at Colin's trial." I consider the harsh gravity of his expression. "You didn't know."

"I didn't work the case," he replies.

"But you've seen this sort of thing happen before, haven't you? You've seen the CPD pit evidence, stop their investigation when they find a suspect they like."

"I really can't answer that," he says. I'm the one to roll my eyes now, because I'm a little drunk. And this posture of professionalism—the military devotion to protocol—is feeling a bit tired. After all, this is Chicago. Nobody follows the rules here, especially not the police. And if Olsen were really as devoted to protocol as he pretends to be, he would never have bought me a drink in the first place.

"So look at the case now," I say. "We know someone else was showering in her apartment, likely the same week she was murdered. If you were the detective on the case, wouldn't you try to find who that was?"

"I would be curious who that person was," he replies, speaking carefully, his mouth tight. "But like I said . . ."

"You weren't the detective on the case," I say, putting the page from the case file back in my bag. Because I know what my next move has to be. "So how do I get in contact with Detective Richards?"

"I might know some guys who still see him."

I glance over at the table of remaining cops behind us. They seem to have lost interest in the TV now that the Cubs have finished losing and are instead taking turns at the dartboard. Occasionally stealing resentful glances in our direction. An entire table full of disapproving chaperones for our little date here at the bar. Perhaps it's because I'm the enemy. Or perhaps because I've allowed Olsen to sit with me, to buy me drinks, after refusing to allow Jimmy to do the same.

It's always mystifying, when guys are annoyed that a woman would prefer the company of another man. As if women must be impartial in their choices. We're not allowed to simply follow our attractions, as men do. Our attentions are tokens to be earned through good works—chivalrous acts like opening car doors or not calling you a cunt even if they think you're really acting like one. And each man is allowed his own righteous anger if we women are not impartial enough, do not justly reward his virtuousness. If we choose wrong, we are stupid, or shallow. Or sluts.

"It's not those guys, is it?" I ask.

"Unfortunately."

"Shit," I reply. "You're going to help me out here, right?"

"I don't know," Olsen replies, leaning in a bit, until I can smell his skin, the sharp sweetness of alcohol. "I get the feeling that helping you might not be in my best interest."

Back in the day, at this point in the conversation I'd have been leading Olsen toward the bathroom by his belt. Because his friends are probably right, whatever they think of me, whatever name they'd call me. I have been all those things, and more recently than I'd care to remember.

But this is different, somehow. I'm different. So instead I lean in too, until I'm just about whispering in his ear.

"You can help make sure justice is served."

"Sure," he says, "but I do that every day."

"How about I let you buy me dinner, then?"

Andrea would not be happy with me. I'm pretty sure this is very much against her journalistic ethics. But fuck it, I want to talk to Detective Richards. And I want to see Olsen again, in spite of myself. I may not be leading him to the bar's bathroom tonight, but that doesn't mean I don't want to have the opportunity again, sometime.

But before he can answer, my phone lights up. I try to ignore the little thrill I feel at the sight of Ava's name on the screen.

"Sorry," I say. "I need to take this." I slip away from the bar, stepping out onto the street. It's raining lightly, so I stand in the doorway, feeling my skin grow damp from the air alone.

"Ava?"

"Someone attacked Colin," she says, her voice warping as she speaks, like the tightening of a guitar string. She's trying to hold back tears. "He's in the hospital infirmary."

"Oh god," I say, any residual lightness from my flirtation with Olsen washing right out of me. "How bad?"

"Bad," she says. "Fractured ribs, probably the radius in his right arm, maybe his eye socket. And that's just what the fucking warden would tell me. He wouldn't let me talk to the doctor treating him."

"Are you allowed to visit him?"

"Not while he's in the infirmary," she replies. "I don't think they want me examining him. The standard of care in these places is basically one step above a fucking Walgreens clinic."

"I'm so sorry, Ava," I say, glancing back into the bar. Olsen is gone from where we were sitting. Fed up, perhaps, with our truncated flirtation.

"We have to get him out of there," she says, and the same throb of emotion is back in her voice. "He can't spend the rest of his life in prison with those animals. We have to get him out."

"We will," I say, with more conviction than I really feel. "Did they notify his attorney?"

"Yeah. We're meeting tomorrow morning to see if we can file an emergency motion . . . I can't remember what he said it was for."

"It's okay," I say. "Just call me after, all right? Let me know what he says."

"I will," Ava says, and I think I can hear her sniffle a bit on the other end of the line, before it's disconnected.

I feel a bit ill. As much as I'm not Colin McCarty's biggest fan, the idea of his lying in a poorly funded prison infirmary with a variety of broken bones is enough to turn my stomach. I think about his splinted fingers during our visit, how he played them off like they were nothing. Now I wonder if they weren't an earlier warning of whatever has happened to Colin now.

The air-conditioning in the bar feels excessive when I step back inside, the night's dampness clinging to my skin. My jacket is still on the back of my seat, and I pull it on, trying to cultivate what little heat is left in my limbs. I'm suddenly excruciatingly tired. I toss a few bills on the bar and look around for Olsen.

I find him back at the other table, back with his buddies, already midconversation. And all the inside information in the world wouldn't be enough to make me walk over there now, have to muster a defense against the antagonism of those men. So when he glances up, I motion to the door and then turn to go before I can see his reaction. Before he has the chance to try to convince me, again, to stay. I leave quickly, heading back out onto the street, walking a handful of blocks before I even think to call an Uber.

Ava's desperation has unsettled me. In quiet moments, when I let myself think for long enough, I understand my aim has only ever been to find out what happened to Maggie. No part of me has ever really believed I could find her alive. So I can't imagine what it must be like to be in Ava's position, feel your sibling slipping away slowly, violently, and be the only person trying to save him. I must serve as a cautionary tale for her, the threat of what is in store for her perfect life, if she loses her fight for Colin. I am what it looks like when that battle is lost. I would be desperate too, if I were in her place.

ELEVEN

Some nights, my mother is there when I kill my sister. My grandmother, too, occasionally. They beg me to stop. They wail until their voices crack, but they do not touch me. They cannot, as I pick up the thing at my feet—a wrench, maybe. A razor blade. They cannot stop me from using it, her throat opening under the blade as easily as the skin of a tomato. They clutch each other and sob as her blood slicks my hands. The man watches too.

I WAKE IN the morning to a call from a number I don't recognize. I answer it, in the haze of half sleep, expecting it to be Ava with more information about Colin's condition in the prison infirmary. Instead, it's the stilted sound of a man's voice.

"Hello, I'm trying to reach Martha Reese?"

"Yes," I say, feeling the word click against the dryness of my tongue. I can't remember the last time I did not wake up cottonmouthed and hungover. I glance at my bedside clock, and it's nearly one in the afternoon, much later than is acceptable to still be sleeping. I swallow and sit up, trying to sound as coherent as possible. "This is Martha."

"My name is Greg Orloff, at Waller Goodman in Milwaukee. You reached out regarding Dylan Jacobs?"

"Yes," I repeat, deciding that speaking as little as possible is the best tack to take here.

"I apologize," he says. "But I couldn't find your name in any of Dylan's records, so I was wondering which case you were inquiring about." He has the speed and cadence of a man who is trying to get through an unpleasant task while performing two or three other unpleasant tasks simultaneously. A bit frazzled, a bit distracted, a bit resigned.

"Oh, I'm just trying to get in contact with Dylan," I reply.

"You said in your message that you were reaching out about an ongoing case," Greg says.

"Right," I say. "I am. About his college roommate, in Chicago. Sarah Ketchum?"

The name clearly doesn't ring any bells for Greg, because he breezes right past it.

"My apologies, I didn't realize you were reaching out regarding a personal legal matter. Unfortunately, Dylan isn't currently employed by Waller Goodman, and we don't have any record of his work regarding legal matters outside the firm." This sounds like an answer he's given more than once, by rote. But, at the very least, he seems more upbeat now that it's clear the call will end quickly.

"I was just hoping you could put me in contact with him," I reply. "Do you have an email address, or a phone number?"

"I'm sorry," he says, and then pauses for a long moment. I

assume he's going to tell me he can't give out the personal information for a former employee, but he doesn't. His voice is halting
when it comes back over the line. "We don't know where he is,"
he says.

And just like that, I'm very much awake.

"What?"

"Dylan," he says. "He's been missing for the last two months.
I'm sorry to be the one to tell you."

"Missing?" I know I must sound a bit dim to Greg. But in actu-
ality, my mind is running so quickly that it's difficult to form coherent sentences. Dylan is missing. The person closest to Sarah
Ketchum at the time of her death—besides Colin—has disappeared. The one person with insight into who might have left
that hair in Sarah's shower is gone. Nauseated excitement shud-
ders through me, the feeling of a stranger's hands in a hotel room,
in a storeroom behind a bar. The part of me that revels in the
terrible things. I know enough, by now, to be ashamed of it.

Milwaukee, I think. I've been tracking disappearances from
Chicago for the past ten years but never paid much attention to
the cases involving men. And I never expanded my search to the
city just two hours' drive north of here. The city where Sarah's
roommate moved after law school. The city from which he disappeared, only a few months after the release of a podcast that
might be connected to his roommate's murder.

The possibilities turn kaleidoscope-fast through my mind,
each one blooming with new color as it takes shape. The starkest,
of course, is a single question: Did we do this? Did Andrea and I set
off a chain reaction—by recording and releasing *Jane Doe*, by es-
sentially reopening Maggie's case on our own—that moved, tidal
and fast, from Maggie to Sarah to Dylan?

"My apologies," Greg says. He seems to be a man who spends most of his time apologizing for things. "All I know is that he didn't show up to a deposition one day, and when we couldn't reach him, we contacted the police. No one here has heard from him since."

"When was this?"

"I think the deposition was on May second," he replies.

"Are they treating it as a criminal case?" I ask, though I already suspect Greg won't be much help. He sounds like the unlucky guy charged with taking on Dylan's work in his absence, not exactly a close friend of his.

"I'm not sure," Greg replies. "The police questioned everyone around the office. But . . ." He trails off for a moment. "Look, I heard from a friend of mine that they found drugs in his apartment. Oxy, fentanyl, a few other opioids. I think the police are treating it like he might have gotten mixed up in something dangerous."

"Is there anyone I can contact who might have more details?" I ask. "Does he have family in the area?"

"Look, we weren't exactly close," Greg replies. "I know he took off a week last winter to move his great-aunt into assisted living, but that's the only time I heard him mention family."

I'm already googling, even as Greg speaks. Buried beneath Dylan's social media accounts and a few Waller Goodman puff pieces—buried to the point where I missed them during my first bout of research—there are three newspaper reports about Dylan's disappearance. Only three. All local Milwaukee outlets.

It's not such a surprise. The disappearance of a young man doesn't have the same dark poetry of a missing girl, none of the romance the media always finds in the idea of women being taken or running off. Those stupid women. Those bad girls. Flocks of them. Like birds. Scattering, with no warning at all.

But it's also clear that Dylan can't have much family, if his disappearance warranted only three mentions in the local press. That's what happens when nobody is out there rattling the cages for you, trying to make sure you're found. You get even more lost.

"Okay, well, I appreciate you calling to let me know," I reply, because I'm already considering my next move. Reaching out to the Milwaukee police for information, certainly. Or perhaps the request would go over better coming from a cop. I think of my conversation with Olsen last night and wonder if my sudden departure from the bar has ruined any chance of his helping me.

Then there's Ava to contend with, who is already distraught over Colin's attack. I wonder if news of another disappearance would go a long way to reassuring her that we're making progress in Colin's case. Or perhaps it would be doubly painful for her, if Dylan's disappearance turns out to be nothing. I know the kind of damage false hope can do. The promise of that Jane Doe in the morgue last year. Maggie, down to the lizard tattoo on her thigh. Everything fit. Everything. And it still wasn't her.

I worry how Ava will react to the same kind of disappointment. She, after all, has much more to lose.

"I'm sorry I couldn't be more helpful," Greg is saying.

"Thanks," I reply, trying to get off the phone as quickly as possible, knowing who my next call will be. "Have a good— I mean, I hope everything goes okay." It's a pathetic effort at civility, but I'm operating at reduced mental capacity as it is, and it's really the best that I can do under the circumstances.

Greg is just saying, "You too," when I hang up and select the first and only contact on my phone's "Favorites" list. Andrea picks up on the third ring.

"You know," she says, without even saying hello, "I'm already looking forward to the days when I can just give her an iPad or sit her down in front of the TV and stare out the window for ten uninterrupted minutes. I'm fully prepared to leverage her mental development and her attention span for it. Whatever, she can tell it to a therapist one day."

"Sarah Ketchum's roommate disappeared two months ago," I reply, and hold my breath—literally, hold my breath—listening for Andrea's reaction. There's a long pause.

"Are you serious?"

"I just got off the phone with a guy he worked with. He dropped off the face of the earth."

"Okay," Andrea replies, "I'll be there in twenty."

Her tone reminds me that we're a bad match in some ways. Because I hear the poorly controlled excitement in her voice, how it mirrors my own. Sometimes I wonder if a better partner would be dispassionate and cautious, slower to process and deliberate in action. Instead, Andrea is more than willing to dive in with me, right into the deep end. Excited because something lurid has happened, because our answers can only come at this cost. Diving with me, right to the bottom, maybe.

"SO LET'S GET this straight," Andrea says as we sit on my living room floor with the pages from the case files strewn around us. Sarah's and Maggie's. Distinguishable based on the typeface—portions of Maggie's in blocky typewriter font, most of it written by hand, while Sarah's is all clearly computerized. Andrea has bags under her eyes and her hair is a mess, a tangle of curls barely held at bay by a cloth headband, but her face is alight with a mania that I recognize. I myself have been compulsively cleaning my apartment since Greg called, my hangover receding the more I go over and over the possibilities of all this. As grisly as they may be, new crimes bring with them new information. New connections. They are useful. The police told us that a hundred times, in that first decade Maggie was gone. To keep our fingers crossed, that a new case would reveal the truth.

I remember being twelve years old, aware that my father no longer slept and instead spent his nights watching the tree line out our back window, as if Maggie were simply lost out there. Apt to turn up some night, stumbling and gaunt and dehydrated, twigs in her hair. Her feet bloodied with blisters from those years of wandering that span of trees, our shortcut home from school. I remember listening to him shuffle to the bathroom and back, praying—actually asking God—for some new girl to go missing. If only to give us some clue as to what had happened to Maggie. That was a lesson I learned, at twelve. That I am the sort to offer up another girl's life in exchange for the answer to a question.

"We've got a hair in Sarah's shower drain," Andrea continues, laying out the case as it stands, "indicating that someone was showering in her bathroom. Probably in the week before her death. So we potentially have a third party in the apartment, who sees Dylan as a threat. Enough of a threat that the killer goes after him now to keep him quiet."

"Which means that Dylan knew him, at least a little, right?" I say. "Even if Dylan didn't make the connection when the hair was found in the shower, the killer still assumes Dylan could identify him."

"So he's met the killer, at the very least," Andrea says, nodding.

"You know, Sarah's father potentially links all three of them," I offer. We've been trying to track down Walter Ketchum since we took on the case, with little success. His last known address was in rural Colorado, and the last familial connection he had in Chicago was severed when Sarah's mother died of lupus two years ago. "I mean, he likely met Dylan at some point, right? And he lived two streets away from us when we were kids. You can see his old house from Maggie's bedroom window."

"I thought he had an alibi," Andrea says, already wary.

"A golf trip," I reply. "But do we know it's solid? What if the CPD ignored something there too?"

"I'm not saying it isn't compelling," Andrea says, placating me but clearly too weary to hide it well. "But let's try and focus on the evidence we have first, before we start exploring the things that may or may not be missing, okay?"

"Fine," I say, as if the word is sharp on my tongue. A blade, spat out, as Andrea pulls her recorder out of her bag.

"I don't think we should wait to get any of this on tape. Tell me again what you told me on the phone."

She presses the record button and sets it down between us, waiting for me to comply. For a moment, I'm obstinate. Glaring at her, unwilling to acquiesce too easily to her directives, as the numbers on the recorder's digital face begin to climb. Because it's not enough, for me, to exonerate Colin. Or to solve Dylan's disappearance. I need the connection. I need Sarah's proximity to my childhood home to be more than just coincidence.

Andrea raises an eyebrow at me.

It takes no time at all for me to crumble under the first sign of her impatience. Still the ignored daughter. The lonely little sister, always wanting approval. I silently curse my own frailty as I begin to recount the whole story for the podcast, from the top. And in no time at all, I'm reminded, again, what a good producer Andrea is. She has a knack for asking just the right questions to keep me from glossing over details or veering off track. It's easy to assume that a listener will have enough information to jump to the conclusions I do, but Andrea always slows me down, makes me explain my thinking, prompts me to reiterate who key players are and which details are important. By the time Andrea shuts off the recorder, any lingering anger within me is gone.

"Here's a question," I say as Andrea shuffles through the paper around us, clearly trying to keep everything in some semblance of order. "Should we be telling the CPD about Dylan's disappearance?"

She glances up at me. "You think they don't know?"

"I think it's amazing sometimes how little police departments share information," I reply, remembering the jurisdictional struggles between Sutcliffe Heights and Rogers Park over Maggie's case. "Especially when enough time has elapsed. Milwaukee might be aware that he's related to a Chicago case, but Chicago might not know he's missing."

Andrea clasps her hands and then holds them against her mouth, and I know she's about to say something she thinks is terrible.

"Would it be wrong of us to wait on that?" she says. "I mean, do we have a moral obligation to share information with the CPD?"

I know what she's thinking, that it would be a boon to the podcast if this is a link we can investigate on our own. And I understand the impulse—after all, Dylan has already been gone for months. Any linkage between Dylan's disappearance and Sarah

Ketchum's murder might not even be taken seriously by the CPD, especially since they all believe Sarah's killer is locked up in prison right now. Still, something pulls at me. A desire to do whatever is necessary to help Dylan. Wherever he is. If he's still alive.

"Okay," I say. "Let's call the tip line in Milwaukee and tell them about his link to Sarah's case. If they want to share information with the CPD, they can. But I want to make sure the people who are looking for him know that there's a broader context here."

"All right," Andrea says. "I'll call it in when I get home."

"So you know what all of this means?" I ask. "If these cases are linked, then Colin is definitely innocent. So all we need to do is prove the linkage, and he's in the clear."

"I know," Andrea says, her words slow, deliberate. "But we need to be careful, Marti. You know? We were just here. Jumping to conclusions, the both of us. Seeing patterns because we needed them to be there. And the fallout from that was . . . it was too much."

"The fallout," I repeat, though I know what she means. My little drop off the deep end. "It wasn't because we got it wrong, Andrea. Is that what you think?"

"If I'm being honest, I think it was probably a mistake," Andrea replied, hands in her lap, fingers tense hooks, winding around each other. "Investigating the Jane Doe. I don't care how popular the podcast is. I never would have suggested it if I thought this might happen." She gives a little wave, the motion of her hand encapsulating me, this apartment. The state of my life. My recycling bin, full of glass. The baby I didn't have.

I take her hand, interlace her fingers with mine.

"I would have fallen apart if it turned out to be Maggie too," I reply. "And even if we'd never recorded a word. At least now I feel like I'm trying. Like I haven't just abandoned her."

"And what if we never find her?" Andrea asks, her voice thin. More possibilities she doesn't want to say at full volume, lest she tempt fate. That knife, ever dangling above our heads, ready to drop without warning. "What if you never find out the truth?"

It's the question that has dogged me since I was eight years old. Not just the mystery of Maggie but of how I could possibly build a life on that unanswered question. A foundation of sand. I did it once, and it took nothing at all to bring it down.

"I don't know," I reply. "Maybe I just do this. Maybe I just keep looking."

"That's what I was afraid you'd say," Andrea replies.

My phone lights up, an unfamiliar number.

"I should get this," I say, glancing up at Andrea. "Someone beat the shit out of Colin yesterday, and Ava told me she'd call."

Andrea hesitates, then gives me a little nod of acquiescence. A promise that she won't be pissed at me for breaking up our little therapy session with a phone call. I stand and answer it.

"I had to bribe Silvia for your number," the man on the other end of the line says. "So you owe me a pack of Marlboro Lights and a caramel Frappuccino." The voice has that same even tone I heard for the first time in the Rogers Park police station. Habitually deadpan, with a slight rasp. My skin prickles as it did last night, when I was close enough to whisper in his ear.

"You know she gouged you, right?" I say as Andrea watches me. "Usually she spills her guts for just the coffee."

"I'll have to keep that in mind for next time," he says.

"So, what can I do for you, Detective?" I ask, growing warm

under Andrea's gaze. I get up from the couch and walk to the kitchen. She follows me, conspicuously trying to listen in on Olsen's end of the conversation.

"You left so quickly last night, I didn't get a chance to tell you."

"Tell me what?"

Now Andrea is in full-on French mime mode, making gestures of exaggerated, mute urgency as I swat her away, trying very hard to keep Olsen from hearing any of the rustling movement that is happening on this side of the line. I finally duck into the bathroom and shut the door behind me, with Andrea on the other side of it.

"I got Detective Richards's email," he says. "And all I had to do was promise my buddy that you would go out to dinner with him."

I go still for a moment.

"Tell me you're kidding. Or I'm hanging up and moving to a different country."

I think I can hear the sly grin in his voice as he replies. "Yeah . . . ," he says. "But I'm not sure I want to unleash you on the man while he's enjoying his retirement."

"Can you reach out to him for me, then?" I ask, jumping at the opening. "He'll remember me. Just ask if he's willing to talk, off the record."

"Why do you think I'm inclined to do you any favors?" Olsen asks, and this time, I know he's flirting. I can always tell when a man is making a chess move he thinks will ultimately get him laid.

"Aren't you?" I counter.

"All right," he says, his voice faux stern, now that he's relenting. "But if I get you a meeting with him, you're buying me dinner."

"Fine," I reply. "I'll even wear my Sunday best."

"Let's not get crazy now," he says.

ANDREA IS WAITING in the doorway to the kitchen when I emerge, a hand on her hip.

"And what exactly were you doing last night?" she asks in her very best headmistress tone.

"None of your business, Mom," I say, dropping my phone onto the coffee table and sitting back down on the floor.

"Is this something we need to talk about?"

"What?" I ask.

"Your sudden affinity for cops."

"I went to a bar to show Olsen the case file. See what he said."

"And?"

"He was a bit evasive," I concede, deciding to leave out any reference to my confrontation with Jimmy and his wandering hands. "But I think he's a good contact to have in the CPD."

"You know he might be keeping you close so he can keep tabs on the investigation?"

"I know." The thought did occur to me. Olsen worked undercover, after all. It wouldn't be much of a stretch for him to engage in a bit of mild flirtation to get me to reveal my cards. "I didn't tell him about Dylan. I haven't told him anything that isn't already public knowledge. And he's reaching out to Detective Richards for me."

"How very helpful of him," she replies.

"I'm very charming, Andrea," I say, ignoring her sarcasm. "Sometimes men just want to help me."

"If that's what you want to call it," Andrea replies. She motions

JESSICA CHIARELLA

to the papers strewn around my living room floor. "So what do we do next?"

"Call in the tip to Milwaukee. I'm going to reach out to a woman I know from this true-crime message board," I reply, an idea forming. "She's had a lot of luck crowdsourcing information about missing persons cases. Maybe she'll be able to help with Dylan."

"I'll reach out to Ava, see if she can give me a list of the people Dylan invited to Sarah's surprise party," she replies. "It might be a good place to start, in terms of men both Sarah and Dylan would have known." She pauses and then pulls her hair into a thick ponytail at the nape of her neck. "Do you think this guy—the killer—knows Milwaukee all that well?"

"What do you mean?"

"It's just, it's a pretty big risk. To travel to a city you don't know to kill someone." Her voice is decisive, like she's simply stating a fact. "Especially after all those years."

"I guess," I reply.

"So the only reason to do it would be if someone started digging around in an old case. And the victim was a loose end that needed to be tied up." She shakes her head, all humor gone from her face. In its place is a look of something like anguish. "Did we get this guy killed, Marti?"

"We don't know he's dead," I reply, because it's a mantra I live by. They're not dead. Nothing is certain until we find them.

184

TWELVE

When I first started lurking on true-crime forums, while I was still married to Eric, I wasn't really looking for help with Maggie's case. I didn't hold out much hope that a decades-old disappearance—one that happened in the nascent days of the internet and without much evidence to speak of—could be solved by the amorphous congregation of amateur sleuths who made up CrimeSolversOnline.

Instead, I was looking for the people there. The ones who, like me, could not let themselves stop. Who could not simply grieve the losses they—or others—had felt. Who were driven to do something to shift the balance of their lives back to a sense of purpose or justice or good. I wanted to feel like the churning energy of my own grief could be put to use.

Of course they already knew about Maggie. The case was famous enough, a pretty, blond sixteen-year-old walking home through a shortcut in the woods. An eyewitness in her little sister, precocious and potentially unreliable. Secrets the two sisters had hidden from their parents uncovered in the investigation. When I first visited CSO, I spent a lot of time reading what was written about me on those message boards. How the local police had largely discounted my story as a potential cover for Maggie's simply running away, while the CSO members believed me to be credible. They seemed to recognize that teenage girls don't simply run off for nothing. Not in a world like ours, where even the youngest of adolescents can feel the press of eyes around her and understand the danger there. The people in the forum seemed to know that a girl needs a reason, most of the time, before she runs.

I never told them who I was, not until *Jane Doe* aired. And even then, there were skeptics, or some people who thought I had been disingenuous in not revealing who I was sooner. But mostly, they seemed to understand. We were all hiding something of ourselves there, each of us with our own reasons to spend hours a day unknotting the threads of other people's crimes. To try, always in vain, to undo the harm that left us guilty for living so unscathed.

ARMY8070 was one of the first people on the forum whom I spoke to at length about Maggie. She spends most of her days on CSO after quitting her job to move home and care for her ailing father. The rumor among the other CrimeSolvers is that before that, she was army JAG. Whatever the case, she's known as the high priestess of crowdsourcing, because she's so adept at using paid social media advertising to generate information on cold cases. From what I've seen of her on the forum, she's also kind. Her messages rarely contain any qualifiers or opinions—she seems almost impatient with wild speculation. She is a woman who lives and breathes facts, and she is the one I turn to for help with Dylan Jacobs's disappearance.

I can set up a targeted advertising campaign on social media, ARMY8070 says when I message her on the forum. It'll probably cost you a couple hundred, depending on how many users you want to reach. But I can pinpoint it by location, so people who live within a four-block radius of your missing man will see it.

I'm not even really sure what I'm looking for, I reply. Strange cars? Strange men? Anything strange?

Let's try something more general, she says. Name, photo, location, potential time of disappearance. A number people can contact with information. Are you prepared to offer a reward?

I'll have to get back to you on that, I reply. Maybe our production company can come up with something. I know I can't. Last time I checked I had a bank balance of $340.

If you send me the info, I can put something together tonight after Pops is asleep, she replies.

Thanks, I reply. I owe you one.

Let's just find him, ARMY8070 types before signing off.

AVA CALLS AS I'm heating up a can of soup for dinner. It's more of an afterthought, as I've spent the past hour compiling everything I know about Dylan Jacobs and sending it to ARMY8070. I've been eating like I'm in college again, meaning most of my calories are coming from vodka and foods that only need to be microwaved. I make a mental note to buy some fruit next week, if only to prevent the possibility of scurvy.

I debate, in the moment before I answer the phone, whether I should mention my discovery about Dylan to Ava. But I can hear the tears in her voice when she speaks, and I decide that the last thing she can afford right now is hope that may come to nothing.

"His attorney got in to see him in the infirmary," she says. "He's in rough shape. One eye's so swollen, he can't see out of it. They fractured his eye socket."

"Jesus, I'm sorry," I say. "Did his lawyer have any idea why this happened now?"

Ava gives a bitter little laugh. "It's prison, Marti," she says. "There doesn't have to be a reason for things to get violent in there. It just happens."

I understand her point, but still, it seems like an excessive amount of violence, if unprovoked. I imagine the hours I've spent in the boxing gym, or grappling on the mats at Bucktown Jiu-Jitsu, and still cannot fathom the amount of force it would take to break a bone in someone's face upon impact.

"Are you working tonight?" she asks.

"No," I reply. "It's my night off."

"Me too," she replies. "Want to get dinner somewhere? Ted is out of town for a conference, and I could really use some company. My treat."

I glance down at the muddy soup in the pot on my stove. There's no contest here.

"Yeah," I reply. "Where should I meet you?"

FOR THE FIRST time since I met her, Ava looks rough. Puffy and worn out and tired. It's almost a relief, to know that she's as human as the rest of us. That the long shifts at the hospital and the strain of Colin's situation do actually have an impact, even if the rest of the time she manages to look as polished as a runway model. We've decided on Chicago Diner, because Ava says she needs comfort food, and she hasn't quite found anything as comforting in the city as fake meat and vegan milkshakes.

"I don't want to talk about it," she says as we shuffle through the narrow aisle and into our booth. "I don't want to think about anything to do with the case tonight." It seems a strange sentiment, given she's chosen me as a dinner companion. But it occurs to me then, between Ted and her job and Colin's case, that perhaps she doesn't have anyone else to call when she's on the precipice of falling apart. It's sort of thrilling, actually, to imagine myself as one of Ava's only friends. If that's what we are.

Plus, it lets me off the hook for deciding not to bring up Dylan in our call earlier. If Ava doesn't want to talk about the case, I don't feel remiss in not mentioning it now.

"So I didn't realize you were married," she says as an unshaven waiter in a stocking cap slaps two menus down on the table.

"Where did you hear that?" I reply, and it occurs to me that Ava and I haven't had much occasion to discuss our personal lives. If we're not talking about the case, I'm not really sure what we have to talk about.

"Andrea. We were chatting when you two came to the hospital to record. She mentioned you were getting a divorce."

"Yeah," I say, thinking of the divorce papers that are still sitting, unread, on my kitchen table. "Eric. We met in college. It fell apart about a year ago."

"What happened?" Ava asks, and it seems like an intrusive question, except that we've spent a decent amount of time already discussing—among other things—her brother's sex life.

"How long do you have?" I ask, trying to dodge. But Ava simply waits, her patience both calming and slightly unnerving. The posture of a good listener, with a keen ear for bullshit.

"I think I got really good at pretending to be normal," I finally reply. "That what I wanted was to be married, and have a beautiful apartment, and take vacations to Thailand, and have babies and take pictures of them for Instagram. And then, this body was dumped outside a hospital, and I couldn't pretend anymore. Because really, I've never wanted anything but my sister back. There's nothing in my life I wouldn't have traded for that." It's a strange admission, when I hear myself say it. More the truth than I will usually admit, even to myself. Most of the time, I pretend the answer to what happened to Maggie will be enough. But really, deep down, I know it's a lie. I will always want her. I want Andrea to be dazzled by her. I want to know what she thinks of Eric. I want to tell her all the things I've done in the name of finding her, because I know she may be the only one who would not hesitate to forgive me.

"So what does that look like?" Ava asks. "When you stop pretending?"

"It generally involved a lot of irresponsible behavior," I reply. Trying to be coy, to hide the pain beneath it. Not regret, not exactly. I think of grappling on the mat, the way it feels to slip free of someone's grip. You can't think about what will happen next. You react, you get free, and then you're faced with your next decision. You stay and fight, or you run. The thing I still can't figure out though, is whose grip I was fighting. "Some drugs. A lot of men. Not, admittedly, my finest hour."

"Sounds like college," she says, though her eyes are wide in a way that looks like she's half surprised, half impressed. And I wonder if she's also lying. If her college experience had little to do with drugs and boys, and was really an endless string of long nights in the library, hunched over biology textbooks the size of shoeboxes. "How long did it take your husband to find out?"

This is the awful part of the story. The part that Andrea and I never really talk openly about. The part that meant the end of my marriage, no matter how much Eric still loved me. I remember that afternoon in Andrea's car, when I was already six days late and half convinced of what was about to happen. When I finally told her the terrible suspicion that had been bubbling like tar in my stomach for days.

"I'm late," I said, watching Andrea for some sort of reaction. Andrea, whose belly grazed the steering wheel as she drove. Andrea was a month away from her due date. So pregnant that the difference between her and me seemed so much more expansive and encompassing than simply the progress of another six or seven months. She seemed transformed, in a way I couldn't imagine for myself.

I had been spiraling downward for five months by then. Lying my way through couple's therapy sessions with Eric, after I'd told him about the podcast but not about the men. Not the hours chasing down leads on CrimeSolversOnline, or the vodka in increasing proportions. Not the days I spent wandering the city, hoping a turn down an alley or a stretch of vacant lot would lead me to my sister. I could not explain to him why I'd kept the Jane Doe from him for weeks, and he had been so disturbed by my withholding that I could not fathom trying to explain the rest. Only Andrea knew, and even she could do nothing to stop me from falling further.

The Jane Doe had finally been identified as a concert violinist and opioid addict from Bloomington, Indiana, a month after my

DNA test. She'd given birth to a son only six weeks before she died. A son who was now being raised by his grandparents. She'd become addicted to Oxycontin after she broke her foot playing tennis, they said, and had been battling with her addiction for years.

Until she found out she was pregnant. She'd stopped using then, at least until he was born. She'd wanted her son to be healthy. I, on the other hand, was six days late and had pounded four cocktails the night before. And burned with the shame of it.

"How late?" Andrea asked. Unflappable as always. Almost preternaturally cool.

"Almost a week," I replied. And then I did the thing I'd been avoiding for months, through all the podcast recording sessions, and in the moments after the DNA results came in, and every night as I lay in bed next to Eric, thinking about my sister. I started to cry. Surprising even myself, that this would be the thing that did it. That sent me into fits. That made me fall apart.

I bent forward, covering my face with my hands as my shoulders shook, as fat, salty tears slipped down my palms and between my fingers. I could feel my nose already running.

"Oh, Jesus, sweetie," I heard Andrea say, her hand on my back as she pulled onto a side street and double parked, punching the button that triggered her emergency flashers. "I thought you were on the pill," she said.

I shook my head, my hair eclipsing my face so she could not see how wretched I'd become. "I stopped taking it. Just before the Jane Doe." My voice broke with hiccupping sobs. "I went off it."

"Why?" Andrea could not hide the incredulity in her tone.

"Because he wants to have a goddamn baby, why do you think?" I said, nearly shouted actually, in the small interior of the car.

"But why would you agree to it?" Andrea asked, her voice gentler now, as she brushed my hair back, tucking it behind my ear.

I dropped my hands from my face, holding them out, palms up. Offering my own bemusement. "I have no fucking idea. Maybe I didn't expect it would really happen? I certainly never expected a body to show up in the morgue." I shut my eyes, dropping hot tears onto the front of my shirt.

"Oh, honey," Andrea said. She would be a good mother, I thought as she gathered me up, let me sob into her shoulder, both of us stretched across the center console. And I, of course, would not.

"A week isn't so long," she cooed into my hair. "We can go get a test right now, and find out one way or another, okay?"

I nodded, wiping wet hands across my eyes, trying to take a deep breath without its hitching.

And I allowed myself to imagine it, doing the wrong thing, just once. Giving birth to a buttery-cheeked boy, with eyes close enough in color to Eric's to make everyone note their similarity, even if the comparison was not perfect. A boy who looked like me in my baby pictures, who had Maggie's childhood laugh. A grandchild for my mother, that final balm. What poetry it could be, to have her hold a child again, to give her back something of what had been taken. Some innocence. Some sense of the rightness of the world.

But I could not allow myself to take up motherhood as a way of keeping myself in check. Because I knew myself better than that; I knew that raising the stakes—making the consequence for my failure huge and terrible: a child, *oh Christ*, a child—would not keep me from failing. I could not be made a mother simply by giving birth. Or, at least, I could not be made a mother that anyone would want. I knew that for certain, because in all my imaginings, I could not allow myself to imagine that I'd have a girl.

"I can't be pregnant," I whispered, angry at myself, my wretched state.

"It's okay," Andrea replied, her hand running up and down my spine.

"I can't do it, Andrea," I said, my voice more certain now, and full of tears. "It's more than I could take."

"You don't have to be pregnant if you don't want to be," Andrea said into the hair at the crown of my head.

"Eric would never understand."

Andrea pulled back then, taking my face in her hands and looking me straight in the eyes. Andrea. The closest thing I had to a big sister.

"Eric would never have to know," she replied.

I DEBATE FOR a moment whether to confide in Ava. It's been a long time since I've told the whole truth of it to anyone. And I worry that when it happens, once one detail comes out, everything else will bubble up. I always want to see how much I can reveal before someone grows disgusted with me.

"He found out after a few months. About as long as it took me to get pregnant," I reply. "It was really the most obvious possible outcome. Right out of an after-school special. By that point Eric and I were barely having sex."

"And you were . . . ," Ava says.

"Having sex with other people. A lot of them. Yeah," I reply, raking my fingers through my hair, trying to fight the embarrassment that always seems to go hand in hand with vulnerability.

"Yeah. I got pregnant once too," Ava says. "During residency. Right after Colin's conviction, actually." I watch her as she speaks and realize how young she is. Only a handful of years older than me. She sometimes looks like a girl who got so good at playing dress-up that the world suddenly forgot she was a child. And I realize how much we have in common, then. Each of us mistaken for the person she is pretending to be.

"I remember thinking that it might kill me, actually kill me, to have a baby right then," she says. "Those were the words that went through my head when I found out. I felt like if I had to do one more difficult thing, I wouldn't survive it. My heart had been so wrung out."

"And Ted understood?" I ask.

"He did," she says. And then, "At least, he said he did. But also I think he knew, deep down, that it was too much for me, after Colin's conviction. I think it was the only time he's actually been afraid for me, that I'd lose it and he'd have to call the men in white coats. So he agreed."

"Ted's a good guy," I say, and I see the fondness in Ava's eyes at the sentiment.

"I'm assuming Eric wasn't as understanding?" she asks, a preparatory wince already creasing her brow.

"I considered trying to hide it from him. Or telling him it was his. But it turned out, I couldn't live with that. Apparently, I do have limits to what I'm capable of," I say. Even now, I can't forget Eric's blankness. The way he repeated my words back to me, as if it were a language he was learning by practicing its foreign sounds before he could grasp its meaning. I wondered for a moment if I had hurt him to the point where even his capacity for language had begun to fail him.

JESSICA CHIARELLA

His anger was a relief. His clasped fists, held before him, resting on his knees. That I could take. His breath hot as it hissed out
of him. But it didn't last, even though I wished it would. He had
never been one for anger, my Eric. It burned out of him, until he
was crumpled forward, his face in his hands. I knelt before him,
on that floor, unable to be the one to comfort him. Begging him
to tell me what I should do.

"Andrea went with me."

"Good friend," Ava says. And I nod, but really, she doesn't know
the half of it.

"She was three weeks away from giving birth to her daughter," I reply, remembering the heavy sweater she wore that day,
how there was no hiding her belly, even despite her best efforts.
"Have you ever seen a woman who is eight months pregnant walk
into an abortion clinic?"

"Protesters?" Ava asks.

"Yeah. I've never seen people like that. It was like dangling red
meat in front of a pack of dogs. And Andrea just grabbed my hand
and walked me through it. Eight months pregnant, and she was
still the strong one."

I stop, because my throat is so tight with tears. But it feels
good, thinking about that day. To remember the depth of Andrea's strength and the far reaches of her compassion. To understand what it must have cost her, to be the one to save me. Because
that's the truth of it. That day saved me. From every sorry, reckless thing that I'd done in the wake of my sister's disappearance,
from being a mother even more grief-ridden and inadequate than
my own. From bringing a child into the world who would be
made to suffer for Maggie's disappearance, as I had suffered, in
penance for being the one to survive.

Ava reaches across the table and takes my hand. And I think of Maggie. I can't stop myself from thinking of Maggie. Not her disappearance, but her. Sitting on my bed with an arm around me, after a group of boys on the school bus told me I was ugly. Finger-combing my long hair, in preparation for a braid. Carrying me across a beach's gravel parking lot to the public bathrooms when I'd lost my sandals in the surf. Always my protector.

"You'd never believe how close I came to getting my tubes tied after that," I say.

"Because you never wanted to go through that again?" Ava asks.

"No," I reply, shaking my head. "Because when I think about having a child . . ." I let the thought hang, sucking a raw patch on my lower lip. Worrying it with my tongue. I think of Olive. "There is so much danger, in loving anything that much."

THIRTEEN

I spend the next few days so caught up in Dylan's case—trying to track down his relatives, reaching out to his friends in Milwaukee for interview requests—that I almost forget that this weekend is the annual benefit dinner for the Chicago Foundation for Missing and Exploited Women. The benefit is always a bit of a painful affair, a hotel ballroom full of wealthy people who want nothing more than to throw money at a sob story, with a slideshow of missing girls playing on a continual loop at the back of the stage. Plus, it's black tie, which means I'd have to rustle up a ball gown somewhere, despite the fact that my bank balance is dipping dangerously toward double digits. And my family, as members of the board of the Margaret Reese Foundation, will be attending.

I try to beg off. Call my mother, leave her a message informing her that I don't have any way of procuring a ball gown this year and asking that she give my regrets to the rest of the board—meaning, mainly, my grandmother and Uncle Perry. Which, of course, prompts a knock at my door the next morning. A messenger, delivering a high-necked Marchesa Notte gown in gold lace, along with a pair of ankle-strap stilettos. Both of which fit like a dream. Checkmate.

I bike to the gym that morning and whale on the heavy bag for the better part of an hour, until my T-shirt and shorts are soaked and one of the trainers asks me if everything's all right.

"Family stuff," I reply, and he gives me a very understanding nod. I feel like I could go for another hour, but I also don't want my arms to be lead tonight, so I unwrap my hands and shake them out—hoping they won't swell from all the abuse—and head for home.

I'M TEMPTED—REALLY tempted—to take the L down to the Palmer House Hilton in the finery my mother has bought for me, just to be obstinate. But it's been a long while since I've spent any time in four-inch heels, and as it turns out, there's no hope of walking more than a block at a time without wanting to amputate my feet at the ankles, so I settle instead for an Uber.

The ballroom is all burgundy carpeting and crystal chandeliers, the bread and butter of old money, and I catch sight of my family's table as soon as I enter. It's just to the right of the center of the stage, as it is every year, and through the crowd I can see my mother chatting with the mayor's chief of staff, who appears to be artfully trying to extricate himself from whatever tirade she's on. Good luck, buddy. I head in the opposite direction, to the bar—intent on a drink before I dive into this night's particular torture—and order a vodka martini.

"Would you be able to help me find my table?" says a familiar voice behind me. I turn to find Detective Olsen, resplendent in his class A uniform, standing behind me.

"What in the hell are you doing here?" I ask as the bartender sets my drink in front of me.

"The chair of the Margaret Reese Foundation personally invited me," he replies.

My mother. Jesus Christ, that woman will be the death of me.

Of course, it's my own fault for not realizing Olsen would be here. After all, Detective Richards attended every year, a guest at the foundation's table. But I assumed that invitation was particular to him and would not necessarily extend to the next man assigned to Maggie's case after Richards retired. After all, Detective Richards was the CPD's favorite detective to send into any dog-and-pony show, especially when press was involved. He had an old-school charm to him, and he was polished enough to move in even the wealthiest and most political of circles. Now I wonder if his charm was a cover, if he was just as ruthless and single-minded as all the rest of the CPD. Still, I think of the blacked-out tattoos beneath the sleeves of Olsen's uniform and wonder how a boy from Canaryville will fare amid the wolves that raised me.

"At least you clean up well," I say, motioning to his uniform. He does. He really does.

"Well, this is slightly different from where I usually spend my Saturday nights," Olsen replies, taking in the splendor around him, his pale eyes pulled dark by the navy of his uniform.

"Don't let the décor fool you," I say. "These people are as vicious as they come. They're just better dressed."

"Apparently." He motions to the raw knuckles on my hand. A couple of them are shadowy, like ink stains faded by repeated washing. "Disagreement over a mutual fund, perhaps?" Olsen says, wry and authoritative, his best patrol cop impression.

"Didn't wrap my hands well enough at the gym," I reply.

"And here I thought I missed you flattening another guy twice your size."

"Not this week," I say. Behind Olsen, on the screen above the stage, a photograph of Maggie materializes. Maggie, grinning at the camera, wet hair blown back, Lake Michigan behind her. I took that photo, at the beach by our house, the summer she disappeared. The last time she went swimming, maybe. I can't remember now.

A cold certainty hits me again, as it always does, especially when I'm caught off guard. The knowledge that I've already seen every photo ever taken of my sister. It's a thought that's occurred to me before, one that spread like the heavy creep of mustard gas, blistering my lungs, as I searched through video after video of blond teenagers bent before rough-faced men with tattooed fingers. Ukrainian amateur pornography, circa 2005, a tip I couldn't ignore. Sick with the fervent desire to see an unfamiliar image of my sister. Equally sick at the prospect of finding it there.

"Hey." Olsen's touch brings me back to the present, his careful hand at my arm. "You all right?" he asks, glancing at the screen behind us.

"Sure." Across the room, I catch my mother watching us. I turn to sip my drink, moving my arm away from Olsen's touch. "You're sitting at my family's table?"

He holds up a place card with the number four on it.

"Are you wearing a bulletproof vest under that uniform?" I ask, and take the opportunity to look him up and down, pointedly. A shifting of power, back into my favor.

"Wouldn't you like to know."

"You think I'm kidding?"

"They can't possibly be that bad," he replies.

"You have no idea," I say. "I'm talking about a group of incredibly privileged, emotionally stunted, phenomenally traumatized people who have a lot of baggage with cops." I lean down to adjust the ankle strap on one of my heels. His eyes flick to the slice of leg that shows through the high slit in my dress and then return to my face.

"Marti," he says, his voice revealing a trace of amusement, "have I mentioned that I spent two years hanging out with actual white supremacists? I promise you, I'm not afraid of your family."

"All right," I reply, taking my drink and hooking my arm around his, leading the way to our table. "But don't say I didn't warn you."

My mother, my grandmother, and my uncle Perry are already seated when we approach. I pause to kiss my grandmother on the cheek as I pass, and then introduce Olsen to the table.

"I didn't realize you two knew each other," my mother says, looking between me and Olsen. I can see the wheels turning in her mind already. The blessing and the curse of my family is that any investigative instincts I have, I've inherited directly from my mother.

"Should we call you Detective?" my grandmother asks, taking his hand between hers. She's statuesque as always, in a dark purple Donna Karan, the very picture of graceful aging, despite her wheelchair.

"Kyle," he says as she gives him a decisive, two-handed shake.

"So you're assigned to Margaret's case?" Uncle Perry says as we take the remaining two seats at the table. "No offense, but you look a little younger than the detectives we're used to." Uncle Perry, my mother's younger brother, works in insurance. He's the sort of man who organizes the world into categories like "alpha" and "beta" and seriously considers himself a member of the former. He actually touches the band of his Omega Seamaster as he speaks, peacocking without the benefit of the bright fan of feathers.

"I spent a couple of years working with the FBI," Olsen says. "It put me on the fast track within the department."

"The FBI," Uncle Perry says. "I used to play golf with the Chicago station chief. Mitch Bresner. You know him?"

"Only by reputation," Olsen replies. "But I was mostly working with the agents assigned to the task force."

"Of course," Uncle Perry says, touching his watch again, as if he's trying to make sure the light reflecting off its face flashes in Olsen's eyes. Still, Olsen maintains his easy calm.

"Did you see the write-up of the foundation's quarterly luncheon in the *Trib*?" my mother asks as the emcee makes her opening remarks and we wait for our entrées to be served. My mother is clearly also growing tired of Perry's preening. Ever the older sister. "Eric made his usual donation, you know," she continues, cannily watching Olsen as she speaks. "I signed your name to the thank-you note as well. I hope that wasn't overstepping."

"That's fine," I reply, hoping to curtail the conversation she clearly wants to have.

"I mean, I wasn't sure if you two are on speaking terms or not. But I thought, what with him continuing to be so generous to the foundation, things can't be so bad, can they?"

I see my grandmother lean ostentatiously toward Olsen and stage-whisper, "Her ex-husband," in his ear. My grandmother, always one to stir the pot for her own amusement. Thankfully, Olsen doesn't betray any surprise at this revelation. Turns out, a man with undercover experience might be perfect for occasions like this.

"We're on speaking terms," I reply. "I just talked to him a few days ago."

"Oh, wonderful," my mother replies. "Did you two discuss . . . you know, next steps? Moving forward?"

"We discussed our divorce papers," I reply, and watch my mother's forehead tighten, her eyebrows threatening to arch. Her hopes of grandchildren evaporating, once more, before her eyes. "And we talked about the next season of the podcast."

"Oh, lovely," my mother says, her sarcasm so thick, it's as if she doesn't quite believe that we'll fully understand her displeasure otherwise. "It's not enough that you have to rehash all our family troubles in public. But now you have to take on other people's problems as well?"

"Do you think that's quite safe?" Uncle Perry asks, ready anew to throw his manly, manly weight around. "I mean, I would make sure to have a talk with your doorman about security measures, if you're going to be working in this . . . field."

"I don't have a doorman," I reply.

"You're not living in a doorman building?" He's turning his concerned gaze back and forth between me and my mom. "What sort of hack divorce attorney did you hire? Did they negotiate on alimony?"

"Not that I really feel like getting into it, but we came to a settlement on our own," I reply.

"That's a no," my mother says helpfully. A few choice terms one should never call her own mother splash through my brain.

"Why in the hell wouldn't you go for alimony?" Uncle Perry asks.

"Because I didn't want his money," I reply as the old anger kicks to life, muscle memory tightening my shoulders, finger-nails cutting creases in my palms. The seed of my impulsiveness, the desire to tear away the foundation of my life with Eric, let the rest crumble. Because I do not want a life that would make these people proud of me. These people, who set up a foundation in Maggie's name because they didn't want to have to look for her. Not if they could pay other people to do it. I want to clear the crystal and fine china from the table with a swing of my arm.

And then I feel it. Olsen's hand, under the table, coming to rest on my knee. His thumb tracing the lower curve of my kneecap. And my rage shivers to a halt.

"Well, I don't think that anyone in this family should be living in a building without some sort of security," Uncle Perry says, as if this is an edict that must now be followed.

"Bartenders don't make enough to afford doorman buildings in Chicago," I reply, distracted by the need to keep still. A meager, last effort, even as Olsen's touch turns my spine to wax.

"Bartenders?" he repeats, in the manner another person might say "porn stars"—all haughty, horrified skepticism. My mother must tell him nothing, content to let his image of her remaining daughter be as flat and staged as the family Christmas cards. My parents and I, baring our teeth at the photographer, clothes all silk and velvet. A ribbon in my heat-curled hair. Grouped so close together, a denial that there was ever space for anyone else in our compact trio. As if we were better off that way.

There is no slack in my leash, no matter what might have hap-pened to Maggie. If I must fall apart—as I have—I am to do it as secretly as possible. Those Christmas cards were my first lesson. Our lives must still be perfect, no matter the damage we've incurred. No matter what the world has done to us.

IT'S AFTER DINNER, after the speeches, after my third drink, when my grandmother motions to me from across the table. A beckoning. I rise from my seat and kneel beside her, so I'm looking up at her, perched in her wheelchair.

"Have you been back to the woods?" she asks, her voice low, so as not to interrupt the conversation of my mother and uncle.

"What?"

"The woods," she says, her eyes glassy, peering into the middle distance, her gaze not quite meeting my eyes, though mine meets hers. "Have you been looking there?"

"For Maggie?" My hands go cold. The blood drops from my head. I grip the arm of her wheelchair, though my palm is clammy against the padded vinyl armrest.

"No." She shakes her head, strands falling from her loose updo at the movement. Her gaze clearing a bit. Refocusing on me. "The other one."

"Who? Sarah Ketchum? She was already found."

"I don't know," my grandmother replies, all her wistfulness gone, replaced with her usual impatience. "It's not like I get name, rank, and serial number with this."

"Okay, which woods?" I ask, feeling suddenly at sea. Wondering if it's possible my grandmother is crazy. Wondering if I should try to catch my mother's attention, alert her that my grandmother isn't making much sense.

"Isn't it your job to find out which woods?" she replies, her voice loud enough to catch Olsen's attention.

"Grandma," I say, almost chiding. Because I don't believe in any of this, not really.

"Fine," she says, waving me off. "Never mind."

But even as I return to my seat, I can't help but replay it in my mind. The scene of the car, parked right at the tree line. Beige, or silver, or blue. The man in the front seat. My sister telling me to run. *The woods*, I think. But people have searched those woods a hundred times over, since Maggie disappeared. She's not there. I know she's not there.

It's only when my mother gets up to speak, with a large school portrait of Maggie projected onto the screen behind her, that I realize what my grandmother may mean. The woods. Back to the woods. And a chill so potent runs through me that I actually shudder, my skin prickling to life under the soft lights of the banquet hall. She means Dylan. It's a sudden, heavy realization.

Dylan Jacobs is in LaBagh Woods.

THE WRONG THINGS excite me. Things that should be horrific send a charge through me, as if all my synapses are wired wrong. My grandmother's words, the potential of finding Dylan dead, in the same place Sarah's body was dumped, should have sickened me. I understand that. I am still the sister of a missing girl, a murdered girl, perhaps. I am not so heartless as to have no reaction to the dark gravity of the situation.

But it is also thrilling. The idea of it, of solving it, of finding an irrefutable connection between the two. Of proving Colin innocent. Of getting justice for Sarah and Dylan and Colin and Ava, instead of letting the question of their fates linger, lost in the fickle winds of the legal system. That possibility puts me in thrall to adrenaline. And, as with panic, as with a cascade of fear or a rush of love, there is a point where you can do nothing but surrender to your own excitement.

Olsen just happens to be there when it hits. Outside the Palmer House, when the rain starts and he pulls me back under the awning while I wait for my Uber.

"So you were wrong about your family," he says. "They're way more interested in torturing you than me."

"A slight miscalculation," I reply. I clear my throat, suddenly very aware of Olsen's hands. One in his pocket, one holding his phone. Calling a ride, probably. "So was that your idea of a distraction?"

"What?" Olsen says, playing innocent, letting it show.

I wonder how much it would take, to shake this man's easy confidence. I imagine telling him the things I never told Eric. Describing the hours I watched those blond teenagers. In green-tiled bathrooms or on rumpled, blotchy satin sheets. Some of them playing for the camera. Some vacant, their quiet a warning of its own. Olsen seems like he could stand to listen to those things.

My ride pulls up to the curb, casting a spray of water onto the sidewalk, and I ignore Olsen's question and take him by the hand, pulling him through the rain and into the muggy back seat. Even though he's already called a car, even though fraternizing with a witness in an ongoing case could certainly get him fired. *What silly games we play*, I think as he kisses me in the back of some stranger's Altima, tasting of heat and rain and cheap table wine. As he kisses me up the two flights of gritty carpeted stairs that lead to my apartment door. As his hand breaches the slit in my skirt while I fumble to unlock my door.

"What do you want?" he whispers as the door shuts behind me and he presses me back against it. Unzips my dress, peels it down to my waist. I have his shirt unbuttoned, but he won't let go of me long enough to allow me to shove it down his arms. Instead he leans down, running his tongue over the lacy edge of my bra. My head drops back against the door.

I used to want escape. To slip the binds of a marriage I could no longer sustain. To tempt fate with my own defiance, to be a slut and see what price the world would make me pay for it. That was what I looked for in those other men. But this is different. An unfamiliar need. Like the memory of a desire I've never actually felt, not even in my earliest of sexual experiences. A desire uncoupled from fear, unconcerned with proving my mettle in a world always canted toward the destruction of girls like me.

I want to be someone else. It's at the root of the games I play and the men I choose and the way I dress. I do not want those people for a family. I do not want to be Eric's ex-wife. Maggie Reese's sister. A girl who searched out sex that scared her a little, always too close to the edge, the vindication of escaping unscathed more potent than any part of the act itself.

I don't tell him any of this. Instead, I kiss him until I'm blinking back darkness, and nothing feels real anymore.

OLSEN WAKES ME up halfway through a nightmare, pinning my wrists to the mattress when I mistake him for the faceless man and go for his eyes.

"Jesus," he whispers when I am finally still. "What the fuck was that?"

I recognize him as my vision adjusts to the dark. "Bad dream," I mumble.

"Yeah, no shit," he replies. He lets go of my wrists and I sit up, combing my hair back off my face with my fingers. Sticky. The sheet beneath me icy and damp. The streetlamp outside my bed-room window casts tracts of murky amber light across the far wall. Sometimes I don't recognize this room. Sometimes I wake and don't know where I am.

"I have to tell you something," I whisper. I feel his fingers brush over my lower back, but I don't turn to look at him. "Sarah Ketchum's roommate is missing."

"I know," Olsen replies. I can feel him watching me.

"You know?"

"Milwaukee police contacted us."

"I think he might be here," I reply. "I think he might be in La-Bagh Woods."

Olsen is still, quiet, for a moment.

"What makes you think that?" he finally asks.

"If the cases are connected, the killer might have buried him in the same place," I say. "If he's dead."

"What makes you think they're connected?"

"You know what," I reply, glancing down at him over my shoulder. Only briefly, not indulging in a longer look. I know he overheard my grandmother at dinner. I don't want to have to say it out loud.

"You never stop, do you?"

"He might have used the same burial ground, since he got away with it before," I say.

Olsen lets out a long sigh, relenting. "Only if he doesn't mind linking the two cases together."

"Except nobody is looking for Dylan here," I reply.

"You're good at this," he whispers, and I turn to look at him then, stretched out in my bed, the sheet bunched carelessly at his waist. There's another cloud of black ink on the outside of one shoulder, and another across the plane of his left pectoral. I reach forward, running my fingers over his chest, over the remnant of that past life. I wonder what's there, underneath that layer of blackness. A swastika, maybe. I wonder if he can feel it still, the horrid shape of it pulsing beneath the newer layer of ink. He runs his fingers up my ribs, over the lizard tattoo, making me shiver.

"Did you ever see the Jane Doe that I thought was my sister?" I ask.

"Yeah," he whispers. "When her husband came to identify her."

Her husband, I remember. She had a husband. She was not Maggie.

"And she had a tattoo like mine?" I ask, because this is the thing that has always made it difficult to accept. Because it should have been Maggie. Because too much fit for it not to have been my sister.

He levers up on his elbow, leaning closer to consider my ribs in the dark, one hand on my hip.

"No," he whispers, shaking his head. "She had a dragon. In navy blue."

"Not a lizard?"

He shakes his head again.

I think of how cruel life is sometimes. How a simple sentence, *She has a blue lizard tattoo on her thigh*, mistaking the word "dragon" for "lizard," sent me reeling from skepticism into certainty. That moment at the bistro, based on nothing but my own misguided hope that the question of my sister would be answered, was the beginning of the end of the life I had. All because of one silly word.

* * *

OLSEN LEAVES EARLY in the morning. I wonder if he feels the way that I do, that there's urgency now, in Dylan's case. That this thread must be caught and held fast, before another chance for answers is lost. Still, he pauses to kiss me before he leaves, a lingering kiss that almost has me working again at the buttons on his uniform. Perhaps trying to make up for his early departure. Perhaps trying to make me miss him.

I don't mind that he leaves without a word. It's easier this way, to be alone again in my bed, the sheets cooling beside me, the morning light strengthening its reach through my window blinds. I don't miss him. I never miss anyone who leaves me by choice.

FOURTEEN

I spend the rest of the day waiting for news about the case. Waiting to hear from Olsen. There is definitely something wrong with me; amid a potential murder investigation, I'm waiting for a guy to call. It's a juvenile feeling, like waiting for the boy you like to ask you to prom. Letting yourself care too much about anything.

I go to the park with Andrea and Olive to distract myself and don't mention Olsen's appearance at the benefit dinner, or what transpired at my apartment afterward. I try not to check my phone more often than normal and remind myself that I spent the past year fucking my way through this city and never expected any of those men to call me the next day. Then I get shitfaced alone in my apartment that night, my phone dark and silent on my coffee table.

I wake Monday morning to the sound of a sharp rapping on

my front door. Jarring enough to already send a surge of adrenaline through me, my sleep-addled brain trying to make sense of it—is this an emergency? Is someone trying to get in? I drag myself from my bed to the source of the sound, put the chain on, and open the door.

"Martha Reese?" A man's voice filters through the gap between the door and its frame. A cop, in uniform, I can see that much.

"Yes?"

"Detective Hardy would like you to come with us to the station. Answer some questions."

His voice is more of a demand than a request.

"Detective Hardy?" I reply, wondering if this is all some sort of mistake. I don't think I've met a detective by that name. "Am—am I under arrest?" I ask, stammering. Trying to remember what cops have the right to do, under these circumstances.

"No," the cop replies, one hand resting on his belt. I eye the gun holstered at his side. I've never really been around guns, so the presence of one on my doorstep is unnerving. The density of its destructive power, right there in front of me. "But we do need you to answer some questions about an ongoing investigation."

"What investigation?" I ask, reluctant to do much more than shut my door and call Andrea to figure out how to handle this.

"The disappearance of Dylan Jacobs," the cop replies. And that's enough. My skin crackles, like I've touched something electric. They found him. Olsen found him.

"Just let me get changed," I reply quickly, and retreat back into my apartment to throw on some jeans.

THE COPS LEAD me down the main hallway of the Twenty-Fourth District police station, to the interview room at the end of the hall. The same one I sat in twenty years ago, looking through mug books with Detective Richards.

I lock eyes with Olsen as I enter, on reflex alone. An older woman in a gray pantsuit stands beside him. She motions for me to sit at the table and then sits down across from me. Immediately, I wonder if I've made a mistake in coming here, in not calling Andrea to alert her that I'm being questioned by police. This feels like an interrogation, like they've brought me in to get something out of me.

I wonder if Andrea was right, if the source of Olsen's interest in me was a desire for information and nothing more. I assumed I'd disproved that theory Saturday night, when he was so eager in the back of that car, when I led him up to my apartment. But now I wonder again if this man—who is so accustomed to pretending to be someone else—is even more ruthless than I expected. I wonder if the details of our night together are now the fodder of some investigative report, hidden by a euphemism, perhaps. *Subject was personally forthcoming.* Or *Subject turned out to be an easy mark.*

"You know Detective Olsen," says the other detective, who has a peppering of dark freckles on her nose and a tight-slicked bun at the back of her head. I try to detect any specific tone in the word "know" that would imply just how we know each other. But she is like a slab of glass. So smooth, I only see my own paranoia reflected back at me. "I'm Detective Dana Hardy. We appreciate you coming in."

"You're with Missing Persons?" I ask before she can start with the questions.

She pauses, her lips pursed. "Homicide."

"Is Dylan Jacobs dead?" I ask, directing my question more to

Olsen than to her. But he's not looking at me, not directly. Feeling guilty, perhaps. "You found his body?"

Detective Hardy shifts in her seat, turns to look at Olsen. I see him, almost imperceptibly, shake his head.

"What makes you think Dylan Jacobs is dead?" Detective Hardy asks. As if this rudimentary information is at all important, as if Olsen has not already brought her up to speed on what I've been doing. My little investigation. I wonder if they're planning to arrest me for interfering with theirs.

"They wouldn't have someone from Homicide on the case unless his body had been found."

"And what exactly is your connection to Dylan Jacobs?"

"During the course of my research into Sarah Ketchum's murder, I found out that Dylan Jacobs, her former roommate, had gone missing from Milwaukee a couple of months ago." I try for professionalism. As if I'm a true journalist, powerful in some noble way. Able to retaliate when threatened.

"This research is for your podcast?"

"Yes," I reply.

"Why were you looking into Sarah Ketchum's murder, when her killer is already behind bars?" Hardy asks with a sort of feigned confusion. We're playing a game here. Talking around the things we all know to be true.

"Because I believe the wrong man was convicted for her murder," I reply. "So it made sense to me, after Dylan disappeared, that the man who actually killed Sarah might have gone after him. To keep Dylan from giving any new details about the case."

"And you think his body was dumped in LaBagh Woods?"

I lean forward in my seat, both of my palms flat on the metal table. Clammy, suddenly.

"You found him in the woods?" *Jesus*, I think. *Leave it to my grandmother to pull the answer out of thin air.*

"Is this your email address, Marti?" Olsen asks, leaning forward and sliding a sheet of paper toward me. It's a printout of an email, with the address at the top highlighted: MReese90@gmail .com.

"No," I reply. "I'm Marti dot Reese at Gmail." I scan the email. It's to Dylan Jacobs, dated April 28 of this year. Asking if he can meet to discuss the second season of *Jane Doe*. My name is typed at the bottom. Gooseflesh spreads in a wave, from the base of my skull and down my limbs. Something harsh and metallic spills across my tongue.

Because I didn't reach out to Dylan until well into July.

"What is this?" I ask. I think of the calls. Someone out there, wanting to scare me. Wanting me to know he's thinking of me. I try to remember when the calls began. Maybe it was April. Maybe before that, even.

"Apparently someone called in a tip to the Milwaukee police. Said Dylan's disappearance might be connected to his testimony in the Ketchum case. Milwaukee was kind enough to reach out, and we got a warrant for Dylan's email," Hardy replies. "And guess what we found? This appears to be an email from you, Marti. Sent only a few days before he was reported missing. Asking to meet."

"I never sent this," I say. "I didn't even know Dylan existed until . . ." I think about the timeline of my investigation. "After the APA awards." I finally meet Olsen's eyes. There's something searching in his expression, like he's trying to figure out if he's gotten me wrong. If I'm secretly dangerous.

I think of the nightmare, of waking in the dark and clawing for his face. What must I seem to him? A feral thing, perhaps. A girl raised on pain, capable of anything.

"If you have access to his work email, then you know I tried reaching out to him just a couple of weeks ago," I say. "Plus, it was my producer who called in that tip. We wanted to notify the Milwaukee police that the cases might be connected."

"Why not call the CPD?" Hardy asks.

"Because he went missing from Milwaukee," I reply, throwing her own feigned confusion back at her. Fuck professionalism. If she wants to play dumb, then so can I.

"When did you start investigating Sarah Ketchum's murder?" Hardy asks.

"Tell me you don't think I had anything to do with this," I reply, ignoring her question. Trying to make them see how ludicrous this all is, because that is the only way they will see the danger in it.

"What year were you born, Marti?" Olsen asks. Quiet, almost regretful.

"Nineteen ninety."

"So this email, MReese90." Hardy reads it out slowly. "It's got the right year, at least."

"Yeah. My birth date is right there on my Wikipedia page," I reply. "And anyway, you can trace the email, right? Find out that it didn't come from me?"

"See, that's the funny thing. The email address was created, and the email was sent, from the John Merlo branch of the Chicago Public Library," Hardy replies. "So there's no way to know who did or didn't send it. Isn't that funny?"

"Hilarious." I can tell my tone rankles her a bit.

"You know," she says, "the best thing you can do to help

yourself is to tell us the truth. Because you're all tangled up in this mess, and stonewalling isn't going to get us anywhere. Help us help you, Marti."

Her concern sounds genuine, for a moment. But I know too much about cops to believe that she's telling the truth. I know how this works. For Colin, for so many other people railroaded through police interrogations. The cops aren't interested in finding out the truth. The fact that they pitted evidence in Colin's case is proof of that. They're interested in making arrests. Closing cases.

I wonder if Olsen is here because they think it will make me more likely to cooperate. If they do, it's a miscalculation. Having him here only makes me angry, a flush of heat in my chest, as if I've inhaled campfire smoke.

"I think I need an attorney," I reply.

Hardy pushes her chair back from the table, scraping it across the tile floor. She folds her arms across her narrow chest. "You really want to play it that way, Marti?"

"Let me get this straight," I say, the anger building within me, a swell of it, difficult to choke back. "You're really so devoted to the idea that Colin McCarty killed Sarah Ketchum that instead of treating these cases as connected—and admitting that there's a man out there who's responsible for the deaths of two people— you're willing to believe that I drove up to Milwaukee and somehow managed to kill Dylan Jacobs?"

"What made you think he would be in LaBagh Woods?" Hardy asks. Setting a trap, I know. I look at Olsen, my jaw tight. Traitor.

"That's where Sarah was found," I reply.

"But, like you said, Dylan went missing from Milwaukee," she says. "That's quite a stretch, to assume that a man who went missing seven years later, from another city, would happen to show up in the same place Sarah Ketchum's body was found."

"It didn't seem like a stretch to me," I reply, even though I know I shouldn't. Not without an attorney.

"But according to Dylan's former colleague Greg Orloff, you've known for more than a week that Dylan was missing. So what made you suddenly land on LaBagh Woods?"

"I guess it was women's intuition," I say, parroting her earnestness back to her.

"Yours?"

"My grandmother's."

"So," Hardy says, clearly enjoying this part, "your grandmother is helping you investigate the case?"

"No."

"Then how did she intuit that Dylan was in the woods, exactly?" Hardy asks.

"You'd have to ask her," I reply.

Hardy smiles, too pleased with herself. "Maybe I will. Maybe she can explain it to me."

"Am I free to go?" I ask, my answering smile crimped and aching.

"Of course, Marti," Hardy replies, as if she's explaining a simple concept to a child. "You aren't under arrest. You're free to leave at any time."

I get up, every bone in my body wrapped tight with rage, to the point where even leaving the interview room, moving down the hall, feels like a strain. I walk past the chair where I waited as a child for news of my sister. Where, twenty years ago, I chewed down the metal eraser end of a number two pencil and used it to

THE LOST GIRLS

scratch Maggie's name into the chair's smooth plastic sheen. I pass it now, the gouges worn smooth and faint with time.

How dare they, I think. *How dare they.*

AS SOON AS I'm out of the station, my first call is to Andrea.

"The CPD thinks I'm involved with Dylan Jacobs's disappearance."

"What are you talking about?" she asks. I can hear the trilling banter of children in the background and know that she's probably at the playground on Ashland and Foster, where she and Olive go most mornings when it's sunny out. I imagine Olive in the wood chips, the Cubs hat I bought her askew on her head. The normalcy of it seems completely incongruous with how I've spent the past hour.

"The tip you called into Milwaukee. Apparently it helped the CPD get a warrant for Dylan's email."

"Okay."

"He has an email from someone claiming to be me, asking Dylan to meet. Just a few days before he went missing."

There's nothing on the other end of the line besides the windy static of the outdoors and the far-off wail of a child.

"I think he's dead," I say. "I think the CPD found him here, and they think I'm involved somehow."

Still, there's only silence. Silence, and the sound of my pulse in my ears. Fast.

"Andrea?"

"I'm here," she says. "Where do you think they found him?"

"LaBagh Woods. I bet you anything they found him where they found Sarah."

"Jesus," Andrea hisses. "Hold on, let me check the news." It

221

takes only a moment. "Fuck," she says. "They've recovered the body of an as-yet-unidentified man from the woods, early this morning. A possible drug overdose."

"Oh god." The world pitches beneath me slightly. I steady myself on one of the trees in the police station's courtyard, its trunk tied with a blue ribbon that's smooth beneath my sweating palm. "The lawyer I talked to at his firm said they found pills in his apartment."

"When was it that you were supposed to have sent this email to him?"

"April," I reply. "Late April, I think."

"We weren't investigating Dylan then," she replies. "We weren't even investigating Sarah yet then."

"So what does that mean?" I ask.

"It means someone heard the podcast and knew that we might start investigating the connection between Sarah and Maggie," Andrea says, her voice projecting poorly maintained calm. "And used you to tie up the last loose end in Sarah's case."

"Dylan."

"Right," Andrea says.

"But why make it look like a drug overdose if you're still going to leave him in LaBagh Woods?"

"I have no idea," Andrea replies. "Trying to cover his MO, maybe? I mean, it would have to be different, right? Killing a guy this time. He wouldn't have had the same weight advantage. And he would have had more time to plan it."

"He did plan it," I reply. "He sent the email so that I'd be linked to the killing. Maybe he used drugs because it's a plausible way I might have killed Dylan," I say, leaning fully against the tree. I feel sick as the ground pitches and rolls beneath me. Shifting, again, as it always does, just when I think I have my feet firmly planted on the ground.

"He's fucking with us," Andrea says.

Despite the heat of the day, I'm shivering. It's the possibility my mother always feared. That publicly searching for the man who took Maggie would send him after me. Would make me a target.

"Where are you right now?" Andrea asks.

"Outside the . . . Rogers Park police station." I have to pause in the middle of the sentence to take a breath. As if I've been running. Or am being chased.

"Okay," Andrea says, all business once again. "I want you to go home, pack some things, and meet me at my place. I think it's better if you stay with us for a few days."

"You think I'm in danger?" I ask. Because I want her to confirm the fear that has taken hold of me. I want to know that I'm not going crazy.

"It would make me feel better, if you weren't alone for a little while," Andrea replies.

I TAKE THE L home from Rogers Park as soon as I'm steady enough on my feet, because I want the insulation of a crowd, to be around people going about their normal business on a regular day, killer or no killer. Though it would serve the CPD right if I get butchered while they're treating me like a goddamn suspect. It would serve Olsen right.

I check my email as the train pushes its way south, in between the brick and stone buildings of Chicago's North Side, as cars crisscross in the streets below. There's a message from ARMY8070. A photo attachment, captioned: **From a neighbor's video doorbell.**

The grainy black-and-white photograph shows a FedEx delivery-man on the porch in question. Circled in red on the street behind him is a dark four-door sedan. It's impossible to discern much about the car from the quality of the photograph, but below, ARMY8070 has written: **Neighbor noticed this Tesla parked on the street, says he remembers it had Illinois plates. May 1. I'm rerunning the ad asking for info on the car.**

According to Greg Orloff, Dylan didn't show up for a deposition on May 2. He would have received the email from the person claiming to be me only three days before.

I send a thank-you to ARMY8070. **What do you think are the chances someone else noticed it?** I ask. She replies almost immediately.

> **It's an ostentatious car, especially for the area. Really not what you want to be driving if you're going to kidnap someone. Chances are, someone else might have seen it.**
>
> **Think we're barking up the wrong tree?** I reply.
>
> **Possibly. But let's chase it down anyway.**

Sounds good, I reply, though a part of me doubts we'd get this lucky. Of course, you wouldn't drive such a recognizable car if you were planning to kidnap someone. And if the email to Dylan from MReese90 is any indication, the person who took him was careful enough to plan his moves in advance. The thought brings back all the anxiety of the past hour, and I glance around the L car in spite of myself. To see if I'm being watched.

My phone rings again as I'm walking from the L to my apartment. A blocked number. I almost send it to voicemail but then reconsider.

"Yes?" I answer.

And of course, there is nothing but silence on the line. Fury, now. Not even panic, as if I've slipped beyond my own capacity for fear.

"I know what you're doing," I say into the phone, my voice so tight it trembles. And then the line goes dead. It takes everything in me not to throw the phone against the asphalt of the sidewalk, watch it spring back up in broken pieces.

FIFTEEN

I pack some things—the essentials only, because I don't really feel like setting the precedent of staying at Andrea's place every time I get spooked by an investigation—and bike over to her apartment. She and Trish live on the top floor of a three-flat, a home that reminds me a great deal of the one I shared with Eric before our divorce. It's got that same new-furniture sheen, with a midcentury-modern sofa in the living room, and a funky chandelier in the entryway, and a well-stocked bronze bar cart in the dining room. The large windows at the front of the apartment are hung with heavy curtains that are always open, because there are so many plants crowded into the little space that the curtains don't have room to close. It's an apartment that blends Trish's love of eclectic pieces and the self-conscious need to reflect seriousness. Adulthood. Andrea's influence. It makes me think of my apartment—the single-income one-bedroom—with its pitted floors and dusty windows and flaking paint. I wonder if it makes me appear pitiable to people like Andrea and Trish, who live in a place like theirs.

I let myself in with my key, as I always do, and am about to announce my presence when I hear raised voices in the kitchen.

"So whoever this guy is, who killed the roommate, he pretended to be Marti to do it?" I recognize Trish's voice, the slight lilt of her British accent—held over from growing up an expat's kid in the UK—which has more or less been ironed out by a decade in the American Midwest.

"Maybe," Andrea replies.

"Maybe?" Trish repeats. "And you think it's a better idea for her to stay here than with her family?"

"You know she doesn't get along with her mother," Andrea says, but Trish cuts her off.

"That's not our problem, babe. Our problem is that you've brought the biggest lightning rod for chaos I've ever met to stay in our home. You enable her. You've always enabled her."

"I'm her friend. I support her, there's a difference."

"Yeah, well now she's wrapped up in a murder investigation. So great that she's staying in our guest room."

A spot of cold guilt forms in my stomach. It's the sensation of swallowing a piece of ice, feeling it drag down the back of my throat. It's a fact that we all try to ignore when we're together, that I won Andrea and Trish in my divorce by virtue of my closeness with Andrea. But it's easy to forget that Trish knew Eric first. Is loyal to him, perhaps, in a way she is not loyal to me. Still, this is probably the best opening I'll get, so I shut the door behind me with a rattling thud.

"Hey," I call into the apartment, and try to project nonchalance as I head to the kitchen. As if I haven't just listened to them arguing over me. As if I can't imagine I'm anything but welcome here.

"Hey, Marti," Trish says, quickly enveloping me in a hug. She smells of lavender, and it makes me think of my mother. The scent of fraught female relationships. "You've had a rough go of it, haven't you?"

"It's been a weird summer," I reply, glancing at Andrea, who is examining the zipper on her hoodie.

"Andrea's been filling me in," Trish says. "The police can't really think that you have anything to do with this, right?"

"I think they're just trying to rattle me," I reply. "They're not huge fans of amateur investigators stomping all over their turf."

"More like breaking the cases they've let go cold," Andrea says.

"Right, well, I'll leave you to it," Trish says, motioning to the nursery. "I think someone is due for a walk around the neighborhood."

"Thanks, babe," Andrea says, giving Trish a smile as she goes to collect Olive from her crib. Grateful. Appeasing. Perhaps a bit regretful as well. As soon as Trish is out of earshot, Andrea turns to me.

"So how much of that did you hear?"

"Enough," I reply.

"She's just being dramatic," Andrea says.

"She's not, really," I reply. "She's right about how crazy this is. She's right about me being a lightning rod for chaos."

"Oh, I wish you hadn't heard that." Andrea winces.

"It's true," I say. "I mean, look at the year I've had. And that was before a murderer was using my name in his email address."

"Still," Andrea says. "It's ridiculous to think that you shouldn't stay here. She's just being paranoid."

"She has a right to be," I say.

"No," Andrea replies, definitive. "I brought you into this, re-member? The podcast. The whole thing. This is happening as much because of me as because of you."

"So what do we do?" I ask, thinking of Olive, thinking of all the ways in which I'm desperate to protect her from every bit of chaos that has touched my life. I can't imagine how I'd feel if I were one of her mothers. But Andrea is resolute.

"We find him," she replies. "If the CPD is looking in the wrong place, we'll find him ourselves. And we'll bury him."

THE RHYTHMS OF Trish and Andrea's place—which are almost entirely dictated by Olive's schedule—are a bit different from what I'm used to. For starters, sleeping until noon is no longer an option. The guest room in which I'm staying is situated right next to their bathroom, so as soon as one of them showers in the morning, the gush of water through the pipes wakes me up. Which would be fine, except my night shifts at Club Rush have had me tiptoeing in after three most mornings, shutting the front door softly and creeping through the apartment to the guest room, avoiding even running the bathroom sink at more than a dribble while I brush my teeth. Olive is up at six, and nothing would make me a more unwelcome houseguest than waking her up before then.

I'm running on so little sleep that I feel half-drunk most of the time. Which is useful, because most of the actual drinking I'm doing is necessarily hidden from Andrea and Trish, after I poured myself a screwdriver at lunch the other day and noticed the concerned glance that passed between the two of them. It's easy to forget how I behaved while I was trying to be normal.

Andrea works from home during the day while Trish goes to her office, so Andrea and I have ample time to walk around Andersonville, the stroller between us, scandalizing the people who pass and hear snippets of our discussions. Mostly about the logistics of kidnapping someone and driving them across state lines to dump their body. Whether Dylan was likely killed in Milwaukee or killed once he and his kidnapper arrived here in Chicago. Whether the feds will get involved, once the medical examiner is able to definitively determine Dylan's cause of death wasn't simply an overdose. How much heroin you'd need to inject into a man of his size to be certain it would kill him. How far from the woods you'd have to park, and how far someone could drag a man's body before the diminishing returns of exhaustion and delay took hold. I worry that Olive is absorbing all of this through osmosis, but every time I lean down to check on her, she's as happy as ever, her little sunglasses hanging off her face, eyes inquisitive behind them. She's listening, though; that much is clear.

Andrea is generally over the moon to have another pair of hands at the ready while Trish is at work, so I spend the afternoons sitting on their living room floor, while Olive plays with her dolls and Andrea does laundry or cleans their kitchen or makes something elaborate for dinner. I mostly search further and further back through Sarah's social media accounts, or read through the true-crime forum's message boards, or wish for a cocktail.

That's where I am when, in my second week at Andrea's, I get an email from ARMY8070.

Better photo of the Tesla, she says in the text of the message. And it is a better photo of the car, this time from the surveillance camera of a local convenience store. The car's back windshield reflects the neon Schlitz sign in the store's front window. But the important detail, the one that makes this photo significant, is that you can also see the license plate number. Illinois plates.

There's no chance you have a PI license or access to DMV records, do you? I reply to ARMY8070. Again, she responds almost immediately.

No such luck. Might have to go through proper channels with this one.

"Proper channels," I say to Olive, wrinkling my nose as she gazes up at me. That can mean only one thing.

I dial my phone, and he picks up on the second ring.

"Detective Olsen," he says, by way of greeting.

"It's Marti."

"Marti," he replies. And then, "I'm glad you called."

"Don't be glad just yet," I reply, and let the words hang for a second, while I decide whether this is really the move I want to make. It is possible that the Tesla is completely unrelated to Dylan's disappearance. It's also possible that Olsen will take anything I give him right to his stern-faced partner. I wrinkle my nose again at Olive, who lets out a high-pitched giggle.

"Where are you?" Olsen asks.

"I'm babysitting for a friend," I reply.

"Staying there?"

"Why do you ask?"

I hear him hesitate before he answers. "I went by your place, a couple of times. It was pretty clear you weren't home."

"Not to worry, Detective," I reply, letting a curl of bitterness into my words, despite the fact that I'm calling Olsen for his help. "There are plenty of places in this city where I can shack up when there's a murderer after me."

I think of the numbers saved in my phone, men whose calls I ignored after the initial thrill had passed. There are a few who might still answer if I call, all these months later, but I say it more to reinforce for Olsen how meaningless the other night was. I say it to reinforce it for me too.

"Look, I understand that email scared you," Olsen replies. "But there's no reason to assume the guy has any interest in you, other than to use your name as bait."

"He's been calling me," I reply, glancing toward the kitchen, hoping Andrea isn't listening to my end of the conversation. I've kept this little detail from everyone, including her.

"What?" Olsen asks.

"I've been getting these calls. For months now, from a blocked number. Someone on the other end, just breathing into the phone."

"How many times?" Olsen asks.

I do a tally in my head. "Twenty-five, maybe?"

"You've gotten twenty-five suspicious phone calls and this is the first you're mentioning it?" His voice is louder now, sharp. Less like the militaristic cool he maintains on the job. More like the moment in bed, as I awoke from the nightmare.

"Oh, was I supposed to say something when your partner was treating me like a murder suspect?" I reply, matching his admonition with my own. "Funny, I guess I didn't get the impression that either of you gave a shit."

"Look, she's not my partner," Olsen replies. "And that's not how I would have played it, if it was my case. But she's old-school;

she was just trying to rattle you. To scare you off your investigation. She doesn't actually believe you sent that email."

"But she thinks I'm responsible for what happened," I say, because it's difficult not to imagine myself at the center of this. That, through the investigation of my sister, through *Jane Doe,* I have set in motion the chain of events that resulted in Dylan Jacobs's death.

"No one thinks that," Olsen replies. I can tell he's lying, but it's a bit comforting, actually. Sometimes it's nice to be shielded from a truth that has such sharp teeth.

"Well, Detective," I say, "how badly do you want to make things up to me?"

AN HOUR LATER, I'm marching into the Twenty-Fourth District police station, sans the police escort this time. Defiant, as always. Silvia gives me a weak smile, obviously well apprised of my interrogation two weeks ago.

"Detective Olsen is expecting me," I say, all business. She nods and motions me back to the bullpen.

He glances up as I approach, but I betray nothing. I feel like the whole station is watching me, as if the air around me pulses with attention as I pass through it. I drop both printed photos of the Tesla on Olsen's desk.

"These are from Milwaukee. The night Dylan Jacobs went missing."

He looks them over and then glances up at me. Surprised, maybe. Or impressed.

"Where did you get these?" he asks.

"Targeted ads on social media," I reply. "A friend of mine is good at crowdsourcing information on unsolved cases."

"You have interesting friends," he remarks, setting the photos back down on his desk. "So, what exactly are you asking me to do?"

"Not much," I reply. "Just run the plates. See which Illinois resident was parked on Dylan's street the night before he was reported missing."

"No way," Olsen says. "There's no way for me to verify the legitimacy of these. I can't treat them as evidence."

"You're doing me a favor, remember?" I say. "I'm not asking you to put them into evidence. I'm asking you to run the plates. That's all."

"I'm afraid that's not a favor I can accommodate," he says, his arms crossed in front of him.

"Don't give me your party-line bullshit," I say, my voice low, though I'm sure the heat of my tone draws the eyes of the people around us. "We're way past that now. You owe me this, for that little song-and-dance in the interrogation room. For throwing me to the wolves, after the other night."

Olsen runs a palm over his mouth. I wonder which parts of the other night, specifically, he's replaying in his head.

"If it ends up on your podcast that I helped you, I'm going to arrest you for interfering in an ongoing investigation," he says.

"If you wanted to put me in handcuffs, Detective, all you had to do was ask," I reply. Just quiet enough to be a warning, too low for the straining ears around us.

He gives his head a weary little shake but then turns to his computer, opening a new window and punching in some numbers. Copying the license plate from the photograph and hitting enter. I watch him go still as his eyes trace over the screen.

"What is it?" I ask, but he doesn't answer. "Kyle."

"I'm going to need to know exactly where you got this photo," he says.

"I told you," I say, getting up from my chair and moving around the desk so I can see the screen. There's a DMV form for vehicle registration, showing a Tesla Model S with a matching license plate and the name of the owner.

The car is registered to Theodore Nelson Vreeland.

SIXTEEN

Ted is arrested three days later. I watch it on the morning news, as he's led out of their Wicker Park condo, the same grand house where I shared a dinner with him and Ava, the opulence of the place making it seem bulletproof. A fortress of wealth, rendered useless. Its monster already inside.

Now he's flanked on each side by a couple of suits—federal agents, most likely—and surrounded by reporters. A jacket, slung over his hands in front of him, covers what must be handcuffs on his wrists.

Andrea sets a bowl of oatmeal in front of me on the breakfast bar and drops some cereal onto the tray of Olive's high chair. Tending to both of her charges, all without taking her eyes from the TV in the living room.

"I actually can't believe this," she says.

"I know."

Olsen has been radio silent since he ran the Tesla's license plate for me, but I know there must be more to the case for the feds to have made such an immediate arrest. I wonder if the Tesla was the first piece of evidence against Ted or the last in a long line of connections, links in a chain that begins with Dylan Jacobs and ends with Ava's husband. Or maybe it begins well before Dylan. Maybe it even begins before Sarah.

"How old do you think he is?" I ask, motioning toward the television. Ted is bending to sit in the back of a police cruiser, a cop's hand on his head, ensuring he doesn't graze it on the doorframe.

"I don't know. Thirty-five? Thirty-eight?" Andrea replies. "You've had a lot more contact with him than I have. What do you think?"

"Somewhere around there, probably," I reply. "So, maybe the same age as Maggie. A year or two older, give or take."

"Is he from here?" Andrea asks, stirring frozen blueberries into her own bowl of oatmeal.

"Evanston, I think," I reply, trying to remember what Ava said when she talked about her husband.

"Evanston? Seriously?" Her movements still.

"I know," I say, shaking my head. "It's not possible, is it?"

"I mean . . ." Andrea is quiet for a moment. "Could the man in the car have been a teenager?"

Again, my recollection is the problem. I shut my eyes, conjuring the memory like an incantation, like I have so many times. It was a man. A man, maybe the age of our father or a bit younger. The man whom I've never been able to recognize, faceless, in the dreams where he makes me murder my sister.

"Maybe," I say. Because I can no longer trust myself. "Maybe it could have been Ted."

"Evanston is so close," Andrea replies.

"I don't know." I remember what Ava said when Colin talked about Sarah's pink dress. A false memory, she called it. Something the brain creates on its own, as vivid as if your eyes had actually seen it. A lie of the mind. And suddenly the person in the front seat of that sedan is a boy, with a square jaw and sandy hair. The golden skin of an athlete who spends his days running across open expanses of well-tended grass. The sort of boy who would easily have enthralled my sister, once upon a time. Just as he tempted me, briefly, in the alley that night.

I rub my eyes, trying to clear away the image in my mind. Because if I'm wrong about this, if I'm wrong about the man in the car, about Ted, about my sister, then I can trust nothing. Not myself. Not anyone.

"Have you heard from Ava?" Andrea asks, and I wonder if she sees the ways in which I could so easily come apart once more. I wonder if this is how it will always be, when the question of Maggie draws close to an answer. I wonder if I'll survive actually finding the truth.

"I can't imagine she'll want to talk to me now," I reply. Now that her husband has been arrested, like reliving the nightmare of Colin's arrest all over again, I'm sure. She's probably coming apart too. And suddenly, I'm desperate to see her. Desperate for her not to be angry with me.

"Maybe she doesn't know you had anything to do with the police identifying the Tesla," Andrea says. "After all, she's the one who asked you to investigate."

Ted, I think. Ted, who cornered me in an alley, warned me to stay away from the case. Threatened me, even. Ted, who cooked me dinner, who made Ava smile.

"So what do we do?" I ask. "Now that we've apparently broken the case wide open?" I know what Andrea's answer will be, even before she says it.

"We should get some recording done," she replies.

WE SPEND THREE hours in the studio, running through the details of the case. Except this time, through the frame of Ted as the killer. Amazingly, after all this time, the pieces begin to fall into place.

The question becomes one of motive. Whether the hair in Sarah's shower drain belonged to Ted. If he was at Sarah's apartment and what may have transpired there to necessitate a shower. Perhaps Ted was feeling neglected by Ava's preoccupation with med school, her insistence on a specialty that would disrupt their lives for years to come, and had turned to Sarah for attention.

"But can we just assume they were sleeping together?" Andrea says. "I mean, isn't that kind of a stretch?"

"Yeah, it's a stretch," I reply. "But it's not out of the realm of possibility. We know, based on Dylan's report to the police, that Sarah hadn't had any houseguests recently. So, it was someone Dylan didn't realize was there. Or Colin. And why else would someone be secretly showering at Sarah's place, if it wasn't sexual?"

"So Ted kills Sarah to keep her quiet about their affair?" Andrea asks, pausing momentarily to adjust the mic in front of her. "Was she that big of a risk to him?"

Olive watches the whole exchange from her baby swing in the corner, an uncharacteristically quiet observer.

"He and Ava were getting serious," I reply. "I mean, you should see this guy. The best of everything. I could imagine him killing Sarah just so he wouldn't lose his perfect life."

"His perfect wife, you mean," Andrea replies.

"So, let's say Sarah leaves her apartment to meet her friends. We know from the court transcripts, and Sarah's case file, that Colin took a cab to his grandmother's birthday dinner at Au Cheval." Andrea nods as I speak. I can feel it, that same lurid energy, the excitement building between us. "But Ava and Ted are on record saying that they arrived separately to the birthday dinner—Ava from their apartment, and Ted from his office."

"His office was only a fifteen-minute drive from Sarah's apartment, according to Google," Andrea interjects.

"Right, so he could have easily been waiting outside when she left. He might have convinced her to get in the car with him and then killed her."

"In the car?"

"Why not?" I reply. "They were never able to determine that she was killed in her apartment. They assumed that Colin probably cleaned up the scene, but there's nothing to prove that she wasn't killed somewhere else. Then all Ted had to do was put her body in his trunk, and he had plenty of time to arrive at Au Cheval ahead of Colin."

"And just sits at the restaurant, with a body in the trunk?" Andrea asks, less a question and more an exclamation of disbelief. Disgust.

"And then after dinner, Ava drove their grandmother home and then dropped Colin off, while Ted supposedly went back to his office to finish up some work. He didn't get home until late. So Ted could have easily driven to LaBagh Woods and buried Sarah Ketchum's body there, without Ava or Colin ever suspecting anything."

"And after Colin's conviction, his perfect life would have fallen back into place," Andrea says, picking up the thread. "He and Ava get married. They plan on having a family."

"Except," I say, "the one hiccup was Ava's constant crusade to release Colin from prison. It undoes her to the point where she can't move forward with any of their plans. She doesn't want to slow down at work or start a family until Colin is released."

I think about our dinner at Chicago Diner, when Ava insisted that Ted was supportive of the abortion she had after Colin's conviction. I wonder now if his veneer of understanding covered something darker, a deep resentment of Colin. A desire to go to any lengths to get his sterling life back on track.

"So when Ava started talking about reaching out to me, about the potential connection between Maggie and Sarah, Ted must have begun to see the danger I posed to him. Ava had the case file with the extra hair listed on it, and that hair had been tested for DNA."

"And Ted's DNA wasn't in the system," Andrea says.

"But an additional investigation could be potentially damning, if he was ever asked to furnish a DNA sample. And Dylan was the loose end. Dylan was the only other person who might have suspected that Ted and Sarah were having an affair. So, Ted went to the library and preempted that part of the investigation. Posed as me in an email, asked Dylan to meet. Killed him. Drove back to Chicago, and once again dumped a body in LaBagh Woods. Which accomplishes two things: it gets rid of any insight Dylan had into Sarah's case, and it discredits me with the CPD. So anything we might uncover would be seen as compromised."

"But wait," Andrea says. "Why dump him here? Why not up in Milwaukee?"

"The same reason everyone assumed Colin dumped her in

those woods," I reply. "They were familiar. He'd done it once before, and Sarah had only been found by chance, days later, after rain had washed away most of the evidence that could have linked her to Ted."

"It seems like such a risk, though," Andrea replies.

"Think about it this way," I say. "Dylan was listed as a missing person in Milwaukee for months. It wasn't until we called in the tip that the Milwaukee PD even made the connection to Sarah's case. And the only reason they started searching in LaBagh was because I suggested it. Dylan would never have been found otherwise."

"So now Ted is going down for two murders, instead of one."

"And if everything goes the way it should," I reply, "Colin McCarty will be released from prison."

"So Ava frees her brother but unknowingly implicates her husband," Andrea says. "That has got to be such a major head trip. I can't even imagine." I feel my phone buzz in my pocket. I glance at the screen and hit the stop button on the computer's recording module.

"Speak of the devil?" Andrea asks.

"I CAN'T BELIEVE it," Ava says when I answer. "I actually can't believe it. That *fucker*." She hisses the word. I can hear the throb of true rage in her voice. It's a bit comforting, actually. I was worried there might be tears. I was worried I might be put in a position of guilt by association. That Ava might have wanted to string up the messenger.

"Was it the DNA?" I ask. "From the shower? Is that what did it?"

"They called me on Sunday and said they found Dylan Jacobs's body. That they needed DNA samples from us, from everyone connected to Sarah's case, for exclusionary purposes," Ava says. "I brought them Ted's brush. Gave them a cheek swab. I didn't even hesitate. What a total rube they must think I am." She laughs a little, a bitter sound.

So it was true, I think. They got Ted's DNA. They must have matched it to something—either the hair in the shower drain or something they found on Dylan. I realize I'm not breathing and pull the phone's mic away from my face. Breathe into my cupped hand for a moment. To keep myself from panicking, hyperventilating.

"I can't imagine how hard this must be for you," I say when I've regained my breath. "I'm so sorry, Ava."

"Don't be sorry," she spits. "That *shit*, that motherfucking *bastard*. He cost me years with my brother. My little brother lost years of his life, because I was too blinded by love to see what was right in front of me."

"It's not your fault," I say, though it's a hollow sentiment. I heard it too many times, as a child, to be able to deliver it with any conviction. And I can understand Ava's rage. I know what it is to have an unbreakable loyalty to a sibling. To be willing to tear down anything else in your life in service to that bond.

"You know Dylan called me once?" Ava says, and I can hear her sniffling. I wonder if she's crying on the other end of the line. "After Colin's conviction. Told me he thought Sarah might have been seeing someone else."

"Dylan told you that?" I ask.

"Yeah. He and Colin never liked each other, but even he had his doubts after the trial. He said Sarah mentioned having a guy over. An older guy, one she had a crush on. Made Dylan swear not to tell anyone." Ava laughs again, and this time it sounds like a sob. She must be crying, I realize. I've never seen Ava cry.

"I never made the connection," she continues. "I never even considered it could be Ted. An older guy. Jesus fucking Christ."

"Did he tell the police about it?" I ask.

"I don't know. I told him to," Ava replies. "But they were so goddamn myopic when it came to Colin being guilty, they probably just ignored him. I should sue the shit out of them."

"Ava," I say carefully, not wanting to betray my own suspicion, "did you ever tell Ted what Dylan said to you? About Sarah seeing someone else?"

As soon as I've asked the question, I catch my mistake. Because this is Ava, and she's quicker than anyone I know.

"Oh god," she says. "You think that's why Ted went after Dylan?"

"I don't know," I say quickly, but my heart isn't in it. I'm guilty of the same things she is, the belief that I am somehow responsible for all the troubles that befall the people in my life. Allpowerful, the two of us. "Let's just focus on Colin right now," I say. "How quickly do you think you can get him out?" I think of his splinted fingers. I think of the beating he just endured. Broken ribs. A fractured eye socket. There's an urgency here. We have to get him out, before something more terrible happens to him.

And a new possibility rises, as if out of cold, soundless depths of water. I wonder if Ted's money, his connections in this city, could buy this sort of violence. If he could slip the right amount of cash to the right person and have Colin killed.

"We have to appeal to the judge and the state's attorney," Ava says. "They're not just going to let him out, not until Ted is convicted. And that could be—I don't know. Maybe years, even."

"What sort of appeal?" I ask.

"We have to put public pressure on the judge to vacate Colin's conviction. Pressure the governor, even. And the state's attorney has to decline to file additional charges."

"Public pressure," I say, as if I'm finally understanding the meaning of those words. "The podcast, you mean."

"You have to finish it. Release it. All of it, as quickly as possible."

"I have to talk to Andrea," I say, glancing out the studio's door to where Andrea is sitting, nursing Olive on one of the seats at the breakfast bar. I can tell she's listening to my end of the conversation though, because her eyes flick to me as soon as I say her name. "I'm not sure how quickly we can get it all edited and released."

"I'll help you with anything you need," Ava says. "Money, resources. I can give you any sort of interview you want. Nothing's off the table."

"Okay," I say. "We'll work on it. We can probably get something pulled together in the next few weeks." I raise my eyebrows at Andrea. She slowly nods.

"We have to do this, Marti," Ava says, a note of desperation in her voice. "I have to fix this."

"I know," I reply. "And we will." As I hang up the phone, I'm struck again by that feeling of power. I've had a part in this, I know. I've had a hand in justice's being done, finally.

CHAPTER
SEVENTEEN

The podcast is a sensation. It has everything that the public wants: a dead girl; two intrepid investigators; a wrongfully convicted kid from a rough, working-class background; police misconduct; and a new murder. And of course, the arrest of an attractive, privileged killer to top it all off. Ted is ubiquitous on cable news, his high-cheekboned mug shot staring out of every supermarket tabloid. Ted Vreeland is suddenly Patrick Bateman. Hannibal Lecter. Jack the Ripper, finally unmasked. "Bundy 2.0" trends on Twitter following the release of each episode.

Andrea cut seven episodes together with the grace of a symphony conductor, always seeming to know when to hammer the details and when to pause for the human element. By the time we release the fifth episode, Ted's trial date is set for the following spring, and every major news media outlet in the country is covering the story.

I can't sleep.

Ever since Ted's arrest, when I returned home to my apartment, the dreams have been getting worse. No matter what I try, I wake in the middle of the night in a pool of my own sweat and can't get back to sleep. I've tried warm milk and Ambien and walking laps around my apartment. But somehow, I always end up on my couch, drinking vodka and watching whatever is on TV between the hours of three and eight a.m.

And it's a problem, because Andrea and I are suddenly in high demand with the press. The word is that Colin will be released from prison any day now, and managers are calling from LA with promises of documentaries and true-crime TV miniseries. A book agent friend of Andrea's is pushing us to write an account of the case that she could sell. Multiple publishers have reached out to me about writing a memoir, the story of my futile search for my sister. That was how one described it. *Futile.*

And then there are the interview requests that come in by the hour. Everyone from the *New York Times* to the *Red Eye.* So being sleep deprived right now, drunk at eight a.m. and hungover by noon, is really not ideal.

Part of the problem, believe it or not, is Marco. Or, more specifically, the thing that Marco said to me last week, just after we released the fourth episode of the podcast. I arrived at Club Rush to find a bored-looking audio technician working on the club's sound system, moving at the pace of someone whose daily dose of caffeine has long since worn off.

"It's fucked," Marco said as I joined him behind the bar. "They say it'll be at least an hour before we can open."

"Great, so we get paid for sitting around," I replied, pulling out my laptop and taking a seat at the bar.

"Without tips, what's the point?" Marco asked.

I shrugged. "Gives me time to work on the side hustle." It was lucky, actually. I was way behind on editing the bonus content we were posting on our website—my responsibility, as Andrea was editing the whole rest of the show. It was mostly extended cuts of interviews, minor-league editing, really. My job was to make sure they were audible, and even that was getting away from me since Ted's arrest.

"Better not let the boss man see you doing that on the company dime," Marco said as I started fiddling with the audio levels of my prison-visit recording with Colin.

"What's he going to do, fire me for neglecting the customers?" I asked, motioning to the empty room before us.

"He thinks you're going to quit anyway," Marco replied. "He thinks you're too good for this place now that you've got your whole citizen-journalist-fame thing."

"He's right," I said, hitting the space bar to listen to the playback, trying to get the levels right during the portion of the recording where Colin first enters. He was further away from the mic than he was for the rest of the interview, as he gave Ava a hug. I was trying to pump up the dialogue while bringing the ambient levels down a bit.

"What's that?" Marco asked, motioning to the laptop.

"A recording of the first time I met Colin McCarty in prison," I replied, replaying the clip again.

"Why's he speaking Portuguese?" Marco asked.

"He and his sister spoke it with their grandmother as kids," I replied. "Apparently they sometimes still speak it now. Especially when Colin is talking about something offensive. Like my tits, for instance." I paused for a moment. "You know Portuguese?"

"Sure, my mom's Brazilian," Marco replied. "Plus, I'm a natural polyglot. You know, in addition to being exceptionally handsome."

"So I hear," I said, replaying the clip again, tweaking the levels just a bit more. "And exceptionally vain."

"Play me the part where he talks about your tits," Marco said, casting a devilish look in my direction. "I wanna hear what he has to say."

"He asks her to bring him women with bigger tits next time. Or something like that—I get the feeling that Ava only gave me a rough translation." I played the clip again, so Marco could listen.

"That's not what he's saying, honey," Marco replied, hands on his hips.

"What do you mean?" I asked. "What did he say?"

"Play it one more time," he said, leaning in close as I did. He nodded, as if confirming his own suspicions. "'Is everything in place?'"

"What?" I asked.

"That's what he's saying. He's telling her he's tired of waiting and asking her, *Is everything in place?*"

"Marco, I swear to god, if you're fucking with me right now . . . ," I said, but Marco only put up both hands in mock surrender.

"Don't shoot the messenger, girl," he said. "Get a fucking translator if you want. They're going to tell you the same thing."

"Are you serious?" I said, replaying the clip for myself, trying to remember the moment. Colin said something I couldn't understand, and then Ava smacked him on the arm, admonished him, introduced him to me. Or maybe she didn't smack him on the arm. I tried to remember. Maybe she clapped him on the shoulder. A confirmation.

"Don't tell anyone about this," I said, glaring at him preemptively.

"Who am I gonna tell?" he asked, pouring himself a shot and then offering one to me. I shook my head. A shot was the last thing I needed. I felt like I might be sick.

IT MIGHT HAVE been nothing. That's what I've been telling myself. It might have been one of those passing, nonsensical moments between siblings. Or Colin might have been asking about the state of the podcast, or his next appeal. But I always come back to a single question: Why did Ava lie to me about it? Why would she tell me that her brother made a sexist crack about my breasts, one that she had to apologize for, if he hadn't? That's the question that sticks with me. The one that keeps me from sleeping. Because I remember that moment, her supposed admission. That was the moment I decided to trust her. Sometimes, I wonder if that moment was engineered to make me trust her.

I don't tell Andrea about it. I don't tell anyone. It feels like a dangerous suspicion to have, damaging in the telling of it alone, like suspecting someone of child molestation or spousal abuse. Plus, I don't even actually know what I suspect. I don't know how to put this into words, other than in its most simplistic, most general form. Ava is a liar. Ava and Colin are both liars.

Still, it's one passing comment, held up against all the evidence against Ted. I remind myself of this as I take hit after hit at the gym, as my sparring partner gets the better of me, as the instructor admonishes me for being distracted. As I hit the heavy bag until my hands swell and ache. As I drink my vodka. I remind myself: They have his DNA. The timeline works. It was his car outside of Dylan Jacobs's apartment the night he went missing. Ted killed him. Ted killed them both. Wake up. Wake up. Wake up.

EIGHTEEN

You'll never guess who left me a voicemail last night," Andrea says as I drag myself into her apartment the morning we release the sixth episode. Despite spending my nights at my own place since Ted's arrest, since the breathy, voiceless calls have stopped, I still spend most days hanging out at Andrea's. Today, I'm not sure if I'm hungover or still drunk. All I know is that I took an Uber instead of biking, because I was certain that riding in traffic in my current state could get me killed. The world around me has developed the habit of shifting at odd moments, stuttering and pulsing, threatening to send me sprawling. Leaving me dizzy, the ground beneath me soft and uneven. I recognize this feeling, where the laws of physics are suddenly pliable, ready at any moment to fail. It's the feeling of a dream.

"Who?" I ask.

"Walter Ketchum," Andrea replies.

I drop my bag on her couch, and it topples off onto the floor. I wince as my laptop inside hits the carpeting. "Sarah's father?"

"The one and only." She places her phone on the coffee table and plays the message on speaker as I lower myself down to the floor and crawl to Olive, who is playing with a set of vividly bright wooden blocks. As the message plays, I help her begin to create what I can only describe as an incredibly impressive—if not terribly structurally sound—princess tower.

"This message is for Andrea Johnson," the voice over the phone intones gruffly. "I'm calling regarding your podcast about my daughter." You can hear something on the other end of the line. Like a shuffling. Or the man clearing his throat.

"What is it?" I ask. But Andrea holds a finger to her lips, just before the voice picks up again.

"I just want to let you know that you should be ashamed of yourselves," he says, his voice tilted in a way that might be the result of either emotion or alcohol. Or both. "Justice had been done in Sarah's case. The man who killed her was behind bars. And because of you two . . . Because of you, I've just been informed that he'll be released by the end of the week. So I'm calling to say, I hope you get what you two deserve. I really do."

The message cuts off, and we're left with dead air.

"Think he was drunk?" I ask, feeling the tight pull of my own hangover behind my eyes, making my stomach swim.

"He sounds it," Andrea replies. "I mean, wouldn't you be?"

"At least he stopped himself short of calling us cunts." I theatrically cover Olive's ears as I say it, which she doesn't appreciate. She gives a little wail of protest, so I release her just as quickly.

"Sorry, sorry," I say, giving her a reassuring pat on the back. "You'll learn all those words eventually."

"The thing is, it might be a problem for us, if he goes public," Andrea says. "It might look like we weren't considering the well-being of the family."

"Andrea, we did everything short of hiring a private investigator to try to find him. It's not our fault that he's only coming out of the woodwork now."

"I know," Andrea says. "I'm just saying, the optics aren't great."

"So what are you proposing?" I ask. Something in me is already dreading the answer.

"I think you should call him back," Andrea replies. "Talk to him about Maggie, talk to him about your experience with Ted. Tell him about your family. I think if anyone is going to be able to talk him down, it's you."

"Can I think about it?" I ask.

"It's Thursday, Marti," Andrea replies.

"So?"

"So, if Colin is going to be released by the end of the week, that's today or tomorrow. We don't have time to wait around."

"Andrea, I'm pretty sure I'm still drunk," I say. It's not news to her.

"He's not going to have the displeasure of smelling you," she replies. "If you're sober enough to balance a bunch of blocks with Olive, you're sober enough to make a phone call."

I look at Olive. She looks back at me with an expression of admonishment for my behavior. When Andrea hands me the phone, I take it.

IT RINGS FIVE times before there's a click on the other end of the line. For a moment, I think it's gone to voicemail, but there's no greeting and no tone. I hold the phone away from my face, but the screen still shows an active call.

"Mr. Ketchum?" I say, and wait a moment for him to reply. He doesn't. "Mr. Ketchum, this is Marti Reese. I was hoping I could talk with you for a moment about your daughter's case."

"What exactly is there to say?" the voice on the other end replies. The weariness in his voice makes me think of my father before he died, in the middle of his successful effort to smoke and drink himself to death in the wake of Maggie's absence. *Like father, like daughter,* I think involuntarily.

"Well, first I wanted to express how sorry we are about what happened to Sarah. I lost my sister too, so I have some idea of how horrible it is to experience the loss of a child from a family."

Andrea is watching my side of the conversation, nodding as I talk. At least I'm not too drunk to be coherently sympathetic.

"That doesn't make you right about this," Walter replies, his tone careful, the way some parents adopt a different cadence when speaking to people their children's age.

"I know," I reply. "And, to that point, I also wanted to try and reassure you a bit, that Ted Vreeland is the man at fault here. I've met him on a couple of occasions. At one point, he threatened me with regard to my investigation. I really do believe that he is a person who is capable of killing, if it means he can maintain his wealth and social status." Even as I say it, I realize that I'm not quite sure all of it is true. Or, if it's true, I'm not sure it means that he's the one who killed Sarah. I think, again, of Ava and Colin. The words that slipped between them at the prison. The ways in which I've been wrong about so much already, so blinded by the pieces that seem to fit.

"I think you and I are just going to have to agree to disagree on that, young lady," Walter replies. It's an oddly comforting sentiment. Like I am, once more, talking to my own father. Always a reasonable man, even through the worst of circumstances.

Olive begins fussing next to me on the rug, and I put my hand over the mouthpiece to muffle the sound.

Sorry, Andrea mouths at me, scooping the little girl up and carrying her toward the nursery.

"Is that all?" Walter asks. And a thought occurs to me, something tugging at my memory. We were trying to find Walter because we had specific questions for him. A name floats up, from somewhere in my alcohol-relaxed brain. A flash of revelation, brought on by the looseness of inebriation.

"Actually, I do have one question for you," I say. "Is Abigail Woods your sister?"

"Who?" Walter asks.

"Abigail Woods," I repeat. "I went to the house you lived in on Galley, and the current owner said that it used to be owned by a woman named Abigail Woods. I wasn't sure if you were related, or if she was your landlord . . ." I trail off, waiting for him to offer clarification. Instead, there's silence on the other end of the line.

"Marti, is it?"

"Yes," I say.

"I'm not sure what you're talking about," he replies. "Where is Galley?"

"Galley Road," I say. "In Sutcliffe Heights."

"I think you might have some incorrect information," Walter replies. "I lived in Palos Hills. I've never lived on a Galley Road."

"But . . . ," I say, about to protest. It was one of the certainties of the case, the connection to Maggie. That our house in Sutcliffe

Heights overlooked Galley Road. That 4603 was within view of our back balcony. But, as I try to remember where I first learned of the connection, I realize that it was Ava who told me Walter had lived on Galley Road. I took her at her word.

I remember this feeling from a year ago, the morning I got the DNA results on the Jane Doe. When I hung up on Detective Olsen and stepped onto the Blue Line heading east, meeting Eric in the West Loop for dinner. Everything around me a hum of static, everything lost in the clatter of the train and the short, staccato hiss of my breaths.

The smell of the L car was the smell of bodies in a confined space, a smell I'd always associated with animals. The spicy brine of the giraffe pen at the Lincoln Park Zoo. Except that day, it felt like the smell was an extra element in the air, like smoke, crowding out the oxygen, making it thin. It seemed like no matter how many breaths I took, I could not get enough air.

I sat down, hard, on the floor of the L car, opposite the doors. Around me, people's legs shifted, crowded in. Though I was sitting, it still felt as if I might tip over with the movement of the train.

"Are you okay?" A man knelt down next to me, so he was in my eyeline. I shook my head but said nothing. "Are you having chest pain?"

I shook my head. Not unless the strain of breathing counted, the physical exertion of trying to open the bellows of my lungs past their capacity, trying to get enough air.

"Trouble breathing?" the man asked. He was bald, with dark skin and dark-rimmed glasses. A wedding ring glinted on one of his fingers. "Do you have asthma?"

Again, I shook my head.

"Is it a panic attack?"

I wondered how I was supposed to know if I was having a panic attack. Maybe it was something you knew only if you'd already had one. Maybe I was really having some sort of episode—a pulmonary embolism or anaphylaxis or the first symptoms of a heart condition no one ever knew I had—and if I agreed that I was having a panic attack, I wouldn't get the treatment I really needed in time to save my life.

As I tried to decide what to answer, the train jerked to a stop and the doors opened at the next station. The man didn't move, instead put out an arm to keep people from crossing between us to get out the doors. I could feel tears leaking from the corners of my eyes.

"Cup your hands over your mouth," he said, miming the motion himself as the doors chimed and slid closed.

I did as he said, breathing into my cupped palms.

"Try to slow down a little. Deep breaths," he said. I could feel the chill of a fog bank rolling in, cold dampness licking across my skin. But, finally, I could take a breath. And then another.

We remained like that, me breathing into my hands, him watching me breathe, as the doors opened and closed, as people shifted around us.

And I remember the feeling of sitting on the floor of the L, of catching my breath as the man—Nate, his name was Nate—talked me down. The feeling of icy vapor wrapping me up. I have that feeling again, talking to Walter Ketchum. Like I'm being swallowed by a cold, dense cloud. Like something has blocked the sun.

"I appreciate your time, Mr. Ketchum," I say, and my voice sounds small, remote, even to my own ears.

"Listen," Walter says. "I understand that you didn't mean any harm. I probably said too much last night in my message. But you have to know . . . I used to tell Sarah, the road to hell is paved with good intentions. And I will go to my grave knowing that Colin McCarty is the man who killed my little girl."

"I'm sorry." I choke the words out. "I am, I'm so sorry." My face is wet, and I realize that two solitary tears have trailed their way down my cheeks. There's a click on the other end of the line.

When I look up, Andrea is standing in the hallway, watching me.

TED IS BEING held in the Metropolitan Correctional Center in downtown Chicago, awaiting trial. He's been held without bail on the recommendation of the state's attorney, as his considerable financial resources and powerful connections in Chicago's business world make him a flight risk. So I have to do nothing but take the Brown Line south to Harold Washington Library and walk a few blocks—past the "Hotel Men Only" sign that Maggie pointed out to me on one of our early adventures into the city, the place where Harrison Ford's character stayed in *The Fugitive*—in order to visit with him.

I probably wouldn't even consider it, visiting Ted, except for the fact that I opened my mailbox last week to discover an envelope with the MCC's return address, containing a half-completed visitor information form. Ted had clearly filled out the inmate section—written in perfect, boilerplate penmanship—and left the rest for me to complete. Even before my conversation with Marco, I was intrigued by what Ted might have to say to me, so I finished the form and mailed it back. Yesterday morning, after I'd gotten home from Andrea's apartment and taken a long, sobering shower, I got a voicemail that I'd been approved for a visit.

The MCC is a strange building, a triangular high-rise made of sandy-colored stone. Its windows are long vertical slits, and from a block or two away, you can see the fencing surrounding the rooftop yard. I remember passing by it countless times when I was younger and thinking nothing of it—just an awkward piece of city architecture amid all the beautiful Chicago buildings that populate the South Loop and Printer's Row. Old printing houses with huge, heavy windows. Dearborn Station's clock tower overlooking all of it. It was only later, when I was older, that I realized the tower only a few blocks away was a jail.

Still, I know what to expect, from my visit downstate with Colin, when I arrive. My purse is screened, and I'm brought into a large communal room, where I sit at a low metal table. Ted enters through a door at the opposite side of the room and scans the space for me before approaching.

"That was fast," he says as he sits down on the other side of the table. He looks strange in his orange prison uniform. Diminished, somehow, without his expensive shirts and his well-tailored trousers.

"I didn't see the point in wasting any time," I reply. "Colin is supposed to be released today."

Ted winces a bit, his jaw so tight the muscle bulges at his ear. "Well, score one for justice then, right?" he says, his voice strained with viciousness. He sits back in his chair, a poor imitation of Colin's jailhouse swagger. He's not cut out for this, and it shows. "I can't talk about my case," he says. "So I'm not really sure why you're here."

"You sent me the form," I reply. "I thought you wanted me to come."

"Right. I guess I never thought you actually would," Ted says, and then gives a little smile, which could also be a grimace. "I guess I just imagined all the things I might say to you if you ever did."

"Well, here's your chance," I reply.

"You're so certain of your own righteousness," he says. "Believe me, I know how that feels. I lived that, for a long time."

"Ted, I'm not certain of anything anymore," I reply. I feel so small here. So wrung out. I want someone to tell me the truth. I want to believe someone when they promise that they're being honest. I lean forward, both of my palms flat on the table between us. "Ted. Please. Did you kill her?"

"I barely even knew Sarah Ketchum. Of course I didn't kill her."

"I'm not talking about Sarah," I reply.

He looks at me blankly for a moment and then breaks into a quick, unironic laugh. When I say nothing, Ted shuts his eyes. Presses a hand over his mouth.

"You're out of your mind, you know that?" he says through his fingers. And then he's leaning toward me as well, his eyes open and fixed on mine. Fevered eyes, like someone delirious with heat. Pupils wide. "I didn't kill your goddamn sister. I didn't kill anyone. This is all insane. I didn't kill Dylan Jacobs or Sarah Ketchum."

"Then who did, Ted?" I ask.

"You wouldn't believe me, even if I told you the truth," he replies, spitting the words at me as if his mouth were full of venom. Still such a handsome man. I wonder how someone like him will fare here, behind bars. The world of rules he's spent a lifetime leveraging to his benefit has no place here. All his rules are gone now.

"If Colin killed Sarah, then who killed Dylan?" I ask, and I can tell he's a bit surprised. That I'm willing to entertain the possibility.

"You're a smart girl," he says. "It's why I sent you that form. Stop being so obtuse for one goddamn minute, and you'll figure it out." He pushes back his chair and stands, heading back out the door through which he came. And I'm left there, sitting alone in a correctional facility's visitation room, with my heart in my mouth.

I ARRIVE HOME from the MCC just in time to receive a text from Ava. A selfie, of her and Colin, both grinning and squinting against the sunlight. Outside, somewhere. So, it's happened. Colin McCarty is out of prison.

NINETEEN

Ava sits down in Andrea's back bedroom, on the chair I usually occupy at Andrea's little studio setup. We've both agreed that Andrea should do this interview. She's more objective. She's not as close with Ava, outside the podcast, never been to her home. Never met Ted.

I don't tell Andrea that I can't stand the idea of interviewing Ava now. I have no way of discerning whether she's telling the truth. About Colin. About where Walter Ketchum lived. And I don't think I can pretend any longer that I trust her.

"Thanks for joining us today," Andrea says once she's turned on the recording setup.

Ava puts on her set of headphones and leans over her mic. "I'm glad to be here. Though I wish it could be under better circumstances."

"Right," Andrea says. "This has to have been a very difficult time for you."

"Well, the past seven years have been difficult," Ava replies. "So this, everything that's happened now . . . I'm sure it sounds strange, but there's a part of me that's extremely relieved that something has finally changed. And grateful too. To finally know who my husband was. When I asked the two of you to investigate this case, I don't think I ever dreamed it would so fundamentally change my life. In large ways and small." Ava glances in my direction, and I give her an encouraging smile. To cover everything that's roiling inside me. To cover the fact that I know she's a liar.

"Let's talk about some of those large ways," Andrea says. "Since we began recording for this podcast, two significant changes have happened in your life. The first: your brother, Colin, has been exonerated for the murder of Sarah Ketchum and has since been released from prison. And the second: your husband, Ted, has been arrested and charged with the murders of both Sarah Ketchum and Dylan Jacobs. Can you tell us, if you can, what this series of events has been like to live through?"

"Well, I think the order of the events has been an important element to it," Ava replies, and I can already hear the warm tones of her voice as if through playback. What she'll sound like to our listeners. How measured and accomplished and articulate.

"Ted's arrest was sort of the first domino to fall, in all of this," she continues. "Which was shocking, and devastating, of course. But as soon as the evidence against him began to stack up—the hair found in Sarah Ketchum's shower drain, the fact that his car was parked outside of Dylan Jacobs's apartment the night he disappeared, traces of his blood on a pair of nail clippers in Ted's travel case—his involvement in both killings became difficult to refute."

"Let's pause for a minute on that last piece of evidence you mentioned," Andrea says, glancing toward me. I raise my eyebrows. This is news to me too. "Dylan's blood was found on a pair of nail clippers?"

"Yes. According to the discovery the police turned over to our attorney, it was discovered in a Dopp kit Ted brings with him while traveling."

"So, what is the theory on how the blood got there?" Andrea asks.

"The police think he might have clipped his nails after he killed him," Ava replies. "To prevent DNA evidence from being found underneath them."

"That's . . . ," Andrea says.

"Horrifying," Ava replies. "Yes. So, for me, it became about coming to terms with that as quickly as possible, so that I could then shift my focus to getting my brother released from prison."

"And what did that process—coming to terms with what your husband had done—what did that look like?" Andrea asks.

Ava blinks. "Well, it involved me breaking just about every dish and plate and glass in my house," she replies. "If there was something breakable and on hand at the moment, you'd better believe I broke it."

I can hear the amusement in her voice, the strain of her own embarrassed self-deprecation.

"But, you know, there's something about being in emergency medicine," Ava continues. "You see life-and-death situations all the time. You see the things that people do to each other, up close. And it makes you realize that most of the time life turns on a dime. It makes you realize how fragile everything is."

"The way that smashing dishes makes everything feel fragile," Andrea says.

"Right," Ava replies, though she's curiously solemn now, all the levity draining out of her. "I think it makes you less surprised by the terrible things, when they happen. Because you see it so often happening to other people. You start to think, *Why not me too?*"

I watch her as she speaks, watch her charisma, how thoroughly charmed Andrea is by her. I've been charmed by her too. I've taken her words as truth. I have counted her as a friend, even.

And I wonder, how dangerous a game have I been playing? I wonder who went to the John Merlo branch of the Chicago Public Library and registered an email address using my name. I wonder who reached out to Dylan Jacobs, drove the Tesla to Milwaukee. Who called me twenty-seven times in the past four months and never said a word.

It all makes so much more sense, if it was Ava. After all, what was the likelihood that Dylan would have gotten into a car with Ted after arranging to meet me? But Ava, with her charm. Ava, the doctor, who promised, above all things, to do no harm.

I watch her animatedly talking with Andrea, and I realize that Ava could probably talk a person into anything.

"I'M ONLY DOING this because it's possible I owe you," Olsen says when he calls me a few days later. It's a welcome distraction. I've been turning everything over in my mind, twisting the possibilities around like wire, every coil tightening my breath, making my heart beat harder. Until I can't tell what is real, until I can't think through the haze of the vodka and the terrible images I've conjured. Ava, pulling up in front of Dylan Jacobs's apartment in her husband's Tesla. Colin, wrapping his hands around Sarah Ketchum's throat. Ted, at sixteen, beckoning to my sister through the open window of a silver sedan. My sister, telling me to run. All of it feels possible. All of it feels as real to me as a memory.

"Doing what?" I ask Olsen, cracking the ice from my tray and refilling my tumbler. Three ice cubes, then vodka. Hoping Olsen can't hear the pop of the ice when the vodka hits it, the way the cubes clink against the side of the glass. It's only noon, after all.

"Getting you a sit-down with my predecessor," he replies.

I set down the glass. "Detective Richards?" I ask. "When?"

"Are you free this afternoon?" he replies.

"Yes. Where?"

"I'll pick you up at two," he says. With half excitement, half regret, I pour my glass of vodka down the sink.

DETECTIVE RICHARDS SITS on an ancient-looking tweed couch, in the front room of his little Edison Park bungalow. He's older than I remember him, even though I must have last seen him only a couple of years ago. There's more gray in his hair and in his mustache. He wears the same sort of polo he used to wear on the job—in navy and gray and dark browns. But the one he's wearing today looks worn in the shoulders, a bit loose in the seams. It's a strange feeling, to be in this man's home. To see the mustard-colored easy chair in the corner, the dusty upright piano, the cluster of half-empty water glasses left forgotten on the kitchen counter. It reminds me that there was so much I never knew about this man. The one who was so good at keeping in touch with my mother, in the years since Maggie went missing. Who always took my calls or sat down with me when I arrived, usually unannounced, at the Rogers Park police station, demanding updates.

I can see Olsen through the picture window, in the slice of light between its lace curtains. Leaning against his car, smoking a cigarette, something I don't think I've ever seen him do before. Must be a habit he picked back up, a holdover from his years undercover. The more I get to know him, the more I wonder how much remains of those days, besides the blacked-out tattoos and a distinct air of violence. Even now, his slouch makes him look more like a loiterer than a police detective. I refused to let him come into the house with me. A condition of my forgiveness, I told him, that I be allowed to see Detective Richards alone.

"How is he doing?" Detective Richards asks, motioning in the direction of my gaze. A wasp that's forgotten how to fly spins and flops and buzzes at the base of the picture window. There are two glasses of overly sweet iced tea between us.

"Well, he doesn't have your bedside manner," I reply. "Or your courtesy. You heard about the Jane Doe last year?"

"Sure. I read the *Trib* review of your show," Detective Richards replies. He says it without affect, like he's not about to compliment or reprimand me. Then again, this man has known me since I was eight years old. He was the one who called my mother the night my father got drunk and wrapped his car around a tree, went through the windshield, and died almost instantly. I don't think this man will ever judge me for the things I do with my grief, in the search for my sister. It's the thing I've always liked best—appreciated most—about him.

"Well, it took him almost a week to call me," I reply. "Karen in the ME's office tipped me off right away. This guy only picked up the phone when he needed a DNA sample."

"He was devoted to doing things by the book, from what I saw," Detective Richards said. "But still, there are worse detectives to have on your sister's case."

"Yeah," I reply, thinking of Olsen's drinking buddies at McGinty's that night. "So I have some questions."

"About your sister?"

"No, about Sarah Ketchum's case." I pull out the case file, set it on the glass-topped coffee table between us. Pull out the two separate evidence lists, the one with the erased notation about the hair in Sarah's drain, and the one without it.

"The Ketchum case?" Detective Richards asks, leaning forward, surveying the documents. "I heard on the news that her killer was released from prison." He rubs a spot on his forehead, his skin reddening beneath his touch. "Don't tell me you were a part of that, were you?"

"I was helping his sister," I reply. "Helping her investigate some inconsistencies in the case."

"God," Detective Richards says, an utterance of exhaustion, as I point to the Wite-Out smudge on the photocopy of the evidence page. His eyes are glassy, red. With age, I hope. I pray, desperately, that this man is not about to cry.

I know what I'm doing. I know he probably thinks I'm being disloyal, in this moment. To him, to the years he spent searching for my sister. I cannot help but feel some shame, hard and sour in the pit of my stomach, in coming here just to accuse him of misconduct. After I've undone all his work in putting Colin away. Still, I have waited too long to leave here without answers.

"There was a notation here, that a hair was found in Sarah Ketchum's drain. Were you aware of it at the time?" I ask.

He considers me, the silver wire of his brows furrowing. "On the record?"

"I'm not really a journalist," I reply. "But if you want, I can promise not to mention you, or anything you tell me, on the podcast." I just need to know, I want to tell him. Fuck the podcast. This is for me.

"Well then, I'll tell you what I told that young man out there," Detective Richards says, motioning toward Olsen. "I can count on one hand the number of cases I've worked where I've been certain. Usually"—he moves his hands in front of him in concentric circles, as if he's waxing on and off simultaneously—"you're fumbling in the dark. And you might find your way to the person, or you might not. On those, you let the jury decide, because it's not your job. But only three or four times have I known for sure, just by looking someone in the eyes, that they're guilty."

He pauses, takes a sip of his iced tea. I watch the small tremor in his hands as he does.

"And one of those times," he continues, "was Colin McCarty."

"You were certain that he killed Sarah Ketchum," I say, my chest tight. I think about losing my breath on that L car, sinking to the floor. I try to take a deep breath without making it obvious to Detective Richards.

"I've been lucky," he says. "I've only seen it a couple of times, in my career. A true psychopath. But I'll tell you, it was chilling. I remember looking into that boy's eyes and thinking, *Nobody's looking back*. It was like, he was a machine that wanted things. And sometimes what he wanted was to hurt someone."

"So you pitted evidence?" I ask, motioning to the case file

again. "The hair in the shower drain? Because you were so certain that he killed her?"

"Yes," he says, and his certainty is unnerving. "I knew all the guys who worked in evidence. They knew enough to trust me when I asked for a favor."

"Even though pitting evidence might have helped with Colin's appeal? Even though it cast doubts on the way the CPD handled the case?"

"He lost that appeal because everyone knew he was guilty. You weren't there, Marti. You didn't see . . ." He trails off. "You have the benefit of hindsight. The remove."

"So if the verdict was so certain, why not include it in the evidence report and take your chances?"

"Because when you have someone like Colin McCarty, you don't take chances," he says. "You don't give the defense a chance to muddy the investigation with questionable evidence."

"What do you mean?" I ask, and he shrugs.

"I've seen a lot of crime scenes in my day," he replies. "And never before have I seen a dry hair lying flat across a drain like that. Not caught in the hair trap. Just lying there across the drain. And it was blond, when Colin McCarty wasn't. Neither were Sarah Ketchum or the roommate. I thought it was one of my guys' hairs, at first. I thought someone leaned over to look in the drain and"—he slaps his hand flat onto the coffee table—"bam. Contamination. False evidence. But do I think it was from someone showering there? No, I don't."

"So you decided not to even test it?" I asked.

"Not if it was planted," Detective Richards replied. "After she was killed. To mess up our case against Colin."

"Who would have put it there?" I ask.

He gives another little shrug. "There was an hour and a half between the time when she supposedly left to meet her friends and the time when the roommate got home. Anything could happen in that span of time."

I think about that span of time, too brief for Colin to have moved Sarah on his own. I've never before considered that perhaps he wasn't alone. Perhaps he called someone, after he killed Sarah. Someone he trusted more than anyone else. Someone who would know what to do.

"That hair is being used right now to bring a case against Colin's brother-in-law for Sarah's murder," I say, my voice coming out choked. As if there is something constricting my windpipe. My own panic, perhaps. "And you're saying, in your official capacity as a former police detective, that you thought it was planted there?"

"That's what I'm telling you," Detective Richards replies, a picture of absolute certainty.

TED LOOKS TERRIBLE the next time I visit him in prison. Peaked, with dark circles beneath his eyes. His skin taking on a yellowish tinge against his orange jumpsuit under the fluorescent lights. I can see the weariness in the way he moves, crossing the room to sit down on the other side of the table. He looks like he's aged a decade. He looks like all the fight has gone out of him.

"I'm taking a plea," he says, before I even have a chance to share what I know.

It feels like getting hit, unexpectedly. A shot to the stomach.

"What?" I ask, everything I had planned to tell him flooding out of me. My plan to expose Ava and Colin. My plan to get Ted out of jail. "What kind of plea?"

"Thirty years," he says, holding up a hand, even as I begin to shake my head. "It's nothing, compared to the time I would serve if we go to court and lose. I could get out and still have some time. A little time, at least."

"Thirty years?" I hiss at him, trying to keep my voice low. "Are you insane? You didn't kill anyone."

"Oh, so you believe me now?" he says, and I know I deserve the bitterness with which he says it.

"I do," I say, because it's the only way I can convince him not to fold. To tell him everything I know. "Ava lied to me about the connection between Sarah and my sister. Sarah's father never lived in Sutcliffe Heights. It was all fabricated to get me involved."

Ted folds his hands on the table between us. "Okay."

"When I first visited Ava and Colin in prison, Colin said something to Ava in Portuguese. She played it off like he made a shitty joke about me, but he actually asked her if everything was in place. I have this on tape."

"Marti—" he says, dragging one of his hands wearily through his hair, a move that strikes me as something a teenager might practice in front of a mirror. I don't let him finish.

"She lied to me, when she didn't have to. He was asking her if everything was in place with Dylan's murder, with setting me up to think that you did it. I know that now. I'm certain of it. Because killing Dylan was the only way they were going to get the CPD to look back at the DNA evidence they pitted the first time around. If there was another body, connected to Sarah, found in the same place Sarah was. They would have no choice but to consider the cases connected."

"So what?" Ted asks.

"*So what?*" I repeat back, feeling my voice rise again, trying to keep the enraged excitement bubbling up in me from boiling over. "So, we can go to the police with what I know. Ava created that email address to impersonate me, because she knew I'd get involved with the case. She knew she could convince me to investigate if she linked Sarah to my sister. And then she drove your car to kidnap Dylan, right? It doesn't make sense that Dylan would have trusted you for a second, when he was expecting to meet me."

"Marti, stop," Ted says, reaching forward now, putting a hand on mine and then pulling it away before the guard has a chance to admonish him. "You think I haven't considered all of this? My wife, the woman I loved, was planning this for years. Setting a trap for me. Ever since she planted that first hair in Sarah's shower."

"So you know she planted the hair?" I ask. I remember her telling me that she brought Ted's hairbrush to the police for DNA. "Which means Colin called her that night, after he killed Sarah."

"He did call her," Ted says. "It showed up in his phone records from that night. He told the police he called her because he didn't remember what time the reservation was."

"And Ava helps him hide Sarah's body in her car, she goes to the restaurant, he follows in a cab. After dinner, they dump the body in the woods. Simple," I say. So simple, yet it never occurred to me, in all the time I spent thinking about it. I feel like a fool. "But the cops pitted the hair evidence that was supposed to implicate you, and Colin was convicted anyway."

"Right. She had to find another way, give them another chance to test the DNA and match it to me," Ted says. "And when your podcast went viral, she saw her opening."

"So that's the story we tell. Publicly. People will believe it, if we lay out the facts of the case."

"They won't," Ted says, shaking his head. "Or, at least, not enough people will believe it. Not when you've been champion-ing Colin's innocence for weeks now. And Ava would do every-thing in her power to stop you."

"What is she going to do? Kill me and dump me in the woods too?" I ask, a bit more cavalier than I probably should be. To hide my desperation.

"She sent that email, didn't she?" Ted asks. "Do you think that's the last piece of evidence she might have fabricated to link you to the case? I mean, can you imagine the cold-blooded dedi-cation it took to frame me? For years, she knew it would come to this. And she did it fucking perfectly. Everything, all the evi-dence, it lines up against me."

"She must have gotten something wrong," I reply, feeling the tears that threatened to fall with Detective Richards welling up again. "I know if I tell a friend of mine, a detective, he'll be-lieve me."

"Will he?" Ted asks. "Or are you just an unstable amateur jour-nalist with a crazy theory?"

I flick away a tear that begins to draw a path down my cheek. I won't give myself over to helplessness, not yet.

"Because that's what it is. It's a crazy theory," Ted says, his hand again reaching to cover mine. "I've gone over it a hundred times. I've gone over it with my attorneys, even. I have nothing but my word and yours to line up against Ava's."

"It'll be enough," I say.

"Marti," he says, his voice soft, as if I am the one who needs to be comforted here. "How many drinks do you have on an aver-age day?"

I shake my head, because I don't trust myself to speak without devolving into tears.

"Add to that the fact that the state just had to release Colin from prison. They're not going to risk looking like they'd go to any lengths to put him away again, not after they hid evidence in his case. I'm sure they're terrified of Ava filing a lawsuit as it is."

"So that's it, then?" I say, not even trying to stop myself from crying at this point. It's too late. The floodgates are open. "You're not even going to try and fight this?"

"With what?" Ted asks. "They have my DNA in Sarah's apartment and Dylan's blood in my travel case. And with Ava against me? Think of the things she could say, if she got up on the stand. Think of the lies she could tell. She could hang me. She would."

"You really think Ava killed Dylan herself?" I ask. Still, almost inconceivable, even as I say it out loud. "You really think she's capable of it? The woman you married?"

He presses the back of his hand to his mouth.

"I think Ava is capable of anything. Especially when it comes to her brother," he says. "She spent her whole childhood trying to protect the two of them from their father. And she blames herself for not being able to stop Colin from becoming what he is."

"What is he?" I ask, but I'm nearly certain I already know the answer.

"I don't know," Ted replies. "I don't know why he killed Sarah. But it wouldn't surprise me if he killed her to see what it was like. I tried to warn you."

The wire inside me tightens further. Constricting my stomach, sending acid into my throat. This is the man I've released, back out into the world. Through my actions, Colin is loose.

"What about Ava? Is she dangerous? Like Colin?" I ask, feeling sick, my heart pounding.

Ted pauses. "No," he replies. "I don't think so. I think she feels enough like a god saving people's lives at her job. That's the awful thing—I don't think she ever would have had reason to hurt anyone, if this hadn't happened. I think we might have been happy. If it wasn't for her fucking brother."

But that's Ava. Devoted to the things she loves, in spite of their faults. Unconditional love, I think, for the first time, can be a truly terrible thing.

"How dangerous is he?" I ask.

"Colin?" Ted asks, shaking his head. "I think he sees other people as insects. Some are fine, just out there, existing. Some he'll leave alone. But if one starts to bother him?" He gives an exaggerated shrug. "Like his sister, I think he's capable of anything. But he doesn't have her intelligence. And he doesn't have her restraint."

"Do you think that's why he got beat up in prison?" I ask, remembering his splinted fingers. The broken ribs. The fractured eye socket. "Because people were bothering him?"

"When did Colin get beat up in prison?" Ted asks, his eyes narrowing as he considers me.

"A couple of weeks after I first met him," I reply. "Right before Dylan's body was found. Ava visited him in the infirmary."

Ted shakes his head. "You're wrong about that," he replies. "We visited him the weekend before I was arrested. He was fine."

"Are you serious?"

He nods.

"Ava told me . . . It's why we fast-tracked the podcast. To put pressure on the state to release Colin. We thought he was in danger."

"Yeah," Ted replies. "That sounds like Ava." He gives an angry little laugh. "I'd almost admire her, if it wasn't so fucking sick. If I wasn't going away until I'm eligible for Social Security."

"If you take a plea, that's it," I say. "There's no hope, then, for correcting this. There's no chance of proving what really happened." I know he can hear it in my tone. I'm begging him to let me try to set this right. To give me a chance to help bring Colin and Ava to justice. But he just shakes his head.

"I can't risk it, Marti," he says. "If I roll the dice in court, that's it. I could get life, I could die in prison."

"We can't just let her win," I say, still pleading.

"She wins," he replies. "That's what she does. She played all of us. It worked out this way because that's what she wanted."

"So what am I supposed to do with that?" I ask, scrubbing the tears from my eyes with my sleeve.

Ted just smiles bitterly. "Get used to it, I guess."

CHAPTER
TWENTY

I can't get used to it, of course. I can't get used to any of it. That I've destroyed my life, that Ted will spend the next three decades in prison, that Sarah and Dylan are dead and my sister is still missing and Jane Doe has a son who will never know her. None of it feels bearable.

I can't get used to it. But I can drink.

Andrea and Trish are visiting Andrea's parents out in the suburbs for the weekend, so I go out by myself. Venture out to Mathilde's, already drinking from a water bottle full of vodka as I get on the L. So much of this started at Mathilde's, after all. Sometimes I think if I hadn't gone out on a run that night, perhaps I never would have had sex with Carey. Maybe I never would have opened the floodgates of my own infidelity. Maybe I would have stayed married, asked Eric to reconsider his desire for a baby, told him about the breadth and depth of the wound my sister had left in me. Told him the truth. That I may never heal from it.

I want to go somewhere familiar. Where I can sit and remember the life I had once, which didn't involve hang-up calls and prison recordings and women zipped into body bags. And I wonder if, by going back to the beginning, back to that first move in the game of chess that followed, I might be able to undo some of it. Or learn something from it, at the very least.

I think I see Carey behind the bar when I arrive at Mathilde's. But it's an unfamiliar bartender, and he shakes his head when I ask after him.

"Doesn't work here anymore," he says over the noise of the jukebox, smelling of hops and cheap body spray.

I order a vodka tonic, which tastes like candy compared to the straight vodka I've been drinking. I drink three at a pretty decent clip, until I sway a bit when I rise from the barstool to go to the bathroom. The girl sitting next to me catches my arm to steady me.

"Thanks," I shout over the music, perhaps a bit too loud. The bartender gives me a look, likes he's anticipating that I might become a problem.

In the bathroom I splash water on my face, considering my dour countenance in the mirror. My hair is starting to grow out of its pixie cut, and now it just looks shaggy, like a child's unruly bowl cut. And I look puffy—my face, my eyes, everything. I'm not sure if it's from the booze or the sleeplessness or what, but it's not very cute. I wish I had one of my wigs on. I wish I'd painted up my face like a goth girl and put on my best leather jacket. I wish I could be the girl I want to be instead of the waterlogged, sad, divorced waif I see looking back at me. Someone gullible.

Someone you look at and immediately know that all she wants is to be loved. Pathetic in her obviousness. Garish in her desire to be noticed, to be wanted. Such an easy mark. For Ava. For Olsen. For anyone.

Before I can think too much about it, I fish my phone out of my purse and call Ava. Even though she's probably at the hospital on a Saturday night. Another twelve-hour shift. Still, I'm prepared to tell her what I think of her. Prepared to tell her that while she's made a fool of me, I've figured her out. I know her for what she is. A killer. A liar.

"Marti?" Her voice comes over the line. "I'm at work, can I call you back?"

"Saving lives?" I ask, slurring a bit. I giggle at the way the words come out, amused by my own ineptness. This seems to give Ava pause, because suddenly she's willing to talk.

"What's going on, Marti?" Ava says, her voice cautious.

"I'm at Mathilde's," I say. "I was thinking I'd come here, be-cause the first guy I cheated on Eric with works here. But he doesn't anymore, though." In my head, the words come out elo-quently. But I can hear in the tone of her response—like she's talking to a child—that I must sound pretty altered.

"Are you there by yourself?"

"I wasn't supposed to be," I reply. "But that looks like how it might turn out. Unless I can find a good pinch hitter."

"Listen, I've got to go in a minute, but how about I call Andrea to come and get you?" Ava asks.

"She's out of town. Family trip. Wish I had one of those." I cackle a bit, to myself.

"Is there someone else I can call?" she asks, but then a group of girls bangs their way into the bathroom, letting in the noise of the bar and the jukebox with them, and suddenly I can't hear anything on the other end of the line anymore.

"Sorry, I gotta go," I half-shout into the phone, before I hang up and go back out into the fray.

TWENTY MINUTES LATER, Colin McCarty comes into the bar. For a moment, my drink-numbed brain thinks it must be a coincidence, that shock of red hair, the inmate pallor. But then he catches sight of me and gives me a strangely boyish wave from where he stands at the bar's entrance, as the bouncer considers his ID. Before I can stop myself, I wave back. I watch as he exchanges words with the bouncer, points in my direction. But the bouncer just shakes his head. After what seems an unreasonably protracted amount of time, I grab my purse and approach the two of them.

"I can't let you in on an expired license," the bouncer is saying.

"Look, man, I just spent seven years in prison. I didn't have a chance to get to the DMV," Colin replies.

"Oh, well in that case, I definitely want to let you in my bar," the bouncer replies.

"Come on, man, can't you give me a break?" Colin says. "How about trying not to be an asshole right now?"

"Now what, exactly, is that supposed to mean?" the bouncer says, standing up. He's easily a head taller than Colin, and likely outweighs him by a hundred pounds.

"Okay, time to go," I say, slipping between them and pulling Colin back through the entrance. "Sorry," I call over my shoulder to the bouncer as we step out onto the street. It's damp outside, and the asphalt is wet. It must have rained while I was inside.

I consider Colin, who looks different, in jeans and a White Sox

T-shirt. Strangely normal. I realize I've only ever seen him in his prison uniform, or in a shirt and tie in courtroom footage.

"What are you doing here?" I ask, my mouth feeling a bit thick as I speak. Everything around me has a strangely pleasant tinge, like the warmth of bathwater. Like the fuzzy thrill of a vivid dream.

"Ava called," he replies, showing his square little teeth as he grins. "Asked me to come get you. She said you seemed a bit . . . *overserved.*"

"Such a polite term," I reply.

"She asked me to take you home."

"Does she think I need a keeper?"

"Do you?" he asks. And I can feel it radiate off him, that shrewdness. The way he seems to be figuring everything out, as he watches me. The look of a predator, I think. Perhaps this is what Detective Richards meant when he described looking in Colin's eyes and finding nothing there but a mechanical intelligence.

I, however, see something else. Something that I assume has everything to do with the fact that I'm a twenty-nine-year-old drunk woman and he is an ex-con, freshly released from prison. He seems to come to the realization at the same moment I do.

"How about I take you home." He says it like he's describing something illicit. And, like every other time I've been in this position in the past year, I feel my heart rate pick up. I wonder what Andrea would think of me. I wonder if this would make my fall from grace complete.

This is the reason I came out tonight, after all. The reason I drank three weak cocktails—no match for my tolerance, after months of straight vodka—and called Ava from the bathroom, leaning into the slur in my words. It's why I slipped a pocketknife into my purse before I left my apartment, a knife I opened and tucked into the back of my pants as Colin argued with the bouncer. Because, somehow, I knew Ava would call her brother. I knew her instinct would be to protect me. Or, at least, to keep tabs on me. To test me, maybe. See if I will go with Colin, or if I've figured out enough already to be afraid of him.

Now there is nothing left to do but move forward. There is nothing left to do but commit to what must happen now.

"Hail a cab," I reply. "I'll give you the address."

HE'S A PERFECT gentleman in the taxi. He even seems cheered, momentarily, when he sees my bottle of water. Up until the point I let him smell it, discover it's vodka. And then he rolls his eyes and takes a long swig from it. He keeps his hands to himself though, holds the car door open for me when we arrive outside my apartment. Waits, patiently, as I fumble with my keys, get us through the front door. Staggering a bit, to make myself look drunk. He follows me up the stairs to my apartment. The presence of the knife, open, throbs at the small of my back as I move.

He's a perfect gentleman, until I let him through my apartment door. And then, so quickly I have to stop myself from reflexively ducking away, he pins me up against the wall, letting the door slam shut behind us. He kisses me like he's forgotten how, like he's acting on instinct alone. It would be just the sort of thing to excite me, if he were nearly anyone else.

I can feel the knife's tip biting into my skin as he presses me back against the wall. My teeth catch his bottom lip as he pulls open my blouse, revealing the red bra I put on, hoping he'd see it. Knowing how pale my skin would look, almost pearlescent in the low light, against the red lace. Walking that edge, waiting to be dragged over.

His mouth moves to my neck as his thigh slips between my legs. I can feel the pinprick of the knife breaking the skin at the increased pressure, and I gasp, my neck arching. He kisses me again as he rests his hand against the base of my throat. He must be able to feel my pulse hammering against his fingers. He must know, as he presses down, just enough, that I'm afraid of him. No matter how good I am at hiding it. He eases back, looking at his hand against my neck. His eyes almost wild, a look I recognize from the first time I saw him. I think of the knife as he pops the button on my jeans. My head drops back against the wall.

Wake up.

"You couldn't just keep quiet, could you?" I whisper, and I know he can feel the vibration of my words against his hand.

"What?" he asks.

"You looked right at the recorder and said it. You asked her if everything was in place."

He eases back, his eyelids lazy, low over his irises. His pupils wide beneath them. Eyes so blue they look fully black in the dark. "Yeah," he says. "My appeal."

"That's not what she said," I reply, feeling his fingers tighten, almost imperceptibly, around my throat. "She said you made a joke at my expense. That you'd prefer she bring women with bigger tits next time."

He lets out a hushed little laugh. "Sounds like something I'd say."

"But it wasn't," I say. "And anyway, you'd already lost your appeal by then."

His fingers grow tighter still around my neck. A warning.

"What are you doing?" he asks.

"You wanted me to know, didn't you?" I say, watching him carefully. Waiting to see if he will give himself away. "That you killed her. Sarah Ketchum."

Something comes alive in his eyes, a swarm of recognition. He releases me for a moment, an unexpected opportunity. *I should move*, I think. I should knee him in the stomach and get him in a chokehold. Land a few punches. Run. But it's not enough. I'm in danger, now that I've turned my cards faceup on the table. Danger if he stays here in the apartment with me. Equal danger if he leaves.

I remain still as he reaches down and slides a hand through the open zipper of my purse, still hanging from my shoulder. Pulls my recorder from my bag, watching its digital screen as the seconds tick by. Recording, ever since I spotted him at the bar. He grins at me, all bared teeth.

"You don't really think I'd be dumb enough to fall for this, do you?" he asks, switching off the recorder.

"I don't know," I say. "I mean, Ava is really the brains in your little operation, isn't she?"

He smiles, and then, in one swift movement, smashes the recorder's digital face down onto the little table in my entryway. I jump at the movement, the violence, my nerves wound tight. He lifts the recorder, the glass of its screen a spider's web of cracks. Gone, just like that, my chance of saving Ted. There is still time to save myself.

I wonder if he'll leave of his own accord. Now, before he implicates himself. Or I wonder if I can escape back out the door, get down the stairs and out into the street before he can catch me.

But even as I think it, I know that either of those possibilities is just as lethal as Colin's standing inches away from me here in my apartment. I'm no safer with Colin McCarty out in the world than in my apartment, especially once Ava understands how much I know about what they've done. No, my only chance is here.

"Ava's smarter than all of us put together," he says, almost a whisper, the edge of a growl.

"Too bad she's saddled with you, then," I reply, shaking my head. "She never would have hurt anyone, would she? If it wasn't for you."

"You're fucking crazy," Colin says. "Your sister running off fucked you over good, didn't it? Ava's basically a saint. She would never hurt anyone."

"My friend who found the photo of the Tesla outside of Dylan's house that night?" I let him see my satisfaction. Let him see that I think I've won. "She found a new one, from a tollbooth just across the state line. It's pretty grainy. But it's of Ava behind the wheel."

It's a lie, of course. I don't have a new photo. I only have my own suspicions. But I know I'm right. I'm certain. And even though I know it will happen, it still takes my breath when he hits me.

I've been hit before, but never like this. Never with bare knuckles, never directly to my face without the protection of headgear or gloves. Sparks bounce across my vision and my stomach roils, and I feel myself make a choking sound at the impact. Choking on nothing, as pain washes across my face and clutches at my skull.

Still, my body is wired for this, to react to these particular circumstances. It takes all the restraint I have to keep myself from stepping into him while he's on his back foot, striking a decisive kick to his knee, using leverage to shove him back while he's off balance. It takes everything in me to stand there, with a hand to my face, look him defiantly in the eyes, and let him hit me again. This time catching my jaw and the corner of my mouth, wheeling my head around. I can feel it when my lip breaks open.

"Who knows about it? Your producer?" he asks, and when I shake my head he hits me hard in the stomach. And I only realize I've collapsed when my palms hit the floor with a decided smack, pain ringing out through my wrists. I barely register it; it is as if my lungs have both collapsed, like a steel belt is wrapped around my diaphragm. I gasp, but my lungs won't open, the pain in my abdomen overtaking everything. As if my stomach is a ripened fruit that has split open on impact, pouring out acid inside me, burning me from the inside out. I can't breathe.

Wake up. Wake up.

He kicks me in the side. Once. Twice. I can feel the pop of my ribs cracking beneath the toe of his shoe.

Panic takes me. Black spots appear before my eyes, like droplets of ink on paper, the beginning patter of rain on pavement. This will only work if I stay conscious. I have to stay conscious. If I black out, that's it.

He grabs me by the hair, dragging me back up onto my feet. Something in the movement opens up a bit of space within me, and air can flow in again. First, in a tiny corner, and then more, until I'm gasping, taking in huge breaths. I flash back, for a moment, to sitting on the floor of the train car. The man sitting in front of me, waiting until I caught my breath.

"Tell me who's seen it," he spits at me, his teeth bared. All animal fury, and it's the only answer I'll ever need. He killed her. He killed Sarah Ketchum. A machine that wants things. A man who sees other people as insects. And I have set him free.

"Please," I beg him as he wrenches my hair back, and I'm afraid the skin will come away from my scalp with the force. I can already feel strands of hair ripping out in his fist. My neck is bared to him. I clutch at his wrist, trying to loosen his grip. Trying to get any relief, as he pulls harder, bends me farther back.

And then he has me by the throat, his hands so tight it's like breathing through a coffee stirrer. I can hear a whistle in my windpipe as I gasp. I can feel the blood, trapped in my head, pounding in my face, unable to get past the grip of his hand. This is how she died; I know that now. He has done this before.

I grip his wrist with one hand, and with the other, I grab the knife from the back of my waistband. The knife, which is already tipped with my blood. And with all the force I can muster, I sink it into the underside of his arm, just above his armpit. It scrapes against bone, and then slides forward and slips in. The hands around my throat go limp, and Colin lets out a sound like he's choking on a cough. Like a sip of water has gone down the wrong pipe. He raises his arm, considering the wound.

And then blood is falling from his arm in thick gouts, almost black, surging along with his heartbeat. He grips the wound with his other hand, as if he can stanch the bleeding, but it's like holding a hand to a running faucet. Blood slips around his fingers, between them. And he looks up at me, as if he's confused. As if he's unsure of what to do now, and I will be the one to tell him. He licks his lips, which are going white, and then lurches to the side, collapsing to the floor at my feet. A marionette with cut strings, just a heap of limbs bending at odd angles.

I gasp for air, leaning back against the wall. Breathing so hard, so desperate for oxygen, that it feels like I may just pass out yet. I sink down next to Colin, settling into a puddle of his blood, my shoes already soaked with it, my hands and my jeans sticky and warm. I lean forward, putting my head between my knees as I gasp, and then retch out hot water and a string of bile onto my shoes and Colin's left hand. I cup my hands over my nose and mouth, just like the man on the L showed me, and I breathe. Breathe, as the voice in my head keeps running on an endless loop. Begging me to wake up.

I wonder how long it takes for someone to bleed to death. Minutes only, I think. The metallic tang of his blood hangs around both of us, the smell of tin and ozone. I could let him go. It could end here. All I have to do is wait.

I sob once, twice, into my cupped hands. A child again, hurt badly enough to be frightened. I want my parents. I want my sister.

Maggie is the one who comes to me. Sitting on my bed, combing through my hair with her fingers. Separating it into sections, preparation for a braid.

Maggie, who wouldn't let my dad spray the spiders that spun their webs on the balcony outside her bedroom. Who took the brunt of whatever violence was waiting in that car, so that I might have a chance to run away.

My fingers fumble at the buckle of Colin's belt, though they're wet with blood and tingling with adrenaline, but finally I'm able to get the buckle free. I yank it from around his waist and wrap it around his upper arm, pulling it tight until the surge of blood from his wound becomes a slow trickle. Pull it tighter still. He doesn't move, doesn't make a sound. My phone is in my back pocket, and I leave streaks of blood on the screen as I dial 911.

OLSEN MUST HAVE heard the call come over the radio, or someone alerted him to it, because he arrives just after the ambulances and the first wave of cops. One of the paramedics is crouching in front of me, giving me instructions that I'm not following very well, while the other paramedics wheel Colin's gurney out the apartment door. The paramedic wants me up, on the stretcher; that much I understand. But I keep telling them to wait. I can't move just yet. Every time I tilt my head, the floor surges beneath me. I'm afraid if I try to move, I will be lost to gravity forever.

"Come on," the paramedic says, and I try to fend him off. I can't go. I can't move. Everything around me is still too fragile; everything could have so easily tipped the other way. I think of the black spots in front of my vision. I think of his grip on my throat. I think of all the points at which it might have turned, might have left me beneath Colin, on the floor. I almost laugh when I think of the call Colin would have had to make to Ava, if he'd killed me tonight. The call, to clean up another woman's body, when he's barely out of prison for the murder of the first.

Olsen shoulders his way in, and I can see in his face how bad it is. It must be pretty fucking bad. The color in his lips disappears when he looks at me. Olsen, a guy who doesn't rattle easily. It seems I found his limit, after all.

He crouches down in front of me. He's wearing a pair of latex gloves. There's so much blood, after all. Colin's. Mine. *I'm part of a crime scene*, I think. *I am evidence now.*

"How bad?" I ask, bringing a hand up to my face, though my hands are still sticky with blood. He must realize at the same time that I do that I'm sitting there in blood-soaked jeans and my bra, because he takes off his jacket and wraps me in it. The warmth of its lining makes me realize how cold I am. My teeth are almost chattering.

"You need a hospital," he says.

There's blood in my mouth, I can taste it, like dirty metal and salt, the skin of a penny. I pray that it's mine and not Colin's. My face feels numb. My body feels numb. I can't feel my fingers, as if I've been out in the cold for too long.

"Ava called him, to take me home," I say, my voice a mumble. There's something wrong with my mouth. At some point I bit into my cheek, hard. Perhaps when his hands were around my throat. There's a wagging chunk of flesh hanging there, inside my mouth. I can't keep my tongue away from it.

"You can tell it to us later," Olsen replies, and his use of the plural is distinct. Us, the representatives of the CPD. Not a man who has been in this apartment before, on his night off. Not a man whom I would very much like to hold me. But I will not ask him to hold me, even if I need it. Even if there is a chance he would.

I allow Olsen and the paramedic to help me up, though the minute I straighten, my ribs feel like a jumble of splintered wood inside me, and I let out a little jerky mewl in spite of myself. When I glance down, dark bruises are already blooming where Colin kicked me. They settle me onto the stretcher and the paramedics make quick work of covering me up and buckling me in. I watch as Olsen remains in the room, his attention now fixed on the pool of Colin's blood on the floor, as I'm pulled away. Always a cop, I remind myself.

TWENTY-ONE

It's Eric they call at the hospital. Eric, who is still listed as the emergency contact in my medical records. I don't even know they've done it until he's there. So quickly, he probably blew every red light he encountered on the way. A trench coat thrown over the running clothes he sleeps in most nights. He comes through the curtains that hang around my gurney, and for a second, I forget that he's not my husband anymore. In that moment he's the boy I knew in college, the one who wanted to do nothing but comfort me.

I cry into his shirt, though my eye is almost swollen shut, and the pain is excruciating. He smooths down my hair, his other hand gentle on my back, and I know he's afraid he'll hurt me if he does any more than that. He probably will, though what does it matter? One pain crowds out another, all competing for primacy. The worst is the part of me that misses him, springing to life again. It's the part I've tamped down with my guilt and my obsession with these dead girls, the part of me that knows I hurt myself too, perhaps irreparably, when I hurt Eric.

"What happened?" he asks, and I can see his face is wet too when he pulls back to look at me. *A good man*, I think. He has always been such a good man, even when he couldn't be what I needed. Even when he could not forgive me.

"He went crazy. Attacked me," I say, though my voice is hoarse and the inside of my cheek is swelling. I can feel the deep gouges of teeth marks with my tongue, and I sound like I've had Novocain, just a little slurred on the damaged side. The muscles in my throat ache when I talk. "I had a knife. I think I might have . . . I think I might have killed him."

"Shh," Eric says, running a hand down the good side of my face, wiping away the tears there. But I see it, when he makes eye contact with the nurse beside me, who is starting an IV, looking for confirmation. I can see that he wasn't told anything upon his arrival.

I want to ask him why he's so surprised. I want to ask him how he, of all people, would not know that I'm capable of this. I woke from my nightmares, night after night, for years with him beside me. I told him, again and again, what I'd done in those dreams. I know now what it was. I know that I was preparing for the moment when I would take hold of a knife and have to use it. To save myself. Always, even in my nightmares, I'm always saving myself.

"What can I do?" he asks. Always wanting to make it better. Always wanting me to be okay.

"Call Andrea," I say, feeling my eyes fill again. The pain overcomes even the steeliest of my principles and all my pettiness. "And maybe call my mom."

* * *

MY MOTHER ARRIVES before Andrea. She starts crying as soon as she sees me, though she tries her best to stanch the tears as soon as they start. Still, it's something, after so many years of being bulletproof. She presses a palm to my good cheek, and it is like waking up after having my tonsils out as a child and feeling my mother's cool hand against my face in the dark of the recovery room.

Eric leaves when my mother arrives, kissing me tenderly on the crown of the head before he departs. It's in that moment, when I catch the brief scent of perfume on his T-shirt, that I realize. There's someone waiting for him, back there. Back in the bedroom we used to share. He left someone to come here. I give his hand a squeeze as he pulls away.

My mother sits with me as we wait for the portable X-ray for my ribs, and the CT scan for my head, and the doctor to pronounce me mildly concussed, with three fractured ribs and some relatively minor soft tissue damage. They decide to keep me overnight for observation, though I'm sure my mother has bribed whoever needed to be bribed to get me an overnight stay in a private room.

Olsen and Hardy show up just as they're getting ready to transfer me. Olsen has the good sense to look grim when he enters. Hardy, on the other hand, looks almost impressed. I can't tell if it's the shape I'm in or if it's because she's heard what I've done to Colin.

"We're just here to take a quick statement," Olsen says.

"Is he alive?" I ask, before he can ask any of his own questions. Olsen and Hardy exchange a look. "Colin. Is he alive?" I repeat. Olsen is the one who finally answers.

"He's in a coma," he says. "They think . . . they think his brain might have been starved of oxygen for too long. He lost a lot of blood at the scene. They don't know if he's going to wake up."

"She's not saying anything," my mother cuts in, her chin pointed upward at Olsen's face. Her distrust of cops is palpable, though this is the first time she's ever been on this side of the exchange. More often, she spent her time browbeating the members of the Chicago Police Department for not doing their jobs to her satisfaction.

"It's okay, Mom," I say, my voice little more than a whisper, wanting nothing but to have this over with. "It was self-defense."

I know what I'm going to say. I've been thinking about it since my last visit with Ted, since he told me he would take the plea deal. Since I made the decision that I could not simply let Colin live out his life after what he'd done. Not when he was likely to do it again.

"Will you just listen to me, for once in your life?" my mother says. "You're not going to talk to anyone until our attorney is present."

"Mrs. Reese," Hardy says, her head tilted in a way that might be slightly deferential, or perhaps only inquisitive. "We just want to hear what happened. We can see your daughter has been through a terrible ordeal, and all we want is to speak with her briefly so we can get all the facts straight as quickly as possible."

"It's fine," I say, though my voice is so hoarse it comes out as little more than a croak. Hardy doesn't wait for confirmation from my mother before she begins.

"Can you take me through what happened tonight?" she asks, flipping open a narrow steno pad.

"I was out at a bar. Mathilde's," I reply, and Hardy and Olsen both crowd in closer, as I can do little more than whisper. "I drank too much. Called Ava Vreeland to see if she could pick me up, but she was at work."

"Why not take a cab? Or an Uber?" Hardy asks.

"I was drunk. I guess I was really hoping Ava would come meet me. I didn't want to go home yet."

"So how did Colin end up in the mix?" Now it's Olsen asking the questions.

"I guess Ava called him. Told him to come get me," I reply. It was a stroke of luck, really, thinking back on it. I never really expected that I knew Ava well enough to be able to anticipate what she'd do in that situation. I had contingencies. I would try again, under different circumstances, to end up in a room alone with Colin. But that it was so easy, and that it came together on my first try, was both thrilling and unsettling. I almost didn't trust it, thought my eyes were playing tricks, when Colin arrived.

"So he took you home?" Hardy asked. I nodded, though the movement made me slightly dizzy.

"And I got this idea that I'd record him."

"Record him?" Hardy asks, glancing at Olsen.

"To see if he'd admit he was involved with . . ." I pause, swallowing hard, blades in my throat. I have to be careful here. I don't know if explaining all of it—how much I really know of what Colin and Ava have done—will put me in danger. With Ava still out there. With Colin in a coma, the near-fatal wound in his arm from my pocketknife.

The more I admit of the truth, the more danger I'm in. From the police, who might see the call to Ava, the concealed weapon, the invitation for Colin to come back to my apartment, as pre-meditation. And from Ava, who might still see me as a threat to her own safety.

"... if he was involved with Sarah Ketchum's murder. To see if he and Ted were working together." I swallow again, hard, motion for the plastic cup of water on the tray next to the bed. Olsen hands it to me, and I take a long drink.

"He found the recorder and smashed it. We scuffled. And I was able to get the knife from my purse," I say, pressing my hand to my torn-up mouth. Tears come easily, burning their way out of my damaged eye.

"So you had the knife on you, at the bar?" Hardy asks.

"I carry it with me," I reply, my voice choked with tears and strain. "My sister . . ." I trail off, motioning to my mother.

"Her sister was kidnapped when she was just a child," my mother says, picking up where I leave off.

"We're aware of the case," Hardy replies in a solemn, folksy way. "I am so sorry that happened to your family. And now this."

But now Olsen seems guarded, his eyes on me.

"How long have you carried a knife?" he asks.

"On and off, I guess, for years," I reply, drinking more water, trying to clear the rasp from my voice.

"And when exactly did you get it from your bag?" he asks.

"I don't really remember," I reply. I know what he's thinking. That it's difficult to take a beating like this and have the where-withal to retrieve a weapon from a bag. Odds are, Colin wouldn't have let me get to it. It's why I had it on me. It's why the knife was open, tucked into the back of my jeans. Still, I feign confusion. "Maybe after he hit me. After I was on the floor."

"So you're able to get the knife," Hardy says. "And you're on the floor. When do you use it? Was he on top of you?"

I know what she's doing. Blood-spatter analysis will show exactly how we were standing when I stabbed him. I've seen enough TV to know that. She's hoping to catch me in a lie, something they can disprove.

"No," I say. "He pulled me up by the hair, had me by the neck, when I . . . used the knife." I show them the bruises on my neck.

"And he didn't see that you had the knife?" Hardy asks. "You were able to get it from your purse, without him realizing it."

"I guess," I whisper. My head is starting to hollow, fill with air, like a stretching helium balloon. The knife. A mistake. I probably should have used something else, something that would not look so deliberate.

"I don't know," I say, but the question is slipping away. I remember the sharp glass edges of my podcast award. Such a poetic weapon; what a missed opportunity. When the thought strikes me, it's so funny that I burst into a fit of giggles. Painful, agonizing giggles, my ribs crackling with pain as I realize I can't stop. Olsen and Hardy glance first at each other and then at my mother. All appear mystified, and a bit unnerved, by my outburst. I clap a hand to my ruined mouth, trying to stop looking like such a fucking maniac. Like I've lost my grip. Fat tears roll down my face. My mother stands, both of her hands up, as if ready to fend off the two detectives, riot-cop style.

"Okay," she says. "I think that's enough for now. I think she's had enough tonight, don't you?"

Hardy nods, considering me like I've spontaneously started speaking in tongues, but she hands me her card.

"If you think of anything else."

I take the card, still choking back laughter. Olsen doesn't look at me as the two detectives leave.

WHEN I SLEEP, I dream of Ava. She comes in the night, slipping by my mother, who sleeps on the nearby love seat, propped up with pillows and covered with a hospital blanket. Ava hovers over me, backlit by the fluorescence spilling through the door to the hallway. I can't see her face in the fuzz of darkness and the pain medicine seeping through my IV, but I know it's her.

"What did you do?" she whispers, her voice almost a moan. "Marti. What have you done?"

I try to speak through my thickened mouth, swollen with blood and sealed with the numbing chill of narcotics. I try to tell her that I only did what she's already done. Pressed my thumb against the scales. Played god, for a moment.

I try to ask her if she's here to kill me.

She sits at the edge of my bed, reaching out and tracing her fingertips, featherlight, over the rawness of my face. My swollen eye, my split lip, down to the bruises on my neck. Her brother's fingerprints left in dark blood under my skin. Her eyes suddenly bright with tears. Angelic, I think, as I reach a tingling hand to her, as she enfolds my fingers in hers. We have both done terrible things; we are joined in that. I wonder where I fall, in her scales of justice, in her ideas of vengeance. I wonder, too, if she is afraid of me.

"Do you know how many lives I've saved?" she asks, a whisper. "How could God begrudge me a single one, for the hundreds I've kept safe for him?" Her hand is soft and dry against mine. She could kill me now. She probably knows a thousand ways to do it.

This is the test of Ted's belief in her restraint. Because if she were going to take another life, it would certainly be mine. It would certainly be now. I, who have taken her most beloved from her. Taken from her the person she would kill for.

"How many have you saved?" she asks, a challenge.

I can't tell her how many. Because I don't know. All the lives Colin would have taken, had he been allowed back out in the world. My own, at the very least. But I think she knows this already. I think she understands, as she brushes at the shining trails on her cheeks. After all, she brought me into this. She used me as a tool for her own ends. My sister's story. That email address. She used me to set the trap that took Dylan Jacobs's life. She should have known that I would not be able to stand it, if I found out the truth.

"Are we even now, Marti?" she asks. A final question.

Even. I understand what she's asking. She's asking me to give her a chance to pay her own penance. To keep to myself the things that I know, so she will do the same.

And I know that, in a just world, she and I would both be locked away somewhere. Because people like us, who are capable of the things we have done, should not be allowed to escape punishment. But I have not believed in justice since Maggie was taken. And so I do not believe that a thing like this can be put right. It can only be endured, in the end.

And so, like a benevolent god, I squeeze her hand in assent.

ANDREA IS THERE when I wake up. Holding my hand, just as Ava did. I think she is Ava still, before I open my eyes and see that she is gone.

"Oh, Marti," Andrea says, looking dawn stricken, a pallor only sleeplessness brings, her eyes a bit deeper set than I remember. My mouth is gummy with dehydration and dried blood, and when I reach for the cup of water on my bedside table, she hands it to me. My face throbs as I put my lips to the straw. It hurts to breathe, like someone slipped a screwdriver between my ribs and is now prying at them, watching them grind and pop against each other. Everyone's right, about how it's worse the second day. I feel like I've been trampled.

"What happened?" she asks.

I shake my head. "Colin," I whisper back, pressing my fingertips to my face. My eye socket feels raw and puffy. I want a mirror. I want to assess the damage for myself.

"But why . . . ," she begins, and then stops.

She knows me, my best friend. She knows that I would not let her daughter grow up in a world in which Colin McCarty walked the streets. She knows that I will walk through fire for her, as she has walked through fire for me.

She takes my hand and leans forward to press her lips to my knuckles. She's seen them swollen and red a hundred times, from sparring, from battering against the heavy bag. They are not so, this morning. They are the one part of me that is perfect, unscathed. They tell her, it seems, all she needs to know.

"WHAT HAPPENED LAST night?" Olsen asks as the nurse removes my IV. It's the last thing to be done before I'm released. Andrea has brought me fresh clothes from my apartment, and I'm desperate to get out of this hospital gown. To get home and shower.

I didn't expect him to return so soon. Part of me didn't expect him to return at all. But here he is, looking like he, too, has had a sleepless night. Looking like I felt, once. Like I knew the truth of something, and nobody else would say it out loud.

"Right to it, huh?" I reply, walking gingerly into the little bathroom adjoining my room but leaving the door slightly ajar as I change behind it. "Are you asking in a professional capacity?"

"Believe me, Marti, I don't want to be asking in my professional capacity," he replies.

"Why is that?" I ask as I emerge from the bathroom, in a T-shirt and jeans that make me feel a lot more like myself. I'm even getting used to my reflection, though it was a tremendous shock this morning. My left cheek is swollen and purple. My eye is black, wrinkled like the skin of a rotting plum. My lip is puffy and split on one side.

"Because I don't want to have to ask you if you brought him back to your apartment last night with the intention of killing him. If you had that knife on you, instead of in your purse. I don't want to ask you how Colin McCarty got the drop on you when Jimmy outweighs him by fifty pounds and I watched you dispatch him with no trouble at all."

"Did you find the tape recorder at my place?" I ask, dabbing some of the antibiotic ointment the doctors have prescribed me on my lip. Olsen eyes me carefully. As if I'm dangerous, the sort to set a trap for someone like him. As if I'm Ava.

"On the floor."

"Were you able to get anything off it?" I ask, because I know Olsen well enough to know that he's dogged in that way. He'll want the answers to every question my little crime scene of an apartment provides, and a big question is what might be on the smashed tape recorder they probably found in a pool of Colin's blood.

"They're working on it," Olsen replies.

"It's like I said," I reply. "I was trying to get him to give something up. Admit that he had some part in Sarah's murder."

"So now you believe Colin did kill her after all?"

"Let's say that I'm certainly willing to entertain the possibility at this point."

"So then who killed Dylan Jacobs?" Olsen asks. "Ted Vreeland?"

I wonder how much I can say. I think of Ava's visit to my hospital room—if it wasn't just a narcotic fantasy of mine, and I'm still not quite sure of that, either. I wonder if linking Ava to Dylan's murder would put me in danger. But Olsen, the bastard, is clever enough to put the pieces together himself, even before I have a chance to answer.

"Or was it the sister?" he asks, and I'm glad I'm on a decent amount of pain medication, because the involuntary clench in my jaw would probably be fucking agony otherwise.

"That's what I was trying to find out," I say, trying to remember what I said to Colin. What they might hear, if they somehow get clear audio off that broken recorder. "I was trying to goad him into giving something up."

"But he found the recorder," Olsen says, not a question.

"Yes."

"And foiled your plan."

"Yes."

"You don't watch much TV, do you?" Olsen asks, and looks almost amused.

"What do you mean?" I reply, though I know exactly what he means. The plan sounds ridiculous, even to my own ears. The sort of thing that would only work on a TV show, and a bad one at that.

"Colin's body doesn't have a mark on him, besides the wound to his arm. It doesn't look like you fought back at all," Olsen replies.

"I was drunk," I reply. "Ask the bartender at Mathilde's last night. Ask Ava."

"Your blood alcohol wasn't that high when you were admitted," he says. "Believe me, I checked. So I can't help but wonder if the only reason you would stand there and take a beating like this"—he motions to my face—"is because you expected him to find the recorder. You expected it to make him angry. And you did nothing while he beat the hell out of you, so you'd be justified in killing him. Those are questions I don't want to have to ask you in my professional capacity."

"I was drunk," I repeat. "And afraid. And trying to do the right thing, despite all of that. So I'm sorry if your asshole of a friend was easy to catch off balance in a bar, but that's nothing like being alone in an apartment with Colin McCarty." This part, at least, is true. I have never been so afraid for my life. I have never been so close to the edge. When my eyes fill with tears, this time, they're real. "He nearly killed me." I look him squarely in the eyes as I say it. "Do you believe that, at least?"

"Yes," Olsen replies. "About that, I believe you."

"Then what does the rest of it matter?" I reach out, take his hand. Because despite it all, I still want him to hold me. It's what I've wanted since the first time I saw him, waiting in those chairs at the police station. I want him to be the one to comfort me.

But he must know what I'm asking. He must know what I want is to draw him into the gray, into the haze in between all this certainty and all his righteousness and all his faith. The place where I live. And he cannot follow me there, I know it, because he pulls his hand back from mine.

"It matters," he replies. "You have no idea how much it matters."

I nod, because there is nothing left to say. Now he's the one who knows the truth that no one else will admit. I've left him there, in that impossible place. And in the way I knew that Eric would never be able to love me after what I'd done, I know that Olsen will never be able to forgive me for this.

Perhaps my penance is not done yet.

EPILOGUE

I sit down in the sunny little café in Lincoln Park and watch the red light blink from the recorder on the table between us. I feel like I should be used to this by now, going on the record, recounting my story for the benefit of an audience. Except this time, it's not Andrea sitting across from me. My best friend, who conducts interviews like a dance, leading me where she wants, letting me show off a bit. The best sort of partner. This, I fear, may end up being a little more like sparring.

The reporter, a young man with horn-rimmed glasses, works for *Vanity Fair*. And I'm hoping against hope, glancing down at the T-shirt and torn jeans that I'm wearing, that he won't start with a discussion of my outfit. Still, I tuck my messy bob behind my ears, just in case.

"So let's start with the obvious," the reporter says, sipping his

Americano. "How has your life changed since the night Colin McCarty attacked you in your apartment?"

"Well," I say, preparing the line I've given to everyone who has asked about Colin in the year since it happened, "I believe even more strongly now that our criminal justice system needs to be reformed. I think if Colin had gotten a fair trial the first time around, and if our prison system had any interest in rehabilitation at all, none of this would have happened."

"So let's be fair," the reporter says, leaning forward and scratching some notes on his pad of paper. "You're the one who helped get Colin McCarty released from prison. And then he turns around and almost kills you. And you're blaming the criminal justice system for that?"

"Colin was released because there was evidence from the crime scene that was never revealed in his trial," I reply. "And because the CPD didn't conduct a thorough investigation of the people in Sarah Ketchum's life. If they had done those things from the beginning, a couple of podcasters would never have been able to help get his case overturned. And we would have a lot more answers now."

"So now Ted Vreeland is in prison for these murders, after accepting a plea deal from the state. But, considering the extreme violence of Colin's attack on you, there have been a lot of questions from the public about whether or not he was actually responsible for Sarah Ketchum's murder. So what exactly are we supposed to believe here?" the journalist asks. He's having fun now, at my expense. Showing me the mess I've made. "Do you think Colin McCarty and Ted Vreeland worked together to kill Sarah Ketchum and cover up their crime?"

It's a fine line I'm treading here, and I know it. It's the dance

I've been doing since Colin attacked me, trying to balance my desire to see Ted released from prison and my need to keep Ava's involvement in the case a secret. Because there are those in the CPD who still suspect me of luring Colin to my apartment to kill him. And if I'm going to move the right pieces into place—if I'm ever going to get Ted exonerated—I can't telegraph my plans for every true-crime junkie in the country. And, more important, I can't telegraph them for Ava.

"I don't know," I reply. "What I do know is that when Colin was convicted of Sarah Ketchum's murder, he was forced into a system that has no interest in rehabilitation and that thrives on violence. And I got so wrapped up in the case that I wasn't looking at it objectively anymore. Just because Colin was unjustly imprisoned, and then released, doesn't mean that he wasn't dangerous. But because I was invested in the hidden evidence in his case, because I'd gotten to know his family, I wasn't able to see the ways in which the prison system had amplified his potential for violent behavior."

"And Ted Vreeland?" the reporter asks. "You know, there's a lot of noise online from people who think he was set up. A lot of people think it was one big conspiracy, to stop the land deal Ted was negotiating at the time, for the old riverfront property on the North Side."

"I've heard those rumors," I reply. "But I'm not exactly convinced that members of Chicago's city council conspired to put Ted behind bars because of a real estate negotiation. It seems like a stretch."

It's lunacy, actually. But people have hit on the right aspects of the case—the fact that Ted Vreeland wasn't ever photographed in his Tesla at the time of Dylan's murder, that someone had the foresight to wipe the Tesla down for fingerprints but didn't clean the trunk where Dylan's body had been. That there was no other evidence of Ted in Sarah's apartment—no fingerprints, no witnesses who saw him entering or leaving, no DNA anywhere else—aside from the hair in the shower drain. Ted appeared to be meticulous in all the wrong ways, if he was trying to hide his crimes. Ways that seemed to point all the evidence conveniently back at him. The online conspiracy theorists are just looking in the wrong place for the person who set him up.

"So what else?" he asks. "How else is life different for you now?"

What isn't different? I think. Eric's second marriage was featured in *Chicago* magazine, its story too perfect not to print. I recognized the name of his new wife right away, the younger sister of Eric's lost childhood sweetheart. They reconnected, after his failed first marriage, over the shared grief they still had for her sister. Summer, his new wife, is four years his junior and claims to have been resoundingly ignored by the boys next door, including Eric, when they were kids. But they were similarly shaped by loss, and when they reconnected at a family Christmas party two years ago, they fell deeply and irrevocably in love with each other. It's a sweet story, the way that sad stories can sometimes be made sweet, but I wonder if Eric recognizes his own patterns. A girl who lost her sister as a child. A girl always trying to be someone else, the one who was lost. I wonder what Summer can learn from what he tells her of me.

"Well, the documentary series with HBO has been a new experience," I reply, because Andrea and I just wrapped a ten-week collaboration with a crew of filmmakers, retracing our steps through every detail of the first and second seasons of our podcast. I was reticent about it at first, considering my own colossal missteps in the case, considering how much I'd have to lie. But the director and his crew turned out to be so enthusiastic about casting me and Andrea as the heroes of the piece that it became easy to tell the story as the podcast presented it, violent ending and all.

"But I guess, personally, there isn't much in my life that looks the same as it did before that Jane Doe showed up in the morgue two years ago," I continue. "Since then, my marriage ended, and I moved into my own place. I went from bartending at a goth club to being a podcaster and the producer of a documentary series. And I'm in therapy for PTSD. I've been doing a lot of work on myself."

"As a result of Colin McCarty attacking you?" he asks, looking intrigued.

"Among other things."

"And what about Colin's sister, Ava?" the reporter asks. "Are you still in contact with her?"

"No," I reply, and try to keep my face even. Impassive. "Last I heard she'd moved away from Chicago. I heard she was overseas, working with Doctors Without Borders, I think."

I sleep a bit easier at night, knowing Ava is thousands of miles away. Colin, on the other hand, is still closer than I'd prefer, hooked to a ventilator in an extended-care facility in Oak Park. One of the best—and most expensive—facilities in the state, from what I read online. Courtesy of Ava, likely funded by the sale of that beautiful condo in Wicker Park. I know exactly what she's doing, tearing her life down, running toward whatever feels alien and penitent enough. I've done the same myself.

I visited Colin only once, posing as a cousin from out of state. I couldn't even enter the room; the feel of his hands on my throat was still so close, so ready to cut off my airway with panic. How ironic, I said to my new therapist, that my own panic does the job just as well as his hands did that night. Keeping me from breathing. It happens too often now, leaving me huddled against walls, in corners, at the mouths of alleys, breathing fast, my hands cupped in front of my face. My body seems to not want me to forget this lesson too quickly.

I watched Colin from the doorway, where he lay in that bed, his body gray and thin and probably stinking, if I got any closer. It seemed a pointless existence to me, lying there unconscious because Ava—for all the steel in her spine, for all her playing god—could not bring herself to let him go. A fitting punishment, maybe, for the lives he ruined. I knew Ava would never take him off life support. She would never be the one to stamp out the possibility that he might one day open his eyes, begin breathing again on his own. I understand her better than anyone, though. It was the same rush of relief I felt when the Jane Doe turned out not to be Maggie. The possibility of getting them back, our lost siblings, is too intoxicating to curtail.

So I watched Colin, looking for any sign that he might still be there, that machine of a brain working away behind his eyelids. Knitting synapses back together, neurons sparking, beginning to dream. Because it is the thing I fear most now, that Colin McCarty might one day wake up.

"And what's next?" the journalist asks, though his eyes have taken on a somewhat vacant sheen, as if he understands he won't be gaining a revelatory insight into my case from this discussion.

"Season three," I reply.

"So you have something in the works already?" he asks, perking up slightly.

"We're mulling some options."

"About Maggie? Do you ever think you'll revisit your sister's case?"

Maggie. I think of the message I got on my phone the previous week, the notification that popped up on Instagram. A DM from a tattoo artist in Ukrainian Village. **Sorry, haven't checked this account in ages. I remember that tat. What do you want to know?**

It took me a moment, rereading my original message, to remember what I'd asked the man. It was about a tattoo of a blue lizard he'd posted, years ago now. I'd sent the message that first night at Mathilde's, killing time as Carey poured me drinks, when I should have been out running.

Is this the girl who got it? I wrote back, attaching a photo of Maggie at sixteen, and then the artificially aged photo the cops have cooked up. The photo that looks unbearably similar to my own reflection. It took a moment, but then he typed a response.

Definitely could be, the tattoo artist replied. **Got a copy of her ID. Looks similar.**

The sort of answer that, a year ago, would have sent me tearing across the city to this man's tattoo parlor, demanding the records of this particular client. Maggie. She might be here. She might be in Chicago.

But then I remembered. If she was here, and she was free to walk into a tattoo parlor and request a replica of her favorite childhood toy—a nostalgia piece about the family she abandoned and the life she left behind—then she also must know I'm here. My photo has been printed in every major newspaper. I am a cautionary tale, the amateur journalist who got more than she bargained for. Who got too close to her subject, lost her objectivity, and was almost killed for it. So I know that if Maggie is out there, she doesn't want to be found. Not by me. Not by anyone.

And anyway, I've had my fill of chasing ghosts.

"I think there are plenty of other girls out there who we should try to find." Even as I say it, I catch my reflection in the café's window and nearly have to look twice. Because now, with my hair a bit longer and darkened with dye, from across the room, I barely recognize myself. Sometimes, when I catch a glimpse of my reflection from far away, I can almost mistake myself for Ava.

ACKNOWLEDGMENTS

I am deeply indebted to my editors, Sally Kim and Gaby Mongelli, for their brilliant insights and steadfast support throughout this process. Working with you has been both a pleasure and an honor. I'm also so grateful for the thoughtful and creative work of the copyediting and production teams at Putnam. Every step in this process has been a true joy, thanks to you. Thank you to my wonderful agent, Richard Abate, as well as Martha Stevens and Rachel Kim at 3Arts Entertainment. I couldn't ask for a better group of advocates for this book.

To Matthew Rickart, I could not have done this without you. Your ideas shaped what this novel became, and I will always be grateful for your generosity. Thank you for helping me find a good story—I hope I've told it well—and for being such an incredible friend. To Susan Curry, for keeping me upright, keeping me laughing, for the gift of your friendship, for your faith and your counsel, and for being my ideal reader—the person I will always strive hardest to impress. To Rowan Beaird, for your thoughtful feedback and for constantly inspiring me with your luminous talent. To Rebecca Johns Trissler for continuing to be such a profound source of encouragement, advocacy, and support. To Michelle Falkoff, Judy Smith, Dan Stolar, Brandon Trissler, and Beth Wetmore, for reading my work and for sharing yours. It is a gift, truly. To Amy Holt and Brett Boham, for the podcasting expertise, and especially to Amy, for being the only person in the world I could stand for a week alone in the Oregon woods. To my uncle, John Diskin, for generously allowing me to pepper you with questions about police procedure, and helping me understand the rules before I so flagrantly broke them. To my incredible friends and wonderful professors at the University of California, Riverside; the two years I spent among you were the most challenging and rewarding of my life. It was a privilege.

To Ashley Weinberg Grebe and Vanessa Bordo Flannes, for being my sisters, my biggest cheerleaders, and my safety net. To my brother, Christopher, for knowing me better than anyone else and talking me through all of it. And finally, to my parents. Your love and support have made all the difference in my life. I'm so lucky to be your daughter.

DISCUSSION GUIDE

1. Twenty years later, Marti is still haunted by her sister's disappearance, both hopeful and afraid of uncovering the truth. Why do you think she is unable to move forward? Do you have any thoughts on what might have happened to Maggie?

2. Marti and Andrea's podcast plays a pivotal role in *The Lost Girls*. Are you a fan of true crime podcasts? Do you think their popularity and the media surrounding them have any real impact on the actual investigations, especially cold cases like Maggie's?

3. Discuss the reasons why Marti agrees to help Ava with her brother's case. Was is the Sutcliffe Heights connection? Or was there something about Ava herself that drew Marti in?

4. Marti begins to spiral after the Jane Doe case, with her

behavior becoming more and more reckless. Do you think this was the reason for her divorce from Eric and the distancing from her family? Or do you think there was always going to be a breaking point for her?

5. Did you believe in Colin's innocence? Why or why not?

6. Talk about Marti and Olsen's relationship. Do you think there's a genuine attraction there? Or is each using the other? If so, in what ways?

7. While Marti was exposed to a lot of police work growing up, all of her own investigative work is done as a civilian. Discuss some of the tactics she used to look into both Maggie's and Sarah's cases. Were any methods particularly interesting or surprising to you?

8. As Marti begins to put the pieces together, she blames herself for Dylan's death. Do you agree with that? What do you think might have happened if Marti hadn't gotten involved?

9. After reading the novel, how do you feel about Ava's decisions? Were you surprised with where her loyalties ultimately lay? What would you have done if you were in her position?

10. What do you think of Marti's decision to hold on to the truth about Colin at the end of the novel? What do you think is next for her?

ABOUT THE AUTHOR

Jessica Chiarella is the author of *And Again*. She holds an MA in writing and publishing from DePaul University and an MFA in creative writing from the University of California, Riverside. She lives in Chicago, Illinois.